Who Killed
Kirby Grindalythe?

Samuel Haskey

All characters in this publication are fictitious and any resemblance to persons, living or dead, is purely coincidental.

This edition published in 2021

1

The right of Samuel Haskey to be identified as the Author of the Work has been asserted by him in accordance with the Copyright, Designs and Patents Act 1988.

Dedication

For my Dad, who's idea I pinched.

And for Pops, who didn't quite get to read this.

Dramatis Personae

KIRBY GRINDALYTHE - A world champion racing driver and rakish playboy. As you may have gathered from the title, he dies quite quickly and doesn't feature all that much.
North Yorkshire

DETECTIVE INSPECTOR MUCH WENLOCK - A world-weary police detective with an ear for lies, a nose for truth and an eye on his pension.
Shropshire

ASHBY DE-LA-ZOUCH - An intrepid sports reporter. On the hunt for the truth or at least a good story.
Leicestershire

UPTON SCUDAMORE - KIRBY GRINDALYTHE's rival on the track.
Wiltshire

HUTTON CRANSWICK - A previous World Champion, killed during a race 4 years ago.
East Yorkshire

SALCOMBE REGIS - A rather unpleasant local pathologist.
Devon

SLAIDBURN - The GREENHOW family butler.
Lancashire

INGLEBY GREENHOW - KIRBY GRINDALYTHE'S estranged wife and heiress to a mind-bogglingly large amount of money.
North Yorkshire

CHEDDON FITZPAINE - A famous politician and mayor. He's a very public figure.
Somerset

SUTTON, MIDDLETON & LITTON CHENEY - Gangster siblings with a reputation for brutality and remarkably good cakes.
Leicestershire, Northamptonshire, Dorset

WRAXAL PIECE - A corrupt police officer who covers up for the powerful from his position in the Major Crimes Unit.
Somerset

GRANTHAM NORTH - Services KIRBY GRINDALYTHE's car.
Lincolnshire

LEIGH DELAMERE - Services UPTON SCUDAMORE's car.
Wiltshire

CORSLEY HEATH - UPTON SCUDAMORE's sister.
Wiltshire

DR CHEADLE - A kindly doctor but frankly a bit of a security risk.
Greater Manchester

LACEY GREEN - A lady boxer whose name does not match her description.
Cheshire

BLUITH WELLS - The owner of the only bookmaking shop in town.
Wales

ACTON TURVILLE - A strange old man who may or may not be reliable or sane.
Gloucestershire

CHERRY BURTON - Woman of mystery.
East Yorkshire

BISHOP BURTON -An ordained bishop and father to CHERRY BURTON.
East Yorkshire

CHERITON FITZPAINE - CHEDDON FITZPAINE's wife.
Devon

NEWTON FERRERS - The mayor's loyal assistant.
Devon

SHIRLEY WARREN - The winner of "Best Fundraiser" at the cathedral for the last 8 years running.
Southampton

PETER & MARY TAVEY - A pair of ridiculous pseudonyms that are seen through instantly.
Devon

DETECTIVE CHIEF INSPECTOR BUDLEIGH SALTERTON - MUCH WENLOCK's commanding officer. Generally referred to as the DCI.
Devon

CHIEF WOODBURY SALTERTON - The chief of police, BUDLEIGH SALTERTON's brother.
Exeter

BURNHAM NORTON - Sent for by CHEDDON FITZPAINE.
Norfolk

WELWICK, SKIRLAUGH & SKEFFLING - Insurers.
East Yorkshire

WOODFORD HALSE - A missing engineer.
Northamptonshire

Dramatis Vehiculum

FFORDE PANTHER - KIRBY GRINDALYTHE's racing car. Fast and red.

FLEMING LYNX - UPTON SCUDAMORE's racing car. Fast and blue.

CHANDLER OCELOT - CHEDDON FITZPAINE's car. Fast and silver.

PRATCHETT MUSKRAT - MUCH WENLOCK's car. Beige and not fast.

ADAMS CIVET - ASHBY-DE-LA-ZOUCH's car. Sporty but thirsty.

RAND PANDA - Rusting death trap inexplicably loved by anorak wearing enthusiasts.

Discography

Peter Gabriel. "Sledgehammer." *So*, Charisma, 1986.

Billy Joel. "Only the Good Die Young." *The Stranger*, Columbia, 1977.

Genesis. "Land of Confusion." *Invisible Touch*, Virgin 1986.

Marvyn Gaye. "I Heard It Through the Grapevine." *In the Groove*, Tamia, 1968.

Baha Men. "Who Let the Dogs Out?" *Who Let the Dogs Out?*, S-Curve, 1999.

Chapter 1

If he'd been paying attention, he would have smelt petrol and exhaust fumes. He would have heard the deafening roar of finely tuned V8 engine, a roar that was drowning out the sound of rapidly rotating tyre on hot tarmac. If he'd turned his head, he would have seen the crowds of cheering spectators, stood dangerously close to the track, urging him on.

If he'd been paying attention, he would have heard the mechanical sound of cog meeting cog as he changed gear. He would have felt the wind whip past his grimy face. He wouldn't have felt any of that wind in his hair as he wore a leather helmet. Nor would it bring tears to his eyes, which were protected by goggles. A grim look of determination set across his lips and jaw line.

He was going fast. Bloody fast, and he knew it. But he wasn't paying attention to that either. All his thoughts were fixated on the tarmac ahead of him and the turns in the road to come.

In hindsight, and unknown to him, this was a waste of time.

He was winning; there were no cars ahead of him, just empty space. Space and time to secure the lap record, the course record and his second World Championship. The prize money alone meant he would never have to race again, not that that idea motivated him. It was the joy he was after. The sheer hell of it.

He took each corner as fast as he dared, and he was a daring chap. Half the lap still to go. The car beneath him purred like a walrus on ketamin having an afternoon nap. It was red, shiny and really, really fast[1]. The twin turbo

---

[1] So not like a walrus at all except the noise thing.

whined as he punched the throttle on the last of the long straights. If he had been paying attention, he would have seen the needle on the speedometer tip into a section that was quite a long way past where anyone would consider sane.

In the wing mirror, a flash of colour stood out where there should have been none. A rival rounded the bend on to the same straight. A brilliant blue blaze of competition glinted in the glorious sunshine. The challenger's thundering engine giving everything to catch the man in front. A competitor, desperate to claim victory for himself.

He was too far behind though, and the driver of the red car[2] knew it. The leader was consumed with the records. He had the skills, the talent and the dashing good looks to break them all. It would be a crowning achievement for a man with an already glittering career. It would bring fame on a previously unprecedented level. Girls the like of which he had previously only dreamed about. Riches that would surpass his wildest dreams. It might even impress his wife.

The straight ended and four more corners remained. The first, a gently banked right-handed lollop. The long nose of the car easily steered round it, taking a racing line that made the race commentator weep with joy at its perfection. The line was so good that it went on to win several awards in some admittedly niche magazines.

No smile emerged on the driver's face. That corner was a distant memory to him. Estranged, like a great aunt that he didn't visit when she lived close by who then moved overseas. The next corner was consuming all his focus. A tight hairpin left. If it had been a boat race, this particular feature would have almost been an oxbow lake[3]. Brakes were pumped in the lightest possible manner. Leather gloves gripped the steering wheel and hoisted it through the required motion. The car followed, the spectators cheered and the accelerator pedal trodden upon with vehemence. Any insects in the

---

[2] The one previously, and erroneously, compared to a walrus.

[3] Finally some use for all those years of Geography in schools!

nearby vicinity would have winced could they have seen such an action. The engine fired and bellowed out a mighty tune called 'Acceleration in G'.

The hair pin left took the race leader into a fairly inexplicable wooded section of the course. Difficult for the spectators to see, the wood was quite dense and houses the most famous corner of the track. In previous years, spectators were allowed to line the track through the wood however it was generally considered bad practice these days as they were:

    a)   unable to see the rest of race
    b)   quite likely to get killed in the event of a crash[4]

At the end of the woods was the final straight and then the finish line. Surrounded by stands on the left and the pits on the right, it wa the place where the more wealthy members of the crowd were sat, waiting with baited breath. Silence swept the seats as all eyes turned to the exit of the wood. Breath, previously baited, was now held. Each spectator heard the beat of their own heart as blood pumped around their expectant bodies. Most of them were veterans of the course and knew how long it should take for a tuned racing machine to fly through the wooded section. Two corners were all that stood between them and their new champion.

The man whose job it was to wave the chequered flag stubbed out the dog end of a cigarette he was smoking (inadvisably close to the pits) and picked up said flag. The soon to be champion gripped the wheel tightly. Two crucial corners remain and both must be taken at dangerous speed should he wish to succeed. But confidence flowed through him; there was no reason to panic. He had raced this track many times - it was his home race. The track was barely a stone's throw from the mansion he grew up in. A big throw admittedly, the sort that would require one of those large chaps from the Olympics, a small stone and a lot of imagination, but you get the idea. He was comfortable.

---

[4] This had been widely disputed until it happened 4 years ago. A previous world champion took the 2nd corner in the wood too fast, span out of control and careened into a stately oak tree, two sycamores and quite a lot of spectators.

And rightly so - the racer took the first corner perfectly. A juddering right-hander that nearly threw the car on to two wheels. The tyres fought furiously for grip and won with aplomb; no fanfare for them yet though, as the second corner beckons.

A small straight first, trees whipping past either side, then a long, sweeping left-hander opened up in front of the steely gray eyes of the soon-to-be champion. He almost allowed his mind to wander to the possibility of after the race. Champagne, photos, one of those big wreathes and a ridiculously oversized trophy. Probably something extravagant in the shape of a swan or female angels with big jugs[5].

He turned in to the bend, a smile emerging on his face. His scarf billowed in the wind behind him and the engine roared one last time as he pushed down on the accelerator pedal...

***

That mighty mechanical roar was heard by all in the stands. Men and women stared, fixated, on the exit of the wood.

Then noises that none expected. A screech. A crunch. A pause. An explosion.

Silence remained in the stands as the onlookers knew not how to react. As if to signal to the gathered mass that their fears were correct, smoke appeared from the tops of the trees. As one, a collective scream from the crowd's more hysterical members broke out. The pit crews sprung in to action and sprinted toward the wood carrying fire extinguishers and anything else they happened to have in their hands at the time. The crew of the standby fire engine[6] dropped their cups of tea and leapt into position before realising that they had left their keys in one of their many pockets. After the key finding farce ended, the siren blared to life and they raced the wrong way up the

---

[5] Amphorae being the technical term.

[6] Health and safety may have been lax but not non-existent.

track back toward the noise, which was unfortunate as the blue rival shot out of the wood exit at the same time, clipped the oncoming fire engine and careened into a barrier. Chaos ensued as the race was brought to a halt and those with the wits and knowhow leapt to the rescue.

One thing was firm in the minds of all: Kirby Grindalythe had crashed.

Chapter 2

KIRBY GRINDALYTHE DIES IN CHAPTER 1 CLASSIC

Read the headline of the newspaper. Sitting reading that paper in Anearby Cafe, Detective Inspector Much Wenlock was not surprised. The Classic, sponsored by the world's largest publishing agent 'Chapter 1', was a famously dangerous race and it wasn't the first time a driver had been killed taking on the challenge. It was early Monday morning and the cafe was practically empty. The creamy, off-white, linoleum clad table tops still gleamed from their early morning clean. Wenlock liked to stop in on his way to the police station as it gave him some peace and quiet to read the paper and drink a cup of the cafe's famously disgusting tea. Also, the tabletops weren't cleaned again that day, so if you stopped in later you were likely to get soggy sleeves.

Wenlock read on. It seemed Grindalythe's red Panther[7] had lost its grip going around the final bend, careering into the same trees as the former world champion Hutton Cranswick had four years earlier. It was fortunate they had stopped spectators going in the wood, thought Wenlock. The article suggested that most believed it to be a racing accident though there were some calling foul play, largely due to the disbelief that Grindalythe would crash on his home course with the title essentially in the bag. To further stoke suspicion, Grindalythe's great rival Upton Scudamore was said to have passed the wreckage without stopping and gunned on toward the finish line.

Wenlock cast his mind back four years, he was fairly certain that Scudamore had been in a similar position when Cranswick crashed....

---

[7] Name of the car, not another inaccurate animal simile

Wenlock dismissed the thought. He was an old and suspicious-minded police officer. Of course it was a coincidence. They were reckless men, driving as fast as they could in machines travelling at speeds that would turn a normal human into a gibbering wreck. Besides, Wenlock never cared much for those rakish playboys. He turned to the sports pages and saw with satisfaction that his preferred football team had lost, the horse he had bet on had gone lame, and that his stocks had nose dived.

He finished and then paid for his cup of what could only have been called tea if you squinted at it. It was going to be a normal Monday.

**

Wenlock drove his beaten up Pratchett Muskrat back to the station. He ambled his way through the front door and nodded to the Desk Sergeant sat behind the duty desk. Bright, alert and ready to take the queries of the public were all things the sergeant was not - she barely looked up from her newspaper to acknowledge Wenlock's presence.

"Did you hear about Grindalythe?" she eventually ventured. A bit too late for Wenlock to give much of a response as he was partially down the corridor, but not late enough that he could safely ignore it. He tracked back down the corridor leaned over her desk and replied.

"Good morning to you too Sergeant. I did, yes."

"Reckon it was a murder?" The Sergeant looked up. She was chewing gum. Wenlock was not impressed.

"I do not," was his curt response. The Desk Sergeant nodded with raised eyebrows and returned to a clearly engrossing 2-page biopic of a missing engineer featuring in her paper. Wenlock headed back off down the corridor to his office. Unfortunately for him, between the front door and his office was the office of his superior. That door was open.

As soon as Wenlock passed said open door, a voice called out.

7

"Ah, Wenlock, good of you to join us. In here please and close the door afterwards."

As Wenlock made to enter the room, he heard the voice of the Sergeant float down the corridor.

"Oh yeah, the DCI wants to see you..."

Wenlock scowled and entered. As instructed, he closed the door behind him, enclosing himself and the DCI in the drab office. The walls were painted a light blue that had long since yellowed and the window behind the DCI didn't really let much light in. In terms of size, you could swing a small cat assuming you tucked your elbows in and you didn't mind braining the animal on an inconveniently placed chimney breast. Wenlock was quite envious; it was the second best office in the building after the Chief of Police's.

"Good morning, sir," Wenlock cheerfully greeted the DCI. The DCI grunted in reply. He too was reading the paper.

"Have you seen the paper?" the DCI enquired. Wenlock nodded to indicate he had. The DCI didn't look up from the paper, didn't see the nod and an awkward silence ensued. Eventually, the DCI repeated his question and Wenlock made a more vocal affirmative.

" I see your team got trounced and the horse you bet on went lame."

"My stocks went down too, sir."

"Sounds like a Monday, eh Wenlock!" the DCI summarised in a jocular fashion before finally putting down the broadsheet and lighting his pipe. He wasn't very good at this and it took a few attempts. Eventually he got it lit and an acrid smell filled the office. Wenlock detested the DCI's pipe and the smell of it so got out a rather foul smelling cigar and lit that himself.

"Was there a reason you wanted to see me, sir?" Wenlock managed once all the smoking paraphernalia had been lit.

"Yes, Wenlock, yes indeed. Have you seen the news about the Chapter 1 Classic? It was on the front page so I doubt you could have missed it. Seems Kirby Grindalythe has been killed!" The DCI said this as if it were a revelation. This confused Wenlock greatly as the previous section of the conversation had firmly established that DI Wenlock had indeed read today's paper.

"Yes, sir, it does seem so," said Wenlock, intrigued to see where the DCI was going with this one.

"Hmm indeed," proclaimed the DCI between puffs on his odious pipe. "A death, and on our patch no less! The Chapter 1takes place just down the road and those fellows down at Chapter 1 publishers (who sponsor the race) are a tad nervous."

"They are sir?" Wenlock, surprised at the idea that the sponsors of a famously dangerous motor race were squeamish about a driver death and that the DCI had managed to fit parenthesis into his speech.

"They are! Even though the race is famously dangerous, they are worried that a death in the race would tarnish their image. A murder even more so!"

That statement surprised Wenlock.

"Murder, sir? Who is suggesting that? Surely it is just an accident in a famously dangerous motor race?"

"Perhaps," said the DCI, "perhaps not. There are many who point out that this is surprisingly like Hutton Cranswick's fatal crash four years ago. With Scudamore close by to both deaths, no less. Makes it seem suspicious. Especially to the press."

"The press sir?" Wenlock queried with a derisive tone. As a long serving officer of the force, Wenlock was no fan of press.

"Yes, Wenlock. It's a slang collective term for the newspapers, the papers, the news media, journalism, the newspaper world, the newspaper business, the print media, the fourth estate; journalists, newspapermen, newsmen, newspaper women, reporters, columnists, commentariat, pressmen, presswomen; in the informal: journos, hacks, hackettes, newshounds, newsies; more dated: publicists; Fleet Street. Used, for example, in statements such as 'rumours began to appear in the press'." The DCI rose an eyebrow and puffed his pipe while Wenlock composed an answer that didn't involve ramming said pipe down the DCI's throat.

"Yes, sir, I meant it in a slightly derisive manner. I meant it to ask 'why are we taking any notice of the press?', sir." Wenlock eventually managed.

"Ah, well there is a lot of them," the DCI replied. He paused before continuing. "And a lot of people do seem to take notice of what they say." Wenlock went to interject but the DCI continued.

"And Kirby Grindalythe was a celebrity. People like it when we investigate celebrity deaths. Keeps us in the news!"

Wenlock thought about which point to protest. As the police, they tended to be in the news quite a lot. Usually followed by words like "incompetence" or 'blunder' or 'evidence tampering'. However, he could see which way the wind was blowing and decided to play it another way. Years of experience in office politics kicked in to action.

"I see, sir. Well, with the death of a celebrity, seems more like it should be given to the Major Crimes Department than the Murder squad to me," Wenlock ventured with an innocent tone.

"Aren't you in Major Crimes, Wenlock?" the DCI enquired, one eyebrow raised.

"No, sir," Wenlock replied with a barely concealed smile. The DCI appeared to give this some thought. Between his pipe and Wenlock's cigar, the office was filled thick with smoke. So thick with smoke that the fire alarm went off and they were forced outside.

***

Eventually, once the smoke cleared and everyone was allowed back in, the conversation resumed in the DCI's office.

"I had a chat with the Desk Sergeant whilst we were outside," Continued the DCI, "She pointed out that until we know it is definitely a murder, it's not a major crime... "

Wenlock sighed inwardly, which is hard to do. He realised he had come up against an intellect far too formidable to penetrate with logic. With great grace, he admitted defeat.

"Yes, sir. Very astute, sir."

"So this one is yours, Wenlock. Don't muck it up."

By reply, Wenlock nodded in resignation.

"Keep an eye out for any missing persons as well while you're at it. There's a bit of a backlog." The DCI was already back to reading his paper. "There's a good chap."

Chapter 3

It was Pandemonium at the race track. Even the death of a famous celebrity couldn't stop the weird anoraks who venerated the classic Rand Panda attending their yearly car festival. Wenlock had to park his Muskrat in one of the overflow car parks[8].

He took the shuttle bus with several Panda enthusiasts, who all informed him that his Muskrat was inferior to the Panda and then discussed amongst themselves the extensive list of repairs they had performed to make their cars road legal that year.

Eventually, he got to the entrance of the race track and the story could continue.

"Are you here for Pandemonium or for yesterday's horrific murder?" asked a fluorescent-jacketed teen staffing the main gate.

"I don't think anyone has announced that it's a murder yet," Wenlock replied.

"Ohhh, but the police are investigating!" said the teen with great excitement.

"Just because the police are investigating doesn't mean it is a murder!" Wenlock was getting slightly narked with all the supposition going on.

"Doesn't mean it's not a murder!" the teen shot back, a bit narked that their juicy bit of information seemed to have been roundly kiboshed.

At this moment, a young lady appeared and butted in on the argument.

---

[8] Specifically in Section K. He wrote it on the back of his hand to help him remember. In a detail that won't be discussed in this chapter, that note washes off. It takes him a very long time to get his car back and makes him late for the events of the next chapter.

"It doesn't mean it's not not a murder," she interjected with a raised eyebrow and wry smile. "You must be with the police."

"No, I work here. That's why it says the name of the race track on my fluorescent jacket."

The lady ignored the teen and offered an outstretched hand to Wenlock.

"I'm Ashby, Ashby-de-la-Zouch. Reporter for the *Everyday Post*."

"DI Wenlock," said DI Wenlock. "How did you know I'm with the police?"

"A hunch," said Ashby enigmatically.

"You're wearing a badge," the teen helpfully pointed out.

***

Ashby walked Wenlock through the race course entrance, through the concourse and down to the track. Pandemonium was a purely static display of rusted death traps, polished to look as if they could run, so there was limited danger of being hit as they walked to the scene of the accident. This was unless someone left their handbrake off or one were to fail, scenarios both possible and plausible.

"So, DI Wenlock, which department are you from?" Ashby started her investigation as they walked the route of the course.

"Murder," replied Wenlock apprehensively, knowing that giving too much away to a newshound was never a wise move.

"So it is a murder!" Ashby exclaimed with glee.

"Not necessarily," Wenlock hurriedly interjected. "I'm here to determine that."

"I see," Ashby said in a disappointed tone. Wenlock could see though that she was already mentally writing the headlines. She felt had a scoop on her hands. Wenlock decided to change the subject.

"Do you own a cat?"

Ashby looked at him like his nose had fallen off.

"Never mind," Wenlock said, realising he needed to change the topic back to the matter at hand in order to drive the story forward.

Their conversation so far had taken them along the track to the exit of the wood that everyone had expected Kirby to blast out of the day before on his route to victory. Now there were several large pieces of tape across the track with words on. The words said "CRIME SCENE". A scrum of photographers and other members of the commentariat buzzed around trying to get a look at the scene of the crash.

Wenlock flashed his badge and a uniformed officer lifted the tape to allow him through. Ashby tried to follow.

"Not so fast, ma'am," said the uniformed officer. Ashby tried again, but slower.

"You can't come through, Miss de-la-Zouch," Wenlock said firmly. "We need to do some serious police work and we can't have reporters coming in and disturbing the scene."

"I actually thought I fitted this scene perfectly," Ashby replied, but she had been to enough crime scenes before[9] to know where the boundary was. "I'll see you around DI Wenlock."

Wenlock waved to her retreating figure (unnecessarily as her back was turned) then turned to survey the wreckage of Grindalythe's Fforde Panther.

It was a write-off. Wenlock didn't have much mechanical or underwriting knowledge but he could tell it would not be repairable based on the way the car was wrapped around a rather handsome oak tree. Bits of the Panther lay strewn about the tarmac in amongst the skid marks and tyre tracks from the race. Members of the police forensic unit were studiously avoiding doing

---

[9] As a reporter. Not as a criminal or victim.

their job of photographing and bagging evidence by having a smoke and flirting with one of the local TV presenters.

Wenlock collared a uniformed officer who seemed to be putting a piece of wreckage in his pocket.

"What do we know so far?" He asked.

"Well, sir," said the officer, "I don't know you that well but I assume we both have basic knowledge bestowed on us by attending school and achieving the education required to get a job with police..."

"About the crime," Wenlock cut the officer off before he detailed the full law enforcement training experience.

"Ah, sorry, sir," said the officer, slightly sheepishly. "The crash happened on the final lap of the race. Grindalythe was going for the title as well as the race and lap record times. He was leading his closest rival in the championship, Upton Scudamore. If Scudamore had managed to overtake him, it would have been he who was crowned as champ, but Grindalythe was well ahead."

Wenlock nodded to motion the officer to continue his summary while he surveyed the scene in front of him.

"Grindalythe entered the woods in front in the Panther but something must have gone wrong with his car."

"What makes you think that?" queried Wenlock.

"Well, it's wrapped around that oak tree now."

Wenlock saw that he had not picked the greatest deductive mind with which to spar wits and so excused himself from the conversation.

"A good summary of the final moments of the Chapter 1. Thank you, officer." The officer nodded and went back to hunting for souvenirs.

Wenlock walked over to the ruined car and gave it a good eyeballing. It had been red at one point but it was difficult to tell now in its advanced state of disrepair. The car had clearly been on fire and then put out[10]. A skid mark led from the entrance of the corner, across the tarmac and then through the grass to the Panther's final resting place.

"It must have been one hell of a fire to torch the car that badly." Another uniformed officer had turned up at Wenlock's shoulder.

Wenlock nodded his agreement. The twisted, mangled wreckage was black and charred. The oak round which it had been wrapped bore scorch marks reaching as far up as the eye could manage through the gloom of the thick canopy.

"Must have a had quite a lot of fuel onboard to have such a big fire," the officer continued. "What doesn't make sense to me is why he would have so much fuel onboard for the final corner of the final lap."

It was an astute point, thought Wenlock. Even in his limited knowledge of motor racing, he knew that no driver would want to carry the extra weight. The cars usually had onboard only the exact amount of fuel needed to get round the course. Wenlock turned round to see who had made such an astute observation. The uniformed officer looked surprisingly like Miss de-la-Zouch. In fact, it was, she was just wearing a police uniform.

"You're not supposed to be here!" exclaimed Wenlock. Now that he looked at her uniform it wasn't even a convincing one. The skirt was ridiculously short and the truncheon hanging from her belt was clearly plastic. Also, no police uniform would allow such a plunging neckline.

"I'm not, but you need help with this one, DI Wenlock. This is going to be a career case and you know almost nothing about motor racing. I was covering this race when the crash happened and I'm a sports reporter for the *Everyday Post* - I know this industry inside out," Ashby exhorted

---

[10] Wenlock could tell it had been put out because it was no longer on fire.

passionately. It would have been a more convincing case had her fake badge not chosen that moment to fall off.

However, Wenlock could not disagree with her. As has been previously described, his knowledge of motor racing was scant. Almost as scant as the skirt that Ashby had on, which he was finding distracting. He decided to administer a test to see if her knowledge was as good as she claimed.

"Prove it," he said, "What's that?"Wenlock asked, pointing at an obscure piece of twisted metal left over from the crash.

"That's an obscure piece of twisted metal," Ashby replied with a knowing smile. She was annoyingly right, as far as Wenlock could tell. He decided to try another line of questioning.

"What's in it for you?"

"A scoop of course!" Ashby replied with a coy smile.

Wenlock heaved a sigh of relief. He had been worried she was going to say money.

"Fine, you can help. First though, you need to get out of that ridiculous get up."

Chapter 4

"Sorry I'm late," said Wenlock, "I couldn't find my car." Ashby was at a table for two and surrounded by empty coffee cups. She and Wenlock had agreed to meet at Anearby Cafe after their deal had been struck. Wenlock took the seat opposite her, removed his coat and draped it across the back of his yellow plastic chair. He lamented the lack of choice when it came to non-alcholic drinking establishments in town as it was past noon and thus the tables were already filthy with the stains of the morning. They sat near the window , the net curtains twitched playfully in the breeze from the open door and the serving staff dutifully ignored all comers.

"No problem," Ashby replied cheerfully, but very quickly. "I think it's time I fill you in on the racing scene inspector. The main players, where they are now and their former position."

"Ex-position,"[11] said Wenlock.

Ashby dove in to her specialist subject with caffeinated glee. "I'll start with Grindalythe. A racing ace and rakish playboy, on course for his second world championship. He was well liked amongst the race going crowds and the media for his pithy quotes, salacious habits and undeniable racing talent."

"Did he have any enemies?" Wenlock asked, ever the alert investigator.

"He had a rival," Ashby answered. "Upton Scudamore. He was Kirby's closest competition and if he had won the Chapter 1 on Sunday he would

---

[11] Rather had to lever that pun in there. If you're a fan of the recent trend in fiction of 'Sexposition', the practise of characters providing exposition against a backdrop of sex or nudity, you can imagine some people having sex during this conversation. Just imagine they are doing it somewhere else as it would violate food safety regulations and this is a respectable establishment.

have claimed the title for his own. It would have been Scudamore's second world championship as well. Kirby and Upton exploded on to the racing scene two years before Hutton Cranswick's death."

Wenlock noted Ashby's poor choice of words but decided to let it slide. He remembered from his sporadic monitoring of the sports pages that Cranswick was the previous world champion, who had crashed on the same stretch of track as Grindalythe.

"How was the relationship between Grindalythe and Scudamore?"

"Difficult," replied Ashby, still exposing at breakneck pace. "They really didn't like each other much. Not surprising given the ferocity of the competition between them. Scudamore blames Kirby for a crash earlier in the season that led to Scudamore retiring from the race, allowing Kirby to get ahead in the championship points. Exactly the number of points that he led Scudamore by at the start of the Chapter 1 Classic."

Interesting, thought Wenlock. Motive for Scudamore... but enough to kill for?

Wenlock pondered this whilst ordering a cup of tea from a haughty waitress who pretended not recognise him, despite his frequent visits. For his trouble, he received a sample from the local pond in a charming, blue, plastic teacup.

Unperturbed by his frankly disgusting beverage, he decided to explore further into the glamorous, but murky, world of motor racing.

"Is there anybody else that didn't like Grindalythe?"

"His ex-wife: Ingleby Greenhow." Ashby replied. "She had been romantically linked both to Kirby and to the ex-world champion Hutton Cranswick."

"Interesting," said Wenlock. "How so?"

"Romantically linked to Cranswick by salacious rumour and romantically linked to Grindalythe by being married to him."

19

"I think I had worked out the last bit myself. When did Grindalythe and Greenhow get together, before or after Cranswick's crash?"

"It was never made official but I reported in the *Everyday Post* that Grindalythe seduced her whilst Cranswick, who was with her *and* engaged to someone else, was recovering in hospital following a minor crash occurring the season before his big crash."

"Do you believe that?" Wenlock employed his policeman's nose for truth.

"Not really," replied Ashby in a flippant manner. "We print all sorts of shit in *The Post*. They probably just hooked up after Cranswick met his fiery doom. It's quite hard to keep track of these racing drivers' love lives."

Wenlock sat back a moment, deep in thought, before framing his next question. This was a lot to digest.

"What caused Grindalythe's marriage to Greenhow to break down? If she is known as Greenhow, I take it she has resumed using her maiden name."

"Kirby Grindalthye was a prolific shagger," Ashby's eyebrows waggled suggestively. "He really did get about. Before an afternoon race two years ago he uttered his most famous quote - you must know it!"

Wenlock indicated he did not and so Ashby told him.

"They asked him what makes you so quick on the track and his answer was: 'Dogging is the elevenses of winners'."

Wenlock laughed involuntarily. He remembered now - it had been all over the papers. Even the better ones.

"He got in so much trouble for it," Ashby giggled girlishly. "I just wish it had been me interviewing him that day!"

When Wenlock had composed himself again, he continued his masterful interrogation.

"Are you sure the carnal relations he was referring to weren't taking place with his wife?"

"Alas for Ingleby, she was not in the country at the time so certainly not. The rumours around the circuit were that he had shacked up with a reporter." Ashby looked vague and evasive as she delivered the last comment. She drank a bit more of her coffee as if to avoid eye contact. Wenlock, ever the investigator, noted the potential golden nugget of information for later questioning.

"It's said," Ashby added mischievously, "that if you were to lay everyone of Kirby's conquests end to end they would fill a race track!"

Wenlock managed to stop himself before he spat his 'tea' over the Formica tabletop.

"Probably a few jilted husbands who also might make the enemies list then" Wenlock commented once he had controlled his unplanned tea-filled expectoration.

"I'd bet!" Ashby replied with enthusiasm. The list of suspects grows, thought Wenlock.

"Anything else I should know?" Wenlock casually pulled the classic question from his prolific book of investigative tricks.

"Again, no official story..." Ashby leaned in close to deliver the next poorly researched claim. Wenlock leaned in to keep in the spirit of things. "Grindalythe didn't remarry so it's said that in the event of his death it would be Ingleby to whom his fortune goes!"

Wenlock went to lean back in his seat but Ashby motioned him to move in closer.

"There's more. It's also rumoured that Ingleby's current fortune is directly as a result of Cranswick's fortune passing to her after *his* death!"

They both leaned back in their seats. This was certainly a piece of news worth thinking on. It looked like Kirby's death stood to profit Ms Greenhow considerably. In addition, though it seemed strange to Wenlock that a man would kill another man just to win a race, it wasn't beyond the realms of possibility that Scudamore was in the frame.

"There is one more angle to explore," Ashby continued her display of in-depth knowledge of the potential suspect list. "Gambling."

"Gambling?" Wenlock queried.

"Yes, 'gambling'," Ashby replied. "The wagering of money or something of value (referred to as 'the stakes') on an event with an uncertain outcome with the primary intent of winning money or material goods."

"I am aware of the definition of gambling," Wenlock sighed, he was getting tired of this happening[12]. "I meant: what is the connection between the death of Kirby Grindalythe and gambling?"

"A lot of money is gambled on these races, and the championship race particularly. If horse racing is the sport of kings, motor racing is the sport of... really, really rich kings... who like to gamble." Ashby smiled as she recovered the sentence. Wenlock could tell she was beginning to crash from her extreme caffeine intake. However, she ploughed on gamely. "Kirby was the hot favourite to win the race and the season. Someone could've made a lot of money by betting against that happening."

"And do anything to protect their investment," Wenlock completed the thought. Suddenly, a smile broke out across his weary policeman's face.

"I'd not seen you smile until now, Detective Inspector. What's happened?" Ashby finally got to ask a question of her own.

---

[12] Unfortunately for Wenlock and possibly for you dear reader, I am not so expect it to continue!

"Well," began the master sleuth, "up to now, I thought this was going to be a ridiculous assignment for a murder investigator like myself. It had sounded like a clear cut case of an unlucky crash in a dangerous race. However, now we have high stakes, motives, romantic sub plots and, between the betting and the jilted husbands, a long list of potential suspects!"

Wenlock paused to take a last swig of his dreadful beverage."Do you know what having a long list of suspects to investigate means Miss de-la-Zouch?" Wenlock asked rhetorically. Ashby shook her head in response.

Wenlock's grin became so wide it threatened to touch his ears.

"Overtime."

Chapter 5

Before interviewing any suspects, Wenlock knew there was a crucial step to take, writ large in all detective books: the trip to the morgue. The morgue was located in the local hospital and Wenlock decided to go there right after meeting with Ashby at the cafe[13]. As she had given him some vital information on the key figures in the racing world, Wenlock felt it was only fair to bring her along to see the body. He also didn't really like having to explain things to others, so it was better that she heard all the gory details first hand.

He and Ashby notified hospital reception of their quest then went down a long staircase leading to the morgue in the basement. A cold and sterile environment greeted them, replete with shiny metal cabinets and bright lighting. Fortunately for them both, the deceased inhabitants of the room were covered on their tables by tastefully placed sheets.

Wenlock hated coming here and mentioned it to Ashby while they waited for the pathologist.

"That's only fair," she said. "It is a place of death. Even animals abhor being near their dead; it's probably the origins of the religious services that lead to our ancestors burning or burying rather than leaving a corpse to rot."

"Yes, that," Wenlock ruminated on this wisdom before adding his own. "Also, the pathologist is an utter prick."

On cue, said pathologist emerged from a side office. He adjusted his glasses and gave a large smile.

---

[13] The tea at the hospital was really, really bloody awful. At least the tea from the cafe didn't taste like it had been through someone else first.

"Hello, DI Wenlock, how wonderful to see you!" The pathologist smarmed."And you've brought me a visitor, a live visitor! How marvelous!" He waggled his eyebrows in a manner meant to look mischievous but came across as pneumatic.

Neither Wenlock nor Ashby offered a response so the bespectacled corpse-botherer bounded across the cold, metallic room and offered his hand to Ashby.

"I wouldn't touch that," said Wenlock. "I don't think he's washed it."

The pathologist gave a pained expression.

"Oh, inspector, please can we be civil?"

Wenlock grudgingly agreed. He motioned toward the pathologist.

"Ashby de-la-Zouch, this is Salcombe Regis - pathologist. Salcombe Regis, this is Ashby de-la-Zouch - a reporter helping me with a case."

Salcombe held out his hand again. Ashby politely declined to take it.

"I've had cold recently. I don't want to pass it on." Ashby lied.

"It's probably for the best," Regis said. "The inspector is correct, I haven't washed my hands!" He let out a throaty laugh that sounded practised rather than natural. As neither Wenlock nor Ashby joined him, he cleared his throat and there was a short awkward silence.

"We're here to see the corpse of Kirby Grindalythe." Wenlock cut to the chase.

"Ooh, my celebrity." Regis rubbed his hands and gave Ashby a conspiratorial wink. "Follow me!"

He lurched off to the other side of the room and motioned for the pair to follow him. Whilst his back was turned, Ashby turned to Wenlock and motioned putting two fingers in her mouth to induce vomiting. Wenlock had to stifle a laugh as they followed the pathologist.

Regis turned and stood over a metal table covered by a white sheet. With a flourish, Regis removed the sheet so Wenlock and Ashby could see what was presumably all there was left of Kirby Grindalythe.

"Is that all there is left of Kirby Grindalythe?" Wenlock asked Regis.

"Presumably," Regis answered.

Wenlock looked over to see if Ashby was affected by the sight. Ashby had her hand over her mouth but otherwise was taking it well. There wasn't much of Grindalythe at all. What was there wasn't even human shaped. It was just a jumble of charred meat parts and something that might have been a femur at one point. Wenlock supposed that helped. It was easier to separate the person he once was from the strange pile on the table.

"Does the, err, corpse tell us anything Regis?" Wenlock asked.

"Frankly, no," Regis responded. "I can tell you that it is almost certainly Kirby Grindalythe on account of the fact it was found in his car. We have sent off for a DNA test to make sure. He probably died on impact, given that he was pretty much obliterated. After which, his remains were barbequed by the fuel catching fire until they resembled this strange pile. The men who brought him in had to scrape him up with a shovel. Gruesome stuff!" Regis was clearly enjoying himself, but his description had got a little bit too much for Ashby. She stepped back from the table and turned away from the remains to be alone for a second.

"For God's sake, Regis!" Wenlock hissed at the pathologist. "Show some respect, the girl knew the deceased!"

"Oh, gosh." Regis put his hand to his mouth in a vaguely pantomime gesture. "I am sorry, Ms de-la-Zouch, I am so sorry," he called across to her.

She gave a weak wave then vomited in a bin.

"We'll probably just leave her to that actually," Wenlock said. He turned back to Regis. "Anything else?"

"Not really," Regis replied. "The burning is consistent with that of the fuel used in the car. The impact was obviously at extremely high speed, I take it you have been to the crash site yourself? There wasn't ever going to be much left of him."

"Is there anything else to identify him? Teeth for dental records?" Wenlock wanted to make sure this wasn't going to be some ridiculous fake, causing him to spend the rest of the case wondering whether Grindalythe was really dead or not.

"A few teeth were found and are being compared at the moment. I'll let you know what comes back from that and the DNA test as soon as I have the answers."

Wenlock and Regis took a second to contemplate the nature of the case whilst Ashby cleaned herself up at the sink.

"Shame, really," said Regis with a rueful smile."I was very much looking forward to cutting him open and looking at his liver - he was an infamous partier. Possibly why he went up in flames so well." Wenlock gave him a disgusted look but that didn't put Regis off. "If you ever find out where the skull is, can I have it please? I'd like to put it in the celebrity tray."

"You really are a massive prick," Wenlock replied.

***

Ashby and Wenlock left the hospital and got some 'fresh' air in the smoking shelter outside.

"Do you think it's really him?" Ashby asked. Wenlock thought he could detect a hint of hopefulness in her voice. "There wasn't much there to identify him by..."

"Hard to know from those remains," Wenlock replied "We'll know for sure when the DNA test comes back. Not overly sure about the teeth thing myself. Someone could always plant a few of his real teeth at the scene."

Ashby started to look upset again so Wenlock offered the only words of comfort he could think of.

"If it is him, then at least it was a quick and painless death. He wouldn't have felt a thing!"

Unsurprisingly, this didn't cheer her up.

Chapter 6

Given the overwhelming rumour and conjecture that would put her at the centre of any attempt on Kirby Grindalythe's life, Wenlock and Ashby decided that the first person worth questioning would be his ex-wife.

It turned out that Wenlock's ex-wife had surprisingly little information of importance so they turned their attention to Grindalythe's ex-wife: Ingleby Greenhow.

After some research[14], they discovered that Greenhow lived out of town in the large country pile that belonged to her family.

They decided to drive there together in Wenlock's Pratchett Muskrat as he could claim the petrol money back from the police. They engaged in light conversation to get to know each other a little better and to help establish their back stories to the reader.

"Have you remarried, DI Wenlock?" Ashby asked from the passenger seat.

"No," replied Wenlock, effectively closing down that avenue of conversation. An awkward silence passed and Much felt he had to fill it out of social courtesy.

"Do you own a dog?"

"No," replied Ashby, equally curtly.

***

Fortunately, Greenhow Manor was not far from the taxidermy shop and the excruciating lack of chemistry was brought to a halt as Wenlock drove them

---

[14] A quick check of the phone book and an amusing anecdote involving taxidermy that might make its way into a spin-off novel.

up the main stretch that led to the house. Wenlock noted it was a textbook example of a country manor, surrounded by open fields with an avenue of trees leading up to the main residence. The front of the house had a gravelled circular drive around a quite unspectacular fountain. The manor itself was in the neoclassical style and symmetric to look at from the front. Wenlock didn't get to see the back so couldn't describe it.

He parked the Muskrat next to the sweeping staircase that led to the front door. They got out of the car and Wenlock, after his earlier mistake, noted down where he had parked in his notebook. Stone lions on plinths flanked the foot of the stairs and eyed the pair suspiciously. To Wenlock, it looked like the lions were guarding their home and its residents from unwanted questions.

Wenlock and Ashby arrived at a towering pair of doors and knocked using the large brass knocker, a curious ornament shaped like a serpent eating a giraffe.

Time passed. Wenlock reached for the knocker to try again but as he did so the door creaked open a small amount and a tired old man in a dusty penguin suit stared back at them.

"Hello?" the aged man managed to croak at the duo.

"DI Wenlock, police. This is Ms de-la-Zouch, my associate. We've come to see Ms Greenhow."

"Oh," the old man said, clearly but inexplicably tinged with disappointment. "I suppose you better come in then."

Though having indicated that entry was on the cards, the old man stayed where he was in the doorway, barring the entrance from entry. More time passed.

"You need to move if you are going to let us in," Ashby added helpfully. Eventually, the old man seemed to get the message and opened the door wide enough to allow entry. He shuffled off in to the main hallway, Wenlock and Ashby followed.

The entrance hall was completely at odds with what they are expecting. No fusty old carpets or dead relative portraits, instead it was modernity personified. It was open, airy, light and white on every wall, save for the one opposite from which they had entered. That wall had been removed entirely and replaced by a huge glass window equipped with sliding doors leading to an extensive veranda, complete with outdoor swimming pool. See-through staircases made of a thick perspex flanked the walls led up to the first floor which, thanks presumably to more thick perspex, seemed entirely see through. The old man in his penguin suit looked completely at odds to the surroundings.

When Wenlock recovered himself, he called to their guide.

"Excuse me, sir, a few questions"

The man eventually turned round, although by this point he had shuffled halfway across the enormous room.

"Yes?" he slowly replied.

"Who are you? And why are you wearing a penguin suit?"

"I am the family butler. My name is Slaidburn. I am not wearing a 'penguin suit', I am wearing a tailcoat."

Wenlock and Ashby looked at each other. Both could see that he was clearly not wearing a tailcoat and was in fact wearing a fancy dress penguin costume. The look to each other was enough to confirm this and communicate the desire between them not to press this point. Ashby continued the line of questioning.

"Where can we find Ms Greenhow?"

"Follow me" the butler called and continued his long, slow waddle across the entrance hall.

"If you tell us the way, we can probably find her," Ashby suggested hopefully. At the rate they were going, she was justifiably worried that Slaidburn might pass away before they ever found the heiress.

"No need," came Slaidburn's slow reply.

***

After an unnecessarily long amount of time travelling through the manor[15], they came to a room on the first floor containing Ms Greenhow. Slaidburn opened the white double doors and announced their entrance.

"Some copper and a bird here to see you, ma'am."

Ms Greenhow was lounging in the middle of the room on a chaise lounge. She was dressed in loose fitting white robes from head to toe. Large black sunglasses hid her eyes from view. The chaise lounge was also white. Wenlock was beginning to wish he hadn't left his own sunglasses in the Muskrat's glove compartment.

"Oh do come in," Ms Greenhow waved them over with a white gloved hand. "Take a seat," she indicated to a small couch on her left. It was going to be a squeeze to fit both Wenlock and Ashby on to it. They managed after several polite apologies.

"You can go, Slaidburn," Ms Greenhow dismissed her butler. Slaidburn shuffled slowly out of the room, closing the doors behind him.

Wenlock took a moment to digest the appearance of his host. Ingleby Greenhow was young, slim, blonde and had the face of a film star. This didn't surprise Wenlock, given that she was the glamorous ex-wife of a championship winning racing driver. It didn't surprise Ashby as she had met her before.

---

[15] Caused by Slaidburn's decrepit shuffle. Wenlock also suspected that he had taken them the long way round.

"Now," Ms Greenhow beamed a radiant smile, "how can I help the police with their enquiries?"

Wenlock had many questions but started with the one that puzzled him most.

"Why is your butler wearing a fancy dress penguin costume?"

"Slaidburn?" Greenhow seemed surprised by this question. "He isn't wearing a penguin costume. He's wearing a tailcoat." Ashby and Wenlock shared a look. It had definitely been a penguin costume. It had a yellow beak. Wenlock decided to drop it.

"I'm DI Wenlock and this is my associate, Ms de-la-Zouch. "

Greenhow eyed Ashby up suspiciously.

"Have we met?" she asked.

Ashby hurriedly replied that they had not. A little too hurriedly and definitely a lie, Wenlock thought.

"Firstly, Ms Greenhow, we're sorry for your loss," Wenlock offered as a way to steer the conversation back to the investigation. Ms Greenhow tossed her hair back and ran a hand through her blonde locks.

"Please, call me Ingleby. Ah yes, Kirby. It seems that this was just one challenge too many for him. Whilst you will know we have not been close for some time, he was still my husband and I loved him dearly." She seemed to stare off in to the distance at this point, as if caught in a memory. Or at least acting like it.

"I am sorry to do this at such a time but, as I am investigating your husband's death, I need to ask you a few questions." Wenlock began the interrogation.

"It is of no surprise to me that you are here," Ingleby gave a winning smile, then she lowered her sunglasses and looked directly in to Wenlock's eyes "After all, he was murdered."

Her eyes were a blue of such intensity that Wenlock left the statement unchallenged and it was up to Ashby to continue the questioning.

"What makes you say that, Ms Greenhow?" Ashby had taken out a notebook and was scribbling furiously. Wenlock tried to sneak a peek at her notes but they were either in an impenetrable journalist's shorthand or merely illegible.

"It is clear, is it not? All the papers are saying it. Even the wretched *Everyday Post* seems to have picked up on it, and that rag prints nothing but tosh." She tossed a conspiratorial smile at Wenlock. Wenlock however was watching Ashby who gave no reaction at this slur to her employer.

"When did you last see your ex-husband?" Ashby continued the questioning.

"He is still my husband," Ingleby shot back. "We are estranged - not divorced; an important distinction." Wenlock noted this also, a different story to the one he had heard so far. Ingleby continued to answer the question.

"I last saw Kirby here at the manor - it must have been two weeks ago."

"What was he doing here?" Wenlock fired in to action. The old bloodhound sniffed a lead.

"He came to see me, said he wanted to talk about insurance." Wenlock could see Ashby scribbling even more furiously than before. "But the subject bores me, so I sent him away." The scribbling abated slightly.

"Did you talk about anything else during that visit?" Ashby asked.

"Oh, the usual rubbish, seeing how we both were. Saying we were both so happy with our lives now that the other wasn't involved. And racing of course." Ingleby appeared to be getting bored and started playing with her hair.

"Racing was pretty much all he was interested in. Racing and bonking of course." She threw back her head and, incongruously to her image, laughed like a camel snorting a ratchet.

Wenlock, after ridding his imagination of Ms Greenhow bonking, decided this was a good time to pursue the infidelity angle.

"You mention Grindalythe's voracious sexual appetite. It is indelicate of me to ask but I understand that was the reason for your separation from your husband?"

"Oh no, not at all." Ingleby gave another smile. "Complete nonsense, printed by second rate gossip rags."

"So you are saying he wasn't unfaithful?" Ashby asked. Wenlock could hear the incredulity in her voice. She clearly believed that Grindalythe had in fact been playing the field. Could it be possible that Greenhow had been unaware?

"No, he was quite spectacularly unfaithful. Really could not keep his hands to himself. An absolute addict." Ingleby lowered her sunglasses conspiratorially. "But that was not why we grew apart."

"Ms Greenhow, if the affairs weren't what caused your separation, what did?" Wenlock was struggling a bit now. He had dealt with many a murder involving a jilted ex-partner. But he had never seen it play out like this before.

"Detective, have you ever dated a professional athlete?" Ingleby asked. Wenlock indicated he had not. Ashby also nodded but in a slightly more sheepish manner that Wenlock suspected may be concealing a half truth.

"They are focussed individuals. Incredibly focussed. Their raison d'être is usually one thing and one thing only - their sport. The honest truth of the matter is that Kirby Grindalythe, when we weren't at it like rabbits, was an incredibly boring man to be married to." Wenlock wanted to interject with other questions but Ingleby was on a roll.

"All Kirby would talk about, was motor racing. We went to watch motor races, he competed in motor races, he trained for motor races and when he wasn't doing those things, he talked some more about motor racing."

"Or chased other women," interjected Ashby, indelicately.

"Indeed. That was him all over. I loved him dearly but you have to understand something." Ingleby leaned toward the duo and lowered her voice. They leaned in too, rapt by the heiress's confessions.

"I loathe motor racing. Detest it. Wasn't that interested before I married him and at no point did it grow on me. I thought I would start to care, but I just couldn't get in to it. Pointless sport. Cars endlessly circling the track round and round and round." Inglebly twirled her slender fingers to make the point. "Stupid, noisy and dangerous."

It seemed jealousy was not a motive that would have driven Ms Greenhow to remove her estranged husband from the picture. However, there was another angle for Wenlock to pursue...

"Ms Greenhow, what insurance did Mr Grindalythe come to speak with you about?"

"Life insurance," she replied. "He wanted to change the details of where his life insurance payout would go in the event of his death."

"Who is the current benefactor?" Ashby asked.

"Currently it's me, I guess he never bothered to change it as we hadn't formally divorced." Ingleby replied in a flat and uninterested manner. Wenlock and Ashby exchanged further knowing glances.

"And he wished to change that state of affairs?" prompted Wenlock.

"Yes, he said that it wasn't really appropriate that I would benefit from his death. He needed me to sign something so that he could change it to someone else."[16]

Even with Wenlock's limited knowledge of the racing world, he could guess that the life insurance payout of a potential world champion would be substantial. Whoever it was would benefit greatly from Grindalythe's untimely demise. While Wenlock's mind pondered this, Ashby leapt in to ask the next and most crucial question.

"Who did he want to change it to?"

"Cheddon Fitzpaine," Ingleby replied cooly.

"Cheddon Fitzpaine?" Asbhy replied with incredulity.

"Yes, Cheddon Fitzpaine - the famous politician and mayor. He's a very public figure. I'm surprised you haven't heard of him."

Wenlock bit his tongue to prevent a laugh, happy it wasn't him on the end of the weak running joke this time. Ashby was unperturbed and continued the interrogation.

"Did he say why he wanted to change the benefactor from you to Cheddon Fitzpaine? Is there a relationship between the two of them that isn't in the public knowledge?" Wenlock noticed that even Ashby, the expert racing reporter, with her unusually deep and sometimes unsettlingly intimate knowledge of Kirby Grindalythe's life, didn't seem aware of this connection.

"I didn't ask to be honest." Wenlock could see that Ingleby was losing interest in the conversation and was starting to stare at her nails instead. "As I said, the subject bores me. I signed the paper and dismissed him from the estate."

Ashby had been scribbling so furiously at this last statement that smoke started to rise from her notepad.

---

[16] I doubt if this is how life insurance actually works but it moves the plot forward.

"You weren't interested in preventing this change of benefactor?" Wenlock asked with some surprise.

"Oh gosh no. I'm minted darling. That pittance wouldn't even make a difference to me." Ingleby stated matter-of-factly. "Great-granddaddy invented soup, which left us rather a sum, and I'm the Chief Financial Officer of a multinational company specialising in mergers and aquisitions on the stock exchange. Also, as I haven't been funding Kirby's blasted motor racing team this year, I'm positively rolling in it."

Wenlock and Ashby struggled to conceal their surprised looks. Ashby even stopped scribbling, which was fortunate as she had been on the verge of setting fire to the couch they were sat on. If her answers were true, both of the likely motives Ingleby would have for wanting Grindalythe dead were gone and it effectively eliminated her as a suspect. Fortunately, she had given them a new lead to pursue. Wenlock decided he had heard enough. He was also struggling to process how Ingleby's great-grandfather invented soup.

"I think we have everything we came for, Ms Greenhow. Enjoy the rest of your day." Wenlock stated, his mind already on the next suspect to interview.

"Again, sorry for your loss." Ashby added to soften the exit. They made their way to the door.

"Would you like me to call Slaidburn to show you the way out?" Ingleby called after them. Both Wenlock and Ashby stated without hesitation they would not.

***

Back in Wenlock's Muskrat, the pair made a summary of their thoughts.

"That did not go as I expected," Ashby admitted.

"She didn't seem all that upset about the death," Wenlock ventured.

"That's true," Ashby agreed. "But where would the motive be? No claim on the money. Not jealous of his infidelity. I doubt she killed him because the marriage had been boring."

Wenlock nodded in agreement.

"At least we have a new lead," he said as he kicked the Muskrat into life. It's mighty two cylinder engine let out a tinny howl at the excitement of the journey ahead. "I think it's time to pay a visit to our esteemed mayor."

"Do you know where he'll be?" Ashby asked.

"I expect he'll be where all politicians are at 11 am on a Monday morning," Wenlock replied.

Chapter 7

Wenlock and Ashby sped to the golf course[17] as fast as the Muskrat could manage. They continued to fail to bond during the journey and mainly sat in awkward silence. Ashby learnt nothing new of interest about Wenlock and all Wenlock managed to establish was that Ashby didn't own a hamster.

They asked at the club shop where they could find Fitzpaine and were told that he was just about to tee off on 8th. They hopped back in the Muskrat and drove over.

Wenlock managed to park on the green of the 7th[18]. True to the word of the club shop attendant, Cheddon Fitzpaine and his party were getting ready to play some golf.

As Wenlock trudged across the grass, he started to recognise the figures Cheddon was playing with. A lot of them were influential local worthies or mildly famous celebrities. All of them looked like idiots because they were wearing golf clothes.

"Mr Fitzpaine," Wenlock shouted louder than necessary, causing the player currently teeing off to wildly miss-hit his shot. "Do you have time to talk to the police?"

"Of course," Cheddon Fitzpaine separated himself from the group and walked over. He had a wide smile fixed on his face and if he was annoyed at the intrusion he made no sign of it. "Anything for our local constabulary. I expect you want to ask some questions about the upcoming budget cuts that will likely affect both your wage and pension?"

---

[17] If you are a politician and take umbrage at this joke, you can imagine it's a Bank Holiday Monday.

[18] He thought the flag would be helpful aid to remind him where he had parked.

Wenlock was about to reply that yes, he would like to know about that as it was news to him. Fortunately for the sake of the plot, Ashby elbowed him in the ribs first.

"Actually, Mr Fitzpaine, this is about the death of Kirby Grindalythe." She got in before Wenlock recovered his breath.

The smile dropped immediately from Fitzpaine's face.

"I see," he replied. "Perhaps we should take a short walk away from my playing companions to discuss this." He motioned to some trees on the side of the course and strode over to them with purpose. Wenlock and Ashby followed, otherwise they would have to shout the rest of the conversation.

"A terrible, terrible thing. So young and so talented. Very tragic," Fitzpaine continued. "Having said this, I am surprised though that you wish to talk to me about it. As far as I can tell, there isn't much of a connection between myself and a world championship winning racing driver." The smile returned to the politician's face.

"Mr Fitzpaine, we have just had an interesting conversation with Ms Greenhow who says otherwise." Wenlock had recovered his breath sufficiently to join the conversation. "She told us that Mr Grindalythe had recently changed the beneficiary of his life insurance."

Fitzpaine didn't reply. The smile didn't drop. He gave a small nod, urging Wenlock on. Ashby took up the story.

"She claimed that he changed the beneficiary to be you."

"I see." The smile dropped again. "Ms Greenhow, the estranged wife of the late Mr Grindalythe?"

Ashby and Wenlock nodded in unison.

"The late Mr Grindalythe, famous for sating his voracious sexual appetite outside of his marriage with an uncountable bevy of beautiful young ladies?"

41

More nodding.

"And the Ms Greenhow who was rumoured to be in an illicit relationship with a previous world champion racing driver, who died in the same place in the same manner?"

The nodding continued. Both Wenlock and Ashby realised they had not touched on this in their interview with Greenhow.

"Ms Greenhow, still married to Mr Grindalythe and yet refusing to fund his latest championship bid?"

The nodding continued, although with some trepidation as it was seeming likely that Fitzpaine was reaching his point.

"Did it ever occur to you she was lying?" Fitzpaine finished. The smile returned.

Wenlock shook his head slowly, still a bit dazed from the earlier rib shot from his companion. Ashby, who was feeling better than Wenlock on account of not having been elbowed in the ribs, managed a more sensible retort.

"Of course. However, she also mentioned some paperwork. Paperwork that I'm sure if we were to request from the insurance company they would be able to provide showing the change of beneficiary."

Fitzpaine's smile dropped once again. This time only a small amount. The effect was unpleasant, now it was more of a grimace.

"Whilst I believe that DI Wenlock here could request and receive that paperwork, you, Miss de-la-Zouch, could not," Fitzpaine hissed through the gritted teeth. "Do not look so surprised, I am aware of who you both are. Also, if you are wondering, yes it was rude of you not to introduce yourselves earlier."

Wenlock did not like where this was going.

"And yes, we have met Ms de-la-Zouch. I believe you have interviewed me whilst I watched the Chapter 1 Classic no less than six times."

Ashby muttered something about not expecting him to remember but Fitzpaine was not in the mood to listen and continued on.

"And as for you, DI Wenlock, we have been introduced after you closed several Major Crimes cases two years ago."

"They were murders, not major crimes," muttered Wenlock.

"Murder is a major crime, Detective." Fitzpaine's more amiable smile returned. "Now, I am enjoying a round of golf with some important people at the moment. One of whom you may recognise as the chief of police and another is a senior editor of the *Everyday Post*."

Wenlock and Ashby dutifully looked over to the group and confirmed that Fitzpaine was correct. The police chief even gave a wave which, in less pressured circumstances Wenlock would have found a pleasant surprise. Fitzpaine continued his lecture.

 "I think that you will find that this insurance business is not a factor in the death of Mr Grindalythe. I think you should not pursue it further. I think with a bit more investigative work that you, DI Wenlock, can successfully close this case as being an accident and you, Ms de-la-Zouch, can write a very good piece of investigative journalism about the dangers of elite motorsport."

Fitzpaine swung his golf club over his shoulder and made to walk back to his party. He called back one last comment.

"After all, motor racing is a very dangerous sport. If I were you, I would focus some more on the technical aspects of the crash, and less on the drama surrounding the life of a colourful character." He gave one last smile, and a jaunty wave. "How about doing something useful, like looking for all those 'missing persons'?"

They waited for Fitzpaine to get out of earshot before discussing his very overt suggestion that they back off.

"That was a very overt suggestion to 'back off'," Ashby started with. Wenlock didn't reply straight away as he weighed up his options.

"Fitzpaine had a point. We have been looking at ruling out motives when possibly the best thing to do is to look at opportunity. Whilst Fitzpaine or Ms Greenhow might have wanted Grindalythe out of the way, neither of them had much opportunity."

"True," Ashby replied. "Fitzpaine was surrounded by people the entire time he was at the race and Ms Greenhow didn't even attend on the day."

"We need to have a look at those with the best access to Kirby's car and access to the track on the day. Do you know who we need to talk to?" Wenlock asked.

"We should start with Grantham," Ashby replied.

"Who is Grantham?"

"Grantham services Grindalythe's Panther. He would know who had access to it on the day," Ashby answered helpfully.

"Let's pay a visit to Grantham and see what he knows."

They trudged back to the Muskrat and set off across the course back to the road. Wenlock couldn't really understand why a man who had been mowing the lawn in the background was very angry with him so he ignored him and gunned it, churning up the green further.

"You're still going to ask for those insurance papers though, right?" Ashby asked from the passenger seat.

"Oh, absolutely," said Wenlock. If nothing else it sounded like they would be good material to have hold of if the salary and pension cuts materialised...

Chapter 8

The Muskrat gently pootled along the winding road that led from the golf course back in to town. The previous conversations between Ashby and Wenlock had been dire and so they sat in silence, each admiring the picturesque countryside surrounding them, lost in their own thoughts.

Suddenly, Wenlock noticed the nose of a very sporty looking silver coupe filling the Muskrat's rear-view mirror. Ashby, previously ensconced in thoughts of lunch, turned to take a look at where the roaring engine noise had come from. The coupe, at the direction of its driver, flashed its lights and beeped angrily. Wenlock swore and made a rather un-police like hand gesture in the general direction of the other car before ceding the road and allowing it to overtake.

As it did so, Ashby exclaimed.

"Fitzpaine!"

Which Wenlock thought was odd. Fortunately, Ashby followed it up with some more details.

"In that coupe! It was Cheddon Fitzpaine overtaking us!"

Wenlock, who had been stewing over his treatment at the golf course by the politician, leapt into action and gunned the Muskrat's protesting engine.

"You're going to try and catch him?" Ashby looked over to Wenlock in horror. "That's a Chandler Ocelot, you'll never keep up in this thing!"

"You'd be surprised." Wenlock muttered as he took the Muskrat ever closer to its top speed along the winding country road. Previously picturesque trees shot past in a now menacing blur. Up ahead, Wenlock could see

Fitzpaine was caught behind a large lorry, waiting for his opportunity to overtake. It allowed Wenlock the short time he needed to catch up.

Unfortunately, in that time, Fitzpaine found his opening and made a risky dart into the lane belonging to oncoming traffic. He zipped past the lorry with a fraction of a second to spare before the aforementioned oncoming traffic closed the gap. Wenlock had to bide his time before making his move to follow. After what seemed like an age but was merely a few seconds, a gap opened up and Wenlock overtook. Ashby gripped the Muskrat's imitation walnut dashboard as Wenlock made a pathetic attempt to follow the far faster silver Ocelot's precarious manoeuvre.

He made it round the lorry before the blind bend. It was more luck than skill but Wenlock was not willing to admit that. He changed up a gear and focussed on closing the gap between him and his silver target.

"Sorry to interrupt," Ashby enquired in a polite but strained manner, "but why are we following him?"

Wenlock was hunched over the steering wheel and concentrating on not ploughing into the side of a tractor that was nudging its way out of a side road. His slight swerve and subsequent correction to avoid the piece of heavy plant caused the Muskrat to briefly skip on two wheels.

"Call it a hunch." His eyes gleamed with excitement. It had been a while since he'd pulled someone over for dangerous driving, and Fitzpaine's little manoeuvres could definitely be counted as such. If he could catch the speeding Ocelot, he might be able to give him a ticket as revenge for earlier or negotiate his way to a tasty backhander. Either was fine in Wenlock's view.

However, at the next bend, it became clear that Ashby was indeed correct and that the Muskrat would not keep up with the silver speedster. The road opened to a long straight, clear of traffic, and Fitzpaine's Ocelot was a mere dot at the end of it. Wenlock knew that, no matter how hard he pushed, there was no way to close that distance. Besides, a bad smell had started to emerge from the Muskrat that Wenlock suspected to be related to his over exuberance.

He eased off and relaxed back in to his seat dejectedly. Ashby, very wisely, decided not to say that she had told him so.

***

A little later they made it to the edge of town and got stuck in traffic. Ashby was idly staring out the window and Wenlock was idly picking his nose when a glint of silver in the queue ahead caught Ashby's eye.

"Fitzpaine!"

Wenlock pulled his finger out and leapt to attention. Ashby was right. Fitzpaine's silver Ocelot was only a few cars ahead in the queue. It had seemed all his dangerous driving had been for naught, foiled by the ring road and the council's unfathomable traffic management system.

"We're following him," Wenlock declared, firmly fixated on the possibility of delivering a ticket to the mayor.

Ashby acquiesced and put the radio on. It was going to be at least another 20 minutes before either car reached the next junction.

***

Fortunately, for the sake of the plot and possible televised version of this novel, Fitzpaine turned off at the next junction rather than sitting on the ringroad for longer. The Muskrat followed, keeping a healthy distance. The silver coupe came off at the first exit of the roundabout and turned into an industrial estate.

"It seems Mr Fitzpaine isn't going to his office," deduced Wenlock, following the Ocelot into the warren of warehouses.

The estate was busy and Fitzpaine's Ocelot had to dodge and weave to avoid trucks being loaded by men in flat caps. Noxious fumes belched from smoke stacks, making it hard for Wenlock to see the turns the silver streak took.

Fitzpaine drove deeper and deeper into the estate. Wenlock gave as much distance as he dared. He was glad he was in an unmarked car; this was not an area traditionally friendly to the local police. He mentioned this to Ashby.

"It doesn't seem like a place that would be friendly to politicians either," she pointed out.

Eventually, Fitzpaine parked at the side of the road next to a large redbrick, but otherwise nondescript, factory. A sign on the wall of the building proclaimed it to be 'The Wholesome Cake Company'. On the sign, a painting of a well-rounded and friendly looking woman in a chef's hat was stirring a bowl of beige mixture with a smile across her jolly face. Her bouffant red hair was not pinned back in a hair net in a flagrant health violation. A smaller sign gave the building's address, the less catchy 'Unit 472A, Bowmore Street'.

Fitzpaine got out of his Ocelot, scanned the street as if for watchers and locked the car door. As he was doing so, Wenlock pulled over as well, hoping that the bland, grimy Muskrat would blend into the bland, grimy surrounds.

Wenlock and Ashby watched as Fitzpaine slipped into a black metal side door embedded in the expanse of factory wall.

"Do you know who owns this factory?" Ashby asked Wenlock in what seemed a strange, slow manner. Wenlock replied that he did not.

"This factory," Ashby be continued in a whisper "belongs to the Cheneys."

Realisation washed over Wenlock like soap. This was an unexpected and unwelcome turn. The redbrick wall began to look less nondescript and more menacing.

"What on earth would Cheddon Fitzpaine have to do with the Cheneys?" He asked rhetorically.

"I don't know," Ashby replied. "I'm as surprised as you are." Wenlock bit his tongue allowing Ashby to speak again.

"This is big, I mean really big. Do you know what the Cheneys are in to?"

"Other than cakes? Extortion, racketeering, money laundering, gambling, prostitution, occasional homicide. As a police officer, I am quite well briefed on their activities," Wenlock smarted.

"Firstly, extortion is a form of racketeering." Ashby replied drily. "Secondly, the gambling that they are into extends very much in to the world of motor racing. They are behind almost all of the illegal bookmaking that goes on."

Wenlock sat back in his seat. If Fitzpaine was connected both to those running the illegal betting rings and to Grindalythe, then something was really up here. He wasn't convinced yet that Grindalythe had been murdered but he was getting suspicious that all was not as it had first seemed. There was too much going on for it to be a coincidence.

"I'm going to need to go back to the office and do some research on this, as well as inform the DCI. If this cake factory does belong to the Cheneys, and the Mayor is somehow involved with them, then this case is really going somewhere and he needs to know about it."

Ashby looked across with a nervous look in her eyes.

"Won't they just shut you down? Fitzpaine is friends with the chief. I'm no expert on police organisational structure, but I'm pretty sure that the chief is more important the DCI!"

Wenlock thought about this for a minute. He hadn't wanted this case at first but now it was looking promising. He could also tell that Ashby was worried about losing her connection to all this. If Wenlock was taken off the investigation, it would make it much harder for her to keep chasing leads. Also, she would have to use her own car instead of getting lifts everywhere. He then began to think about his expenses and came to a decision.

"I have to tell him. He'll understand. If there is a link between Fitzpaine and the Cheneys, it needs to be investigated. It might be innocent, he might just be..." Wenlock faltered. He couldn't really think of a legitimate explanation for a politician to be sneaking in the backdoor of a gang-owned cake factory on a Monday afternoon. "Look, I'm just going to tell him and do the research first. I'm driving so, unless you want to get out of the car and catch a bus home, it's my call."

Chapter 9

I get out of the car. Wenlock was being a coward and he knew it. The people deserve to know the truth about what happened to Kirby. No, the people need to know the truth! I shut the car door behind me as quietly as I can and sidle across the street toward the factory entrance that Fitzpaine slipped through moments before. I hear Wenlock slowly reversing the Muskrat behind me. At least he was quiet whilst making his exit; hopefully no-one inside the factory heard him leave.

The door is my first challenge. There isn't another way in to the factory on this wall. It is a large red brick building, several stories high with a tall chimney at the other end. For a factory making cakes, it seems to be belching out a surprising quantity of noxious fumes. My knowledge on the mass production of baked goods is scant but maybe it would make a great environmental damage scoop? I shake the thought out of my head so I can focus. I need to follow Fitzpaine through the door. It could be locked. There could be people on the other side of it. There is no way of knowing . I take a last look at the street around me, thankfully still deserted. There is no alternative: I have to try opening the door.

It isn't locked. I feel the handle give and the lightness of a door unburdened by its latch. No light escapes from the room inside - it must be devoid of humans. I open the door as slowly as I can and only wide enough to fit myself through. Inside it's almost pitch black. No window to the outside world. The only place the light comes in from is 3 murky panes of glass, not cleaned in many years, running along the top of the wall to my right. It's a small room, cut off from the main factory. As my eyes adjust to the gloom, I see it is some kind of store room. Dusty shelves surround me, packed with old boxes and frightening looking equipment that has no place in the world of cakes.

Fitzpaine is clearly not here. Fortunately, there seems to be only one route through the shelving so this must have been the way he went. I pick my way through as quietly as I can, afraid that someone might be waiting for me around every shelving stack. I hear a distant throbbing of machines at work but nothing more.

After what seems like an age of creeping around the moulding boxes, I reach another door. It's slightly ajar and I hear nothing on the other side. I nudge it open. The door leads to a narrow corridor with a flight of stairs at the end. The stairs double back on themselves to lead up into the higher reaches of the factory. I've come too far now to stop so I push ahead. I take each step one at a time, listening after each one to see if I can make anything out. Nothing but that distant mechanical rumble.

I make it past the first flight of stairs to the switch back. Another flight of stairs, leading ever upward. I feel compelled to continue - I have no choice if I want to know what Fitzpaine is doing here. I climb the stairs quietly, but as quickly as I dare. I contemplate what might happen if I am caught. The Cheneys have a frightening reputation. Rumours of their savagery to those who have crossed them fill a page of print every week in the Everyday Post, not that all of it can be believed...

Eventually, the staircase ends. Another doorway. This door has a frosted glass panel about half way up and I can see light through it. It doesn't look like a room on the other side. I crouch and approach the frosted glass from below. I slowly bring my eyes up to the level of the glass, I can just about make out what lies beyond the door. It looks like a gangway, suspended over the factory floor. The sound of machinery is much louder now that I am close to the door and I can see movement beyond it. If I cross the gangway surely I'll be exposed? There is no alternative, Fitzpaine must have come this way. I have come so far; I don't think I could face slinking back and telling Wenlock that I chickened out. I take a deep breath and open the door, again slowly and only enough to allow me through.

I was right: it is a gangway, made of a metal and suspended over the cake making machines below. The machinery throbs, whirrs and occasionally whistles. Fortunately, there are few workers on the shop floor; automation has taken hold in the food processing business. Those who are down below are busy with their respective tasks and show no interest in the gangway suspended high above them.

I take my first steps along the gangway. It is solid and doesn't creak. The noise from the machines masks my footsteps. I can see the gangway runs to a suspended cabin that overlooks the factory floor. There is a door with another frosted glass window guarding the entrance. The glass is dark suggesting no light on behind it.

I edge further along the gangway. I'm now closer to the suspended office than the door I came in from. It will be a long run back if I am seen. One of the machines below lets out a particularly large metallic clang and I stop in my tracks. None of the workers below look up - it must be part of the usual routine. I let out a breath I did not realise I was holding and continue. I make it to the door. As before, I crouch low so my silhouette can't be seen from the other side. I am about to peer through when a whistle sounds through the factory. Not a mechanical noise - this is a signal. A light turns on in the room ahead of me and the door begins to open. I don't have time to panic, only time to get behind the door as it swings outward toward me. Fortunately, whoever is the on the other side does not open the door fully and I have enough space on the gangway to hide behind the now open door.

A figure walks on to the gangway. I can't see them but I can smell the foul cigar they are smoking. I hear the creak as they lean on the railings to peer down at the factory below. Seconds pass. The figure gives a grunt of satisfaction, deep and definitely male. He has seen what he wanted and returns back in to the cabin, closing the door behind him. I breath out for the first time in minutes and fight the rising panic. It takes a little time for me to get myself back under control. I look down and see that the shop floor is now almost deserted, the whistle signalling a break of some kind. I wait a moment more before plucking up my courage to peer into the frosted window again. I can see that the room beyond is another storage room with two doors. The suspended cabin is only small so there cannot be many other rooms. Fitzpaine must be behind one of them!

I let myself into the store room. Immediately, the noise of the machinery dies down and I can hear a male voice from behind one of the doors. I creep across the room to try and hear what is being said. I arrive just in time to hear Fitzpaine finish his sentence:

"...and that's why I had Grindalythe killed on the track! Thank you all for helping me out in this. I couldn't have done it without you sending your chaps down to the pits to spike his petrol with cleaning fluid. No one will ever suspect a thing!"

I nearly fall over in surprise. This was it! The truth! It couldn't be plainer: he killed Kirby! The world would know. I felt the need to rush back, to tell Wenlock and drag the entire police force down here. Politician kills racing driver! What a scoop! Wenlock would interrogate him and find the reason, or I could do it myself! I could sneak back to the back door from which he came in and ambush him on the street as he leaves! I stand up and take a step back to the door I came in through, but too loudly. The conversation on the other side of the door stops. I hear a female voice I don't recognise.

"Did you hear that?"

I freeze. Do I run? If I run, they are sure to chase. If I stay, still they may think it was nothing.

Footsteps. Toward the door I have been listening at. I decide to run. It's too late. The door opens. I make it to the other side of the small store room before the shout goes up. Cigar smoke fills my nostrils. I start to open the door to the gangway but the cigar holder is on me. He is fast and he is strong. The struggle is short before he has a hand across my neck. He throws me backward on to the floor.

"What have we here?" I hear Fitzpaine ask with a sneer. "An intrepid reporter! On your own are you, where's your tame Pig?"

There are four people in the room and they all laugh. Not with much humour. I get a chance to look up. Fitzpaine was one of them and with him were the three Cheneys: Sutton, Middleton and Litton. I'd seen enough pictures of them in the paper to know their faces.

"How much do you think she heard?" it was Sutton Cheney, the oldest. Still smoking the cigar, he had been the figure on the gangway and the one that caught me.

"Anything was too much," that was Litton, the youngest Cheney, I remembered seeing a picture of one of her victims. It had stopped me sleeping for days.

Fitzpaine steps forward; he grabs my hair and pulls.

"I asked you a question. Are you alone? Is DI Wenlock with you?" he hisses. He doesn't wait for an answer. "She accosted me earlier today. Her and a police detective. He might be in the building still."

"I'll deal with it," Sutton nods curtly and left the room. I start to sob; there is nothing I can do to stop myself.

"We're not taking any risks." It was time for the final Cheney to weigh in: Middleton. Known to be the worst of the three. Middleton was linked with more heinous criminal acts than her sister and brother combined.

"Agreed, can you do it without causing suspicion?" Fitzpaine this time. Middleton smiles at Litton in a way that I don't like. Then they both smile at me which I really don't like.

"Well, then, I'll leave you ladies to it." Fitzpaine lets go of my hair and straightens his jacket. "Enjoy yourselves," he throws back as he departs. I don't think the comment is meant for me. The Cheneys advance. They're both much bigger than I. I try to run to the nearest door but Litton grabs my arm. Her nails dig in like razors.

"Don't be going anywhere now," she whispers to me. "We've got all afternoon!"

Chapter 10

"On second thoughts," said Ashby. "If I followed him in, I'd be on my own, with no legal right to be there, in a factory owned by notorious gangsters and with a politician who has already threatened me once today. "

"Also, this doesn't seem like an area with a regular bus service to get back in to town," she added.

"I'm glad you made that decision," Wenlock replied. "Largely because whilst you've been daydreaming I've driven back to town." Ashby looked out of the Muskrat's window and saw this to be correct. They were nearly back at the police station.

"I need to see the DCI. I think it's best that I do that alone. You can wait in the car if you like or I can drop you somewhere?"

**

Ashby elected to be dropped back off at her own car. Wenlock grumbled slightly that this was the other side of town but eventually consented. After dropping Ashby off, he made his way back to the station.

"Is the DCI in?" Wenlock asked the Desk Sergeant, who was still chewing gum.

"Probably," she replied unhelpfully.

"Have you seen him go in to his office?" Wenlock decided to press the point.

"Yes."

"Have you seen him leave?"

"No."

"Are there any other ways by which he could enter or leave?"

"Not without setting off an alarm."

"So he is in his office," Wenlock concluded. This elicited a long winded response from the Desk Sergeant in which she outlined to Wenlock that whilst she could be certain that the DCI had entered and was sure that he had not left, he still may not be in the room. She continued that this uncertainty came from the uncertainty principle, as highlighted by the famous thought experiment known as "Schrödinger's cat"[19]. Until it is measured whether or not he is in the room, he is both simultaneously in and not in said room.

Wenlock replied that her grasp of the concept was shaky at best and decided to go and find out if the DCI was in or not himself.

Fortunately for the plot, he was in his office as expected, behind his desk and still reading the newspaper from earlier today.

"Hello, Wenlock," he said cheerfully. "How is the investigation going? Figured out who did it yet?"

"I'm still not convinced it is a murder sir," Wenlock replied candidly as he took a seat. "However, I am certainly beginning to suspect there is something going on. It's why I came to see you."

The DCI looked puzzled and became interested enough to finally put down his paper. Wenlock outlined the investigation so far. He started with his investigation at the track, the visit to his ex-wife, then the more fruitful visit

---

[19] In which Dr Schrödinger posited about a cat shut in a box with a vial of poison. Whether or not the vial of poison cracked and killed the cat depended on whether a radioactive atom had decayed and emitted radiation or not. The cat is therefore simultaneously alive and dead until the box is opened and it's state measured.

It's a bit more complicated than that obviously. I'd suggest looking it up for the full details. I can't really fit them all in this footnote.

to see Ingleby Greenhow. He explained the insurance money link to Cheddon Fitzpaine and finally he described following Fitzpaine to the cake factory known to be operated by the Cheneys. He left Ashby out of the story. Partnering with a reporter probably wouldn't go down well.

"So, as you can see sir, the investigation is getting a little more complex."

"Gosh," said the DCI. "That really does sound like you're on to something. Good work, Inspector!"

"I thought it best to inform you sir before continuing to pursue this line of inquiry. I mean, the involvement of a politician would usually mean handing the case over to Major Crimes." Wenlock squirmed a little as he said this. He was invested in the case now and didn't really want to lose it, but he knew how these things went. Cases with politicians in them invariably went to Major Crimes who invariably failed to find any evidence of wrongdoing by those in power. He knew that saying this was risky, but he had to know the DCI was onside.

The DCI sat back in his chair and looked thoughtful. He lit his pipe and set the fire alarm off again. After some time and another pointless argument about quantum uncertainty with the Desk Sergeant, they returned to the office.

"Well, I'm all for it. Carry on, Inspector. You're doing a great job." The DCI gave a big smile. "The police need to be shown to be transparent and, frankly, I'd love nothing better than to find an excuse to bring the Cheneys down. They've been a menace to this town for too long. As for Fitzpaine, I voted for the other chap. Cleaning up corrupt politicians can only result in some good press for us!"

Wenlock was surprised by this approach but not unpleasantly so. He decided that it might be time to introduce the idea that he had been receiving some help.

"I've also enlisted some local expertise to help me with the case. Ashby de-la-Zouch, a sports reporter for the *Everyday Post*."

"A reporter, how excellent Wenlock! A masterstroke of public relations. It's about time the world got to see us in action, and if this case is going the way you describe it will play very well, even if *The Post* is an odious shitrag." The DCI's smile became even wider - it's edges peaked out from under his ample moustache. Wenlock relaxed. He had never seen the DCI so happy. He decided to chance his arm a final time.

"This looks like it will be a difficult investigation, sir, lot's of leads still to chase and time is of the essence..."

The DCI held up a hand to stop him.

"It goes without saying, Wenlock, any overtime request you make will be approved. I want you to stop at nothing in finding the truth. The people need to know what happened to Grindalythe and the connection between Fitzpaine and the Cheneys. Good luck, Inspector - and do let me know if you see any missing persons on your travels."

They stood up and shook hands. The phone rang and the DCI said he had to take it. Wenlock left the office with a grin on his face. He hadn't had a case this good in a long time. Unlimited overtime! He was about to leave the station when the Desk Sergeant called to him.

"The DCI wants to see you in his office."

"No," replied Wenlock patiently. "I wanted to see him in his office."

"No, he just called me. He wants to see you in his office, now," the Desk Sergeant countered. "The DCI said he wanted to see you 'Straight away and with no arguing about cats in boxes this time.'"

A frown crept over Wenlock's face. This was unlikely to be good. He went back down the corridor. This time the office door was closed so he knocked.

"Come in," came the reply, from the DCI. Wenlock opened the door, the DCI was sat at his desk and not reading his paper.

"Take a seat please, Inspector."

Wenlock did as he was told.

"Can I help you, sir?" Wenlock ventured.

"I understand you have been investigating the Grindalythe case, is that correct?" the DCI asked politely. He looked serious. His entire mouth was concealed by moustache.

Wenlock replied that it was and the DCI should know this as he assigned it to him and they had recently discussed it at length.

Something was up.

"And this case led you and a Miss Ashby de-la-Zouch to a conversation with Mr Cheddon Fitzpaine at a golf course. Is that also correct?"

Wenlock confirmed it was. He didn't like where the conversation was going.

"Please can you explain to me the events leading up to this?"

Wenlock decided it was best not to query why he needed to repeat himself. He started from the beginning and even described the butler in the penguin suit. The DCI did not respond for some time. He didn't even light a cigar.

"Detective Inspector Wenlock, I fail to see from your description of events how you, as a murder unit detective, can continue to investigate this case. Firstly, there is insufficient evidence that Kirby Grindalythe was murdered. Secondly, you had no right to approach or tail Mr Fitzpaine based on the evidence collected so far. Thirdly, you have deeply involved a reporter in your investigation which is a gross breach of protocol."

Wenlock's face fell. He put two and two together. The phone call the DCI had received as Wenlock had left the room...

"I have no option but to remove you from the case. It shall be handed over to Major Crimes as is right and proper. You shall be involved again *if*, and I stress 'if', it is found by Major Crimes that Grindalythe was in some way

61

'murdered'." The disdain in the DCI's voice as he said the last sentence suggested that this was not a likely outcome of the investigation.

"Sir!" Wenlock protested before being cut off again.

"Inspector Piece from Major Crimes will be taking over the investigation."

"Sir!" Wenlock protested again. "Wraxall Piece is an odious dirtbag! Notorious for his zero percent conviction rate! He's nothing more than a toady used to hush up the crimes of high society."

The DCI indicated a man stood to Wenlock's right. A man who Wenlock knew to be Wraxall Piece. It had been impolite to call him a 'odious dirtbag' but Wenlock didn't care. It was accurate and Piece knew just what Wenlock thought of him. Wenlock didn't have time to wonder how Piece had appeared in the room.

"Inspector Piece here will be taking over the investigation and that is final. If you're not careful, Wenlock, I'll assign you to 'Missing Persons' for the rest of your career. Now, tell him everything you have told me." Wenlock threw up his arms in frustration, both at the loss of the case and at the prospect of repeating himself for the third time.

The DCI put on his hat and made to leave the office, clearly unwilling to hear the story over again. "I am going for lunch," he paused at the door.

"When you said the butler was wearing a penguin costume at the Greenhow residence, you mean a tail coat I assume?"

"No, sir, penguin outfit, sir. With a beak."

The DCI looked puzzled.

"What kind of penguin?"

Wenlock had to think about this before replying.

"Probably a rockhopper, sir."

The DCI seemed satisfied at this. He said one more sentence before leaving the room, putting the cherry on the shitcake for Wenlock.

"One more thing Inspector, all overtime is cancelled."

Chapter 11

The sun had dipped well below the urban skyline by the time Wenlock left the police station and got back in his beige 'speed' machine. As he drove the familiar roads to his home, he mused to himself. Being pulled off the case wasn't a great shock. He had felt the sinking feeling the second Fitzpaine's name came up that the case wouldn't stay in his lane.

On the other hand, he had argued against taking the case in the first place. Really, he should be relieved that his original thoughts had been confirmed and he could go back to his day job, solving the ordinary murders that plagued the lives of ordinary people.

Unfortunately, there wasn't a lot of murder investigating to be done at the moment[20]. Things had been quiet. There wasn't a sniff of overtime on the horizon, thought Wenlock. He also wondering if he'd get to claim his mileage back. His misery deepened.

He would still need to meet Ashby to tell her what had happened, a small gesture for the small help she had been. Maybe she could team up with Piece and convince him to do a proper follow up on what they had found out so far? Wenlock doubted it. DI Wraxall Piece had been in Major Crimes for 4 years without making an arrest. If Wenlock had been in charge, he would have ridden the force of Piece years ago. It was unthinkable that anyone could investigate high profile crime for that long and not catch a single tax-evading sports personality or corrupt bureaucrat.

***

Wenlock met with Ashby at their appointed meeting location the next day: a local lamp shade shop. When setting the meeting place, Ashby explained to

---

[20] Unfortunately for Wenlock. Fortunate however for the local population that they live in an area with a low murder rate. Lots of missing people though...

Wenlock that she didn't get a lot of time outside of work to shop for soft furnishings so it seemed a practical and inconspicuous place to have a conversation[21].

The shop could charitably be described as 'cosy' but, in its defence, was well stocked. Lampshades were available in all shapes, sizes, and colours. A haughty looking shop assistant kept a beady eye on his few customers from behind his till fortress, ensuring none decided to do a spot of light-fingered home revamping. Ashby was deep in the bowels of the Aladdin's cave, weighing up the social acceptability of a heinous polka-dot Empire Box Pleat.

"They've pulled me off the case," Wenlock snarled - he didn't bother with a hello. He had a pretty sore head from spending the previous evening commiserating with himself.

"Oh," said Ashby, seemingly unsurprised at this turn of events. "That seems a bit early. We'd barely got started," she said, hanging a potential lampshade on the tester lamp.

"Yes, I thought that too if I'm honest. It was strange. The DCI seemed fine with us continuing at first. I thought on this last night and to be honest I expected he would let us go a bit further before objecting," Wenlock said with a frown. "When I first went to see him, he encouraged us to continue. He seemed to get a phone call that changed all that."

"Probably from the chief, threatening his pension or something even more valuable to him. Does the DCI have moustache?" Ashby asked, hanging some more lampshades.

"He does!"

"Did he demand you turn in your badge and gun?" Ashby asked, trying one more lampshade and seeming happy with it.

---

[21] To fully appreciate this chapter I suggesting looking up the verb 'lampshading' if you aren't already familar with the practise.

"No, he just took me off the case. Also, I don't have a gun."

"How disappointing. Not even the offer of 24 hours to solve the case?"

"No, he was quite clear that it was immediate. He did threaten to assign me to 'Missing Persons'."

"They do seem to always be busy." Ashby was well aware of their plight; missing people took up a few pages each week in the *Post*.

"Indeed, but because they're so woeful at finding people the overtime was cancelled years ago."

"Anyway, who are we going to interview next? Grantham as we had planned?" Ashby took the lampshade off the test stand and headed to the till to pay.

"What!?" Wenlock replied in shock, startling other fans of lighting accessories perusing the wares of the store. "It's over Ashby. I'm off the case. If I carry on, they *will* demand my badge! Wraxall Piece has been assigned to follow up," he added glumly.

"But you're not going to take that are you? I mean, this is a proper mystery. Surely a once-in-a-career-case!" Ashby was about to pay for the lampshade but then had a change of heart.

"I'm not really the cowboy cop type, I'm more of the by-the-book variety," Wenlock replied, hanging a fetching lime green lampshade that had caught his eye. In doing so, he realised he hadn't redecorated in a long time.

"Damn it, Wenlock, we can't give up now. A famous racing driver murdered, a corrupt politician, organised crime! It's the holy trinity of mystery, Much!" Ashby berated him, much to the amusement of the haughty cashier.

"You just want the story. This is my career at risk, my entire life!" Wenlock shot back. "If you're so keen on investigating this, you just go on ahead but I can't be a part of it." He realised that the first lampshade he hung had been disgusting rather than fetching and tried another.

"Fine!" Ashby shouted. "I will!" She stormed out of the shop. Wenlock followed, much to the chagrin of the shop assistant, who had hoped at least one of the two was going to buy a lampshade.

By the time Wenlock had left the shop, Ashby was already in her car and reversing out of her parking space. She sped off, definitely breaking the local speed limit. Wenlock watched her go and felt helpless. If he'd had a speed camera on him, he could have got a bonus for issuing her a ticket. He went back to the parked Muskrat and decided what to do with the rest of his day.

***

Ashby knew she couldn't stop now. The story was too big. It would be far more dangerous to continue without Wenlock giving her an air of legitimacy but this was too great an opportunity to turn away from. She also couldn't stop because she was on the dual carriageway and stopping meant receiving points her driving license couldn't handle.

She would continue as she and Wenlock had planned. If she backed away from the Fitzpaine/Cheney angle and made discreet enquiries on what actually got Grindalythe killed in the first place, that might help them to forget about her and lull the more influential suspects into a false sense of security. With Wraxall Piece assigned to the case, they would know they had nothing to fear from the police.

She took the exit toward the racetrack and managed to park near the entrance. It was quiet there now Pandamonium was over. Even with the car smashed and Grindalythe dead, she knew Grantham would still be at the track with the team. He was always there; she figured he probably didn't have anywhere else to be. Like Kirby, racing was his life.

Chapter 12

Ashby was correct. Grantham was exactly where she expected. She had walked to the team's garage in the pit area so many times that her legs had led her there automatically. It was strange heading down there and knowing that Kirby would not be waiting for her.

The large main door to the garage that gave the car access to the track was closed so Ashby let herself in the through the mechanics' entrance. The garage was dingy inside but a single bulb glowed at a workbench in the corner. Grantham's unmistakable lanky frame, including ever present flat cap, was hunched over the bench, operating a loud power tool. He hadn't noticed her enter so she paused to take the room in. It was strange seeing it so empty. Usually the red Panther would fill most of the space. Hunkered on its four outsized wheels, it's chrome work reflecting off the photographers' flashbulbs. Without the car, the garage looked sad, like a house without a family or a gin without tonic.

When Grantham had finished torturing some unsuspecting piece of metal, he turned off the power tool and straightened up from the work bench, unfolding like deckchair to reach his full height. Ashby took the opportunity of the new peace that settled on the workshop to announce her presence.

"Hello Grantham."

Grantham jumped with surprise and turned around to face her.

"Oh! Hello, Ms de-la-Zouch! You startled me there," he said in his thick, generic, regional accent. He gave a smile of recognition. It soon turned to a frown of curiosity. "You know Mr Grindalythe isn't here don't you?"

"Yes, Grantham," she replied, kindly. "I know what happened to Kirby. I'm actually here to ask you a few questions, if you don't mind?"

"I'll answer what I can." He said slowly and thoughtfully. "But please, nothing on the Huguenots - I'm very weak on French ethnoreligions. Not great on mollusc biology either."

"No Grantham, I want to ask you some questions about what happened to Kirby. There are people who think it wasn't an accident."

Grantham picked up a nearby rag and gave his hands a wipe before replying. The rag was probably filthier than his hands at that point so the end effect was just mixing two different kinds of muck together. He walked over to a different bench, picked up a kettle and put it on a small, one-ring gas burner that looked like it had once been part of a blowtorch.

"I'll do what I can, Ms de-la-Zouch. I don't know how much I can help though. All I ever did was look after the car."

Ashby refrained from pointing out that Grindalythe had died in the car. It probably wouldn't help the situation. She knew how much time the two of them spent together in this garage working on the Panther. She doubted they had ever been close on a personal level, they were two very different characters, but professionally they had been inseparable.

"Would you like some tea?" Grantham asked. Ashby replied that she would and whilst Grantham busied himself with the tea making process she allowed her mind to wander back in time. To how often she had come down to interview Kirby and the two of them had not noticed her entrance, so engrossed they were in the car. The times she had visited much later on the same day to find them still stuck on the same topics, figuring their way through problems and tweaking subtle bits of the Panther's finely tuned machinery. Totally focussed on the quest of the next race. She had struggled to pull Kirby away from the car. When she eventually managed to, Grantham would keep working. The more she thought about it,she realised that she had never seen him outside this garage. He always seemed to be here.

Grantham broke her reverie by handing her the tea. Rather than in a mug, it appeared to be inside a hollowed out piston that had been crudely fashioned into a watertight vessel. The liquid was the colour of the previously mentioned rag and when sloshed it in the cup the contents moved too slowly to have been made purely with water.

"Just how you'd always have it," he said with a weak smile. Ashby smiled back and wondered how the hell she was going to avoid drinking the oily brew this time.

"How have you been holding up?" she asked him.

"Oh, I've been OK, Ms de-la-Zouch. Just carried on, really. Bit hard working on the car, with it not being here and all but there are still plenty of bits that need doing. Lots of stuff still needs fixing or mending or repairing." He took a sip out of his own cup[22] and grimaced. He probably thought that was how tea was supposed to taste, thought Ashby.

"You've known Kirby for much longer than I. How did you meet?" Ashby realised she had never really had much of a conversation with Grantham, usually when she had come down to the garage she and Kirby had left the room almost immediately.

"There's a question, Ms." Grantham replied. "I first met Mr Grindalythe right here."

"At the track?" Ashby queried.

"Oh no, Ms! In this garage. Y'see, Mr Grindalythe's father, also Mr Grindalythe, was in racing too. He employed me to look after his car when Mr Grindalythe was just a wee babber. I worked for Mr Grindalythe for ten years before he passed on and Mr Grindalythe picked up the racing game himself."

---

[22] Ashby didn't recognise what it had been fabricated from but it appeared to have its own built in heating system.

Ashby took a minute to process this sentence before replying.

"Gosh! So you've known Kirby since he was a boy!"

"From a boy, into a successful man," Grantham said proudly. "In that time, not a single soul has worked on Mr Grindalythe's cars but me."

" Kirby didn't trust anyone else with his car," Ashby added kindly but also truthfully. "He always said you were best. I saw a lot of the other team garages in my job and I can agree with him."

"Why thank you, Ms." Grantham might have blushed underneath his grimy visage; it was hard to tell.

"Grantham, can you talk me through what happened to the car between the last race and the one this weekend?" Ashby began to hone from conversation to investigation.

"Of course, Ms." Grantham's face lit up as the conversation turned back to his best subject. "Mr Grindalythe brought her back in after the race, I gave her a once over to plan the work I'd need to do that week and order parts. She was in good working order, though a little worn as it's near season's end. Nothing a little T-L-C couldn't solve, mind. Mr Grindalythe had taken care of her."

Grantham paused for another sip of dark fluid.

" I worked on her in the garage all week. Had to top up the oil filter, rewire the radiator, torque tighten the alternator, inflate the spark plugs..."

Ashby had to stop him or he would continue describing faux mechanical nonsense for the rest of the day.

"So you got the Panther back up to working order before race weekend?"

"I did, I tuned her up and got her ready." Grantham interrupted his list of tasks, seeing that summary was what Ashby wanted. "I fueled her up to Mr

Kirby's specification - we always put more in than most of our competitors as the Panther can handle it."

Ashby made a mental note that this explained the larger than expected fire that had toasted the car and it's unfortunate driver.

"All functioned as usual? Nothing to suggest things might have been off?"

Grantham looked shocked at this question.

"I looked after the Panther as if it were my own child. I wouldn't let Mr Grindalythe get in a vehicle that I myself wouldn't spend the night in!"

Ashby ignored the slightly odd response and took it to mean that the car seemed fine.

"Could anyone have tampered with the car between you working on it and the race?" The key question.

"Absolutely not Ms. I was with that car from the moment it finished the last race to it leaving the garage for the Chapter 1 Classic." Grantham was adamant. "I watch anyone who comes near the car very carefully. There's all sorts who might want to hobble Mr Grindalthye's chances."

"But you must go home Grantham. You must sleep!" Ashby worried where this was going.

"I do, Ms, I do! I sleep here and lock myself in!" Grantham pointed to a pile of rags in the corner that Ashby had previously assumed was an over flowing bin/fire hazard. "Food is brought to me by Mr Grindalythe when he comes to work on the car, or I order it in. No-one visits this garage without me knowing and no-one came to visit last week, except Mr Grindalythe himself. Even then, I don't let him alone with the car. No telling what he might do to her..."

Ashby made a mental note that she needed to call social services when she left the garage, Grantham was going to need a lot of help over the next few weeks. It was pretty conclusive though. No-one could have tampered with

Kirby's car in the run up to the race. Not without Grantham knowing about it.

"Oh, wait. There was one strange thing that happened though..." Grantham thoughtfully rubbed his chin with his hand, smearing together the various substances about his person.

"Go on." Ashby urged him.

"Well, the day before the race I heard a knock at the garage door. I went over to see who it was and it was Leigh Delamere!"

"Upton Scudamore's mechanic?" Ashby knew Leigh by sight. She had interviewed Grindalythe's rival Scudamore plenty of times and, like Grantham, Leigh was usually near her driver.

"Exactly. I thought it was strange. After all, Leigh Delamere services Upton Scudamore's car. What would she be doing here?" Grantham continued his story.

"What did she want?"

"She wanted advice of all things! Surprising, it was. She was having trouble with the brake manifold of Scudamore's blue Lynx. She asked if I would come and take a look. Said she was desperate and I was the only one around who she thought could help."

"But Scudamore was Kirby's biggest rival. Why would anyone on his team come to you for help?" Ashby interjected. Grantham looked a little sheepish at this.

"To be honest, Ms de-la-Zouch, between us mechanics we sometimes have to help each other a little. Wouldn't do to have a one horse race due to a technical issue. You haven't really won if you haven't beaten the best!"

"I see," Ashby noted this, might be worth a scoop later down the line... "Did you go with her?"

"I did, only took five minutes. Wasn't all that complicated really, she just needed to overbraid the solenoid. Thinking back, I'm quite surprised she didn't think of that herself."

"So the car was out of your sight?" Ashby's journalistic sense were tingling. This sounded like a lead.

"Surely, no! I locked the door... didn't I?" Grantham replied uncertainly. Ashby saw the realisation hit Grantham like freight train full of steel girders, masonry and body building equipment. "Oh, Ms de-la-Zouch! What if I didn't? Anyone could have got in!"

"It's possible Grantham. Could they have done anything to the car in 5 minutes?"

"All sorts, Ms. That's why I never leave the car alone! I'd trust the other mechanics but on race day there are all sorts of folk milling about!" He almost began to breakdown and cry.

Whilst it was possible that this was how someone tampered with Kirby's car, Ashby didn't feel it was fair to make the poor man blame himself on this one. She put a hand on his knee to comfort him[23].

"It's probably nothing, Grantham. You would have noticed if they had done anything to the car before the race, I'm sure."

"Oh, I hope so, Ms. The mind comes up with all manner of undetectable faults they might have concocted."

"Like washing up liquid in the fuel tank?" Ashby chanced her arm.

"I suppose," Grantham replied with a frown. "Though the car wouldn't have got far into the race had that been the case."

---

[23] This was a mistake. The level of grease on Grantham's overalls meant she never managed to get that hand truly clean again.

Ashby was disappointed but not surprised. After all, the information had come from a daydream of her own devising. She decided it was time to end her questioning; she had the information to continue the investigation and pursue her next lead. She needed to speak to Leigh Delamere and Upton Scudamore. She needed to find out if Delamere had lured Grantham away from the Panther on purpose.

"And to think, Ms, we nearly didn't get to race this year," Grantham spoke up unexpectedly.

"What do you mean?" Ashby asked.

"Well, with Mrs Greenhow no longer sponsoring the team, Mr Grindalythe almost didn't have the backing to race! In one sense, maybe it would have been better if he never got it..." Grantham replied wistfully before adding, "on the other hand, if he hadn't raced this year it probably would have killed him anyway."

Ashby thought on this and how Ingleby Greenhow had mentioned it earlier. It chimed with the estranged wife's lack of interest in motor racing and changed marital status. Ashby reflected that even she had been unaware of the lack of sponsorship until Ingleby had brought it up, which made her a pretty shoddy sports reporter.

"Who stepped in to help, Grantham?"

Grantham scratched his head or at least smeared grease on his hair before replying.

"Don't truthfully know. I didn't really care much about the business side." Grantham paused before adding. "Oh, and I wasn't supposed to tell anyone about the money troubles... I suppose it doesn't matter now."

She stayed a little longer to comfort Grantham and drink another sip of the 'tea' before saying goodbye and suggesting he get a shower.

On her way out of the race track, she stopped by the Scudamore team garage. It was locked tight and no-one answered when she knocked.

Ashby didn't know Delamere well and had no idea where to find her when not at the track. Fortunately, she had a very good idea about where to find Scudamore. He had clipped a fire engine and run into the barrier at the end of the Chapter 1. An accident like that could only put him in only one place.

Chapter 13

"Which room is Upton Scudamore in please?" Ashby politely asked the hospital receptionist. The receptionist looked up from her crossword and gave a look that suggested Ashby smelt of durian fruit[24].

"That is not information I am able to divulge madam."

Ashby winced, firstly at the madam but secondly at her own naivety. She had gotten used to working with Wenlock, his DI badge opened doors. She was going to have to get inventive to access Scudamore. It was time to use some of her old reporter tricks...

"I'm his sister," Ashby ventured, a classic move.

"I see." The receptionist pulled a file from a large folder on a shelf behind her. "Can I confirm your name please?"

Ashby cast about in her mind. She had written a bio on Scudamore in the *Post* some years ago. She was sure she could remember the sister's name. She remembered she was no longer a Scudamore as she had married...

"Corsley Heath!" Ashby exclaimed as her memory returned, probably a little too enthusiastically. The receptionist did not look impressed.

"You're looking very well, Mrs Heath." The receptionist gave the compliment in a way that Ashby did not like.

"Thank you?" Ashby replied, uncertainly.

"For someone who has been dead for 2 years." The receptionist shut the file abruptly.

---

[24] If you know the smell... you know.

Ashby cursed herself. That was the reason for the bio.. A poor attempt. She needed to get her head back in the game. She decided to walk away from the reception with the little dignity she had left.

It was a large hospital - going room to room in search of Scudamore wasn't a practical option. Especially not now that she had been rumbled by the receptionist. What she needed was someone on the inside, someone who worked at the hospital and had access to the records.

***

"Why, Ms de-la-Zouch, how pleasant to have you back in my humble dominion! I trust you are feeling a little less queasy? Many apologies for my previous crassness - I get a little cooped up down here." Salcombe Regis smarmed his way across the morgue to greet Ashby. She had, with reluctance, headed back down the hospital stairs to the pathologist's lair. Unfortunately, Regis was the only hospital employee she knew.

"Hello, Mr Regis. Much better thank you," Ashby replied. She looked around the room and saw with relief that Kirby's remains had been removed from the table. No doubt stored in one of the many metal drawers lining the walls of the morgue. The thought arose to her unbidden that he wouldn't take up much space in one of those drawers.

"Please, call me Salcombe. Is DI Wenlock also joining us? I have the results of the DNA test and dental record check." Regis continued, making a dramatic show of looking for the absent detective.

Ashby had forgotten about these. She had come to terms now with the idea that Kirby was definitely dead and had not faked it. The good news was that Wenlock's removal from the case hadn't reached the ears of the pathologist. She leapt on the opportunity this presented.

"Ah, no DI Wenlock isn't with me, he asked me to pick up the test results instead. He's interviewing another suspect," she lied, convincingly this time.

Salcombe paused for a second, obviously in thought on how to proceed on what was likely a gross breach of protocol.

"Now, he should know that I can't just go giving records out willy-nilly to non-authorised personnel." Regis confirmed Ashby's suspicion.

"He said you'd say that." Ashby replied quickly. After the experience with the receptionist, she had thought ahead this time. Admittedly, she had planned on using this tactic to extract the location of Scudamore's room but it should hold for both uses. "He said 'If that prick Regis doesn't hand over the results, tell him the next time I see him I'll stick my boot so far up his arse that when I wiggle my toe it'll make his glasses fall off'."

Regis let out a loud, and forced sounding, laugh. He even clutched his belly. Quite the amateur dramatist, Ashby thought.

"That does sound like the inspector. I have no interest in having my glasses removed in such a manner and so I shall take your word for it. Allow me to get the files." He bustled off into a little side office. Ashby decided this would be a good time to strike with her true purpose. She followed him in to the office. It was tiny, overflowing with paperwork and stank of stale coffee. She could see a cup on the side that hadn't been cleaned in so long the bacteria inside had evolved to develop arable farming techniques.[25]

"DI Wenlock also asked if you could tell me which room Upton Scudamore is in? He wants to interview Scudamore later today."

At this, Regis stopped digging through his paper mound and looked up.

"He did, did he? Why would he think I know that?" Ashby had to think fast, she recalled some of the comments Regis had made earlier.

---

[25] There appeared to be a kind of mould town hall in the middle and several well ploughed fields radiating out from it. Small mould huts dotted the fields, presumably built by tiny bacterial hands. One could imagine a little mould family settling down in such a place and living a long and happy life, waiting only for the invention of mould mechanisation to ease their hard mould lives.

"Wenlock said 'Reception won't tell you without a badge but that little prick Regis will know where Scudamore is, he loves a celebrity. The creepy prick'." To really sell her whopping fib, Ashby made it look as if she was using great effort to recall the DI's exact words. Regis straightened up from his digging and gave Ashby a smile that made her skin crawl. She wasn't sure if it was because he showed too many teeth or too few.

"That does sound like our friend the inspector. Scudamore is in room 210 on the second floor. He has a private room, being a special guest," Regis coupled the words 'special guest' with a leer. "A police officer stands outside his room to stop unwanted guests. I tried to pop in to say hello but they would not admit one!"

Ashby thought on this. Why would Scudamore need a police officer as a guard? Although he is a celebrity, surely a full time guard was unnecessary?

"Thank you for the information, Mr Regis. I'll have those tests too, please."

"Of course, right away," he went back to digging, "and, please, do call me Salcombe."

"I'd rather not," was Ashby's curt reply.

***

Once Ashby had the location of Scudamore and a wedge of official looking files in her possession, she escaped the morgue as fast as she could. She managed to politely, but firmly, turn down the pathologists offer of a tour of his famous lungs collection. She didn't even ask if it was the collection or the owners that were famous. Her trip back upstairs gave her time to think on how to get in to Scudamore's room. She'd have to use another of her favourite tricks. All she needed now was to get her hands on a white coat.

Chapter 14

Ashby walked back up to the main hospital from the morgue. She considered trying to borrow a coat from Regis, but even the idea made her itch and squirm. Instead, she went back up to the main reception, essentially a large waiting room. A heavyset orderly guarded the door leading into the hospital proper, ensuring that only those whose names were called made it through. Having a coat was not going to be enough to get past the orderly, one had to be summoned. She observed the room for five minutes and so far no-one had been called forth. She inwardly cursed hospital waiting times and settled in near a coffee machine for a long stakeout...

***

After an hour of observation[26], Ashby understood the pattern. A doctor emerged from the door, called the patient's name, and they would disappear together into the bowels of the building. Ashby figured out what she needed to do to get inside.

She needed to make an appointment.

To make an appointment, she needed to be ill.

A new plan came to her. Fortunately, there were toilet facilities available in the waiting area and she sauntered in to the ladies as casually as possible. Inside, she used her makeup to cunningly disguise herself as a dead person. She was slightly annoyed that due to several days of hard investigative journalism it took a lot less time than she thought it would to achieve a pallid skin tone, dark rings under her eyes and the overall look of someone who belonged in the hospital.

---

[26] In which one person made it through the door. Ashby's main conclusion during this time was that the health service is in dire need of further investment.

She left the bathroom and marched over to the reception desk. Luckily a new, and judging by the gentle patter between her and the patients entering the waiting room, more pleasant receptionist was on duty.

"I'm ill." Ashby stated to the receptionist. The receptionist, slightly to Ashby's annoyance, agreed instantly.

"What have you got?" the receptionist asked with a seemingly pleasant smile.

"I don't know, I'm not a doctor." Ashby replied.

The receptionist noted this response on her notepad.

"Would like to see a doctor?" the receptionist continued the interrogation, smiled fixed in place.

"Ideally, yes please."

"Then go to your GP," was the response. It seemed this receptionist, whilst more social, had been trained by the same school as the previous one. The receptionist shut her notepad and dismissed Ashby with a cold and definitely not pleasant smile.

Ashby was going to need another new plan. As a trained and experienced journo, one came to her instantly. She used a talent she had previously only employed as an extremely vile party trick. A trick that had won her few friends, and she actually regretted every time she did it, but finally had its use.

Ashby's party trick was the ability to vomit at will and without mechanical intervention. A trick she used to great effect on the receptionist. Following this drastic and rather unpleasant move, several nurses appeared from nowhere and ushered Ashby through the doors and past the orderly.

She was in.

***

Her next challenge was that Ashby was now held in a small room and being subjected to a rather invasive check up by a tiny, but incredibly strong-fingered, nurse. Ashby wasn't sure why the symptom she had presented all over the receptionist called for a rectal examination but she had to concede she wasn't a trained medical professional.

The nurse eventually left the room to run some tests on the samples she had quite forcefully gathered, giving Ashby an opportunity to continue her quest for answers. Once the sound of the nurse's footsteps died out, Ashby gathered her clothes and slipped out in to the corridor. She guessed her gown would allow her to blend in to the milling patients and get her to Scudamore's room.

A few hours of wandering the corridor later, it turned out she was correct. Ashby found room 210 without a hitch. The hitch she did find was in the form of a burly police officer guarding the room as Regis had described. It was clear that she was going to have to revert back to plan A and acquire a white coat to get past.

In her hours of corridor wandering, Ashby had found exactly what she needed. In fact she had found a plethora of them. All the white coats she could ever need. Unfortunately, they were all being worn by doctors.

Ashby saw that the room next to 210 was empty. A doctor was walking toward her at a brisk pace, reading a chart and not paying much attention. A new plan formed in Ashby's mind.

"Excuse me, I have a problem in my room." Ashby called to the doctor. He looked up from the chart. He was a kindly looking soul and Ashby felt bad for what she was about to do.

"Can I help you, miss?" The doctor gave her a smile. His friendly eyes exuded warm spirited and compassionate humanity.

"Yes, I'm cold. Can I borrow your coat please?" Ashby gave a mock shiver and her best puppy dog eyes, laying on her performance as thick as she dared.

The doctor seemed to think about this for a minute.

"I don't see why not." He took his white coat off and handed it over. Ashby put it on and went in to the empty room so as to convince the doctor it was from whence she had come. The unsuspecting doctor set back off on his round, sans coat.

Inside the room, Ashby discarded the gown and changed back into her normal clothes, which she had miraculously kept vomit free[27]. She removed the makeup she had used to look ill and reapplied a more normal layer so that she looked a bit less ill. She gathered the report Regis had given her on Grindalythe's remains and set off to fool the police officer guarding Scudamore's room. The officer gave her a quick glance before returning to his important inspection of the wall opposite him.

"Hello," she said to the officer, "I am a doctor, let me in." Unsurprisingly, the officer didn't comply.

"I'm only allowed to let in Doctor Cheadle," the officer replied.

Ashby checked the name tag of the coat she had borrowed. She was in luck.

"I am Dr Cheadle." Ashby pointed at the name tag stitched to her coat. "See, it says so on my coat."

Whilst the officer seemed surprised at this news, he inspected the stitched name and seemed happy enough to let her in. She closed the door behind her and made a mental note to never accept protective custody from the police.

Inside room 210 there was only one bed. In that bed was Upton Scudamore. Every inch the image of a professional racer. Lean and high cheek-boned, even laid up in a hospital bed he looked ready for a photo shoot. His dark, wavy hair was carefully coiffed and his pencil moustache shaved to a fine

---

[27] Another part of her party trick. Did not help endear her to fellow party guests.

point. Ashby noted that his leg was in plaster but otherwise seemed fine. He was smoking a cigarette, which probably wasn't allowed.

"Hello, Ashby." He said in an affable manner. "What are you doing here? I thought you were a journo, not a doctor! When did you retrain?" Ashby looked around and could see there was no one else in the room. Scudamore had been appointed a very comfortable existence with his own bed, bathroom and a window looking out over the hospital car park.

"I haven't. I'm still a journalist, Upton. You should know I'd never quit whilst there are still stories to chase!" Ashby replied earnestly.

There was an awkward silence after Ashby's weird overeagerness. Upton's (almost) ever present, charming smile returned and he struck back up the conversation.

"How can I help you, Ashby? I see you've snuck in to my room dressed as my doctor, most ingenious! Certainly must have fooled the flatfoot on the door. Come to get the scoop on Scudamore's rapid recovery?" He waggled his eyebrows at her in a knowing manner.

"Something like that," Ashby replied. "I'm doing a piece on the Chapter 1 Classic."

The cheerful grin Upton had been wearing dropped away from his face.

"I suppose you'll be focussing on what happened to Kirby?" Scudamore sounded disappointed. He turned away from Ashby and gazed morosely out of the window near his bed.

"It's certainly part of it, Upton - he did die!" Ashby responded, slightly shocked that the racer could be so self-centred.

"Of course, of course. And so close to winning as well. Terribly, terribly sad."

Ashby thought that Scudamore didn't sound particularly sad about it.

"Can I ask you some questions, Upton? About the race? I want to tell it from your perspective. I'll do a section on your recovery as well! A double header."

This cheered Upton up somewhat. He was one of the few drivers that truly enjoyed the press side of the racing and Ashby knew she could use this to her advantage.

"Go on then Ashers - only for you! How could I say no when you worked so hard to get in here!"

Ashby gave him a big, fake smile and got started with her questions. Speaking about the difficulty getting in reminded her of the most pertinent.

"Why do you have a police officer guarding you? Surely even you aren't getting mobbed by fans so badly that you need the police here?"

"Nothing to do with the fans, Ashers, let them come. The bobby outside is by order of DI Wraxall Piece. Sent over to protect me since the race. He's worried that whoever offed Kirby might take a pop at me!" Scudamore replied jovially. He clearly wasn't taking the threat too seriously.

However, it gave Ashby some serious thoughts. Were the police once again treating Kirby's death as a murder? Or was the officer outside more to deter people like her getting in to the room and talking directly to Scudamore? In the meantime, it was time to hear Upton's rendition of the Chapter 1. He needed little prompting to tell his side of the story.

Chapter 15

"Started race day like normal. I woke up at 6 and downed a pint of tomato juice. I did 54 sit-ups, 68 star jumps and 103 squats. Nothing like some exercise to get the blood pumping. After the routine, I ate breakfast: more tomato juice then toast and eggs. Delicious, can't recommend my housekeeper enough. Her eggs are sublime, particularly when poached. After breakfast, a short drive to the track."

Scudamore paused only to puff on his cigarette. He was going in to a bit more detail than Ashby really needed. He had already described the night before the race and treated Ashby to a fairly graphic description of his pre-race urine test. However, things were finally starting to get interesting.

"I arrived at the track around 9 and went straight to the garage to see how Leigh was doing with the Lynx. Things weren't going well down there, some sort of brake manifold bother. Unusual for her, never normally has any issues on race day. Anyway, I went for a coffee with some reporters. Actually, I think I ran into you there, Ashers, didn't I?"

Ashby managed to get a nod in before Scudamore resumed his flow.

"We chatted about my chances. I wasn't favourite but I felt I could take Grindalythe. Must say, you lot didn't fancy me but I knew I had a little something to give me the edge!" Scudamore gave a conspiratorial wink.

"What did you have? I don't remember you saying!" Ashby found herself moving close to the edge of her seat. Scudamore was saying all the right things to keep her interested. This could be it, the link between Scudamore and the crash!

"Pressure!" Scudamore roared, slapping the hospital bed for emphasis. "Grindalythe had all the pressure on him and I was worry free. Felt that the pressure would get to him. All the occasion, figured he would make a bungle of it. One mistake from him was all I needed to take the podium, and the season, from the rotter. I was excited, by gosh." Scudamore's pencil moustache practically quivered to convey said excitement.

Ashby, however, slumped back in her chair. She had been hoping for something a bit more incriminating or sabotagey. Upton did not seem to notice Ashby's reaction, he took another drag on his cigarette then continued his tale.

"After the chat with you lot, I went back to the garage to see how Leigh was getting on with the Lynx. Ran in to one of those Cheneys on the way there, actually. Bit of an odd thing as they aren't usually around the pits on race day. More the champagne and socialising sort."

"Which one?" Ashby perked up. Scudamore had a think before replying.

"The big one, I think. No idea of the name. We didn't talk really. Just a polite hello."

"Man or woman?" Ashby asked.

"Hard to tell," replied Upton. Ashby thought that was fair enough. She had seen the Cheneys at the races before and they were quite difficult to tell apart. Especially for someone as self-obsessed as Scudamore. The interesting thing was that a Cheney had been down in the pits, possibly going to meet Delamere...

"After I ran into the Cheney 'sibling', I caught up with Leigh. She said she needed a bit longer with the car."

"Where is Leigh at the moment?" Ashby asked, as casually as she could manage.

"I imagine she is still in the garage. That's where I normally find her." Upton replied dismissively. "Now that you mention it, she hasn't been to visit me! Bit off that, thought she might have popped in."

"Do you know where she lives?" Ashby asked. Scudamore gave her an odd look so she hurriedly added a reason. "I'd like to interview her, how she feels seeing you crash and all that."

"Erm, no, I don't actually. Never thought to ask to be honest," Upton replied. Ashby sighed inwardly but managed not to let it show. At least she had heard about the proximity of a Cheney sibling to the pit area. Ashby noticed that Upton looked thoughtful for a minute, an unusual occurrence.

"You might be able to find her at Anearby Boxing Gym." He added after the thinking ended. "She has mentioned to me that she trains there occasionally." Ashby made a mental note of this and Scudamore continued his story.

"Anyway, Leigh asked me if I could stay out of the way a bit longer so I complied and went to the Champagne tent. Had a lovely drink with Cheddon Fitzpaine and the rather tasty Ingleby Greenhow. They had been chatting to each other so I thought I'd join in. Some waffle about compound interest - not interested, didn't really listen."

More connections, thought Ashby.

Upton ploughed on with his description of events.

"Finished the drink and made my way down to the start line. Leigh had got the car there on time and we were ready to go!"

Scudamore then went on to give a very detailed description of the race, corner by corner. Ashby, who had seen the race herself, nodded politely at the appropriate moments. A curt summary of the description was that Scudamore spent the entire race well behind Grindalythe. Upton painted it as a heroic chase against a technologically superior foe. Ashby started to pay attention again when Scudamore got to describing the last corner of the last lap.

"...So I blasted out of the hairpin. I had him in my sights! The woods are the worst bit. Some of the toughest corners. After two hours of hard racing, it's only natural that one could lose concentration, especially in the gloom amongst the trees! I knew this would be my chance. Kirby had charged in at pace but I was right behind him. I took each corner as hard as I dared. I had to be quick - it was my last chance."

Ashby held her breath. The next part was going to be painful to hear.

"I heard the crash as I took the first corner of the woods. I didn't see it happen; it was a split second before I rounded the bend and was confronted by the wreckage. I was going too fast to stop. Nothing I could do but dodge the car parts in the road. I could do naught but continue. I thought he had made the mistake I was looking for and as long as I kept going victory was mine! Still would have been if it hadn't have been for that fire engine charging me down."

Ashby went a bit numb. Even Scudamore hadn't seen the crash. No witnesses at all.

"...Something the poilce should investigate really, see if those firefighters were employed to sabotage me!" Scudamore had continued but Ashby wasn't paying much attention. There wasn't much more Upton could add and she knew this, she had watched him crash into the fire engine and then get loaded into an ambulance. One more question then it was time to leave the hospital.

"Did you know Kirby's team were in financial trouble at the beginning of the season?" she asked.

"I did not. That's news to me!" Scudamore's eyes widened with surprise. "He always had access to all that lovely Greenhow money from his scrummy wife!"

Kirby must have kept it very quiet if even the other drivers didn't know thought Ashby.

"Thanks, Upton. Very useful. Keep your eyes on the papers at the weekend!" Ashby stood up and hurried to the door.

"What about the piece on my recovery?" Scudamore asked, clearly disappointed at having to stop his story.

"Oh, yes." Ashby had forgotten. "How are you getting on with the recovery?"

"The doctors say I'm doing remarkably well for a man who has been in an accident like mine. Heart like a horse they say..."

"Great." Ashby said to cut him off and made it through the door. "I can work with that."

"You don't even know what's wrong with me!" Scudamore called back, hurt laced in his voice, but it was too late. Ashby had already closed the door and set off down the corridor.

Chapter 16

Anearby Boxing Gym was in a rough part of town. Ashby was glad to have a lead on Delamere but she was not looking forward to the visit. The gym was famous for its links with the local underworld. It wasn't a place that outsiders were welcome.

The rough part of town was not near the hospital and so Ashby had to drive, rueing her inability to claim back mileage on her woefully uneconomic Civet. By the time she pulled up outside, it was opening time for the gym.

Not that there was much sign of this from the outside. The Boxing Gym entrance was a rusty black metal doorway atop a flight of rusty metal stairs. The stairs were at the end of a dingy alley that was sandwiched between a shop that looked like it sold big, black curtains[28] and a shop advertising illegally imported sausages. The only indication of the gym was a sign above the rusty black metal door that read 'Boxing Gym' with a caricature of a kitted up boxer knocking several teeth out of another man. Worryingly, the man in the sign receiving the punches was not wearing boxing kit.

Ashby watched the club door to get a feel for the comings and goings of the gym. Even though a cheery sign over the handle said 'Open!', there were neither comings nor goings for an hour. She was going to have to go in there with no knowledge of what was on the other side. Not for the first time, she wished Wenlock was still with her. Not as physical protection, Ashby had long ago clocked him as being a bit of a softy and he was far from physically imposing, but his presence at least meant someone to watch her back. Most importantly, he had a badge of authority that still meant something, even in this part of town.

---

[28] It probably didn't sell curtains - the only thing in the window was a big, black curtain across it so you couldn't see inside. It didn't look like the kind of place the honoured a returns policy and certainly didn't give credit.

On her petrol-thirsty drive to the gym, she had stopped home and picked up her own gym kit, Ashby's idea being that she might be able to blend in with the regulars and try to spot Leigh. If Leigh wasn't there, she hoped to befriend a local who would point her in the right direction.

Ashby grabbed her kit and made her way down the alley, up the stairs and to the gym entrance. It was going to be tough, it had been awhile since she had used a treadmill and the stairs were pretty steep.

***

There was no receptionist at the front desk. In fact, there was no front desk, just a small corridor with three doors. On the left, a door marked 'MEN', opposite was a door marked 'WOMIN' and at the end of the corridor a door marked "GYM". Ashby figured 'WOMIN' was where she needed to start.

The ladies changing room was small and seldom cleaned. Ashby got changed, touching as little of the room as possible, before heading back through the corridor to the main gym.

It was exactly as she imagined. A large room with wooden floors, inadequate lighting and punch bags hanging from the low ceiling like pieces of fetid meat at a butchers that the health inspector did not dare visit. On closer inspection, it appeared some of the bags were in fact carcasses of animals Ashby did not recognise. It stank of sweat, cigarettes and vulcanised rubber. In the centre of the room was a raised ring occupied by two towers of meat - who were very much occupied with tenderising each other. A small, wizened man at the ringside was shouting barely comprehensible encouragement at one or both of them. Ashby assumed he was a trainer but frankly he could have been shouting out his shopping list for all she could tell.

All around the main ring, training fighters hit punch bags or each other with varying degrees of success. In the far corner was a weights section, with the sorts of dumbbells that wouldn't look out of place being dropped on the heads of cartoon characters.

What there wasn't, Ashby noticed, was much in the way of cardio equipment. To keep with tradition there did appear to be a boxer using a skipping rope in the corner. Ashby thought that this seemed like a good place to start - she didn't fancy the rest of the equipment just yet as she hadn't had her induction.

She wandered toward the skipping figure who, on closer inspection, turned out to be a woman. She was skipping slowly but methodically and looked to be in it for the long run. Ashby could tell that the skipper definitely wasn't Leigh, but given how small the changing rooms were there couldn't have been many other female members of the gym and thus it was likely this lady would know of the missing mechanic. Ashby took up the spare rope next to her target and began with some long lazy loops. She covertly surveyed her intended informant to see what she could glean. The other skipper was a good head taller than Ashby and built like a boxer, which was unsurprising given the circumstances. She was shock blonde and her hair was cropped so closely to her skull that Ashby could see her think.

Ashby's surveillance did not go unnoticed. The other skipper caught her eye and started to intensify her swings. Ashby kept pace with ease and so her counterpart swung faster still. Ashby decided it was time to signal intent and brought out her special moves. She kept the pace and stuck a Straddle Cross in there to signify she was no amateur. This elicited a raised eyebrow from her newfound gym buddy who copied the move and added a Side Swing to the sequence[29]. Ashby repeated the Side Swing and responded with a Side-to-Side Skier. This seemed to be enough for her shaved companion who slowed it down and indicated getting some water. Ashby wound up the rope and followed her to a bench at the side of the gym.

---

[29] If you're curious as to what these moves are, I recommend looking them up with the aid of an online search engine or a popular video player. Or a book if you're really imaginative. Not this book though, I'm not going to describe them here.

They are all real though.

"Nice moves," the taller lady said.

"Thanks. Not bad yourself," Ashby replied.

"I'm Lacey, Lacey Green. Nice to meet you."

"Ashby-de-la-Zouch." They shook hands and took a long drink from their water bottles.

"Haven't seen you in here before. You just joined?" Lacey asked.

"Doing a taster day," Ashby replied, "seeing if it's for me."

Lacey looked a bit surprised at this. Ashby realised it was unlikely that Anearby Boxing Gym did taster sessions. Fortunately, the other lady didn't push the point. Ashby began her investigation.

"Not many other women in here. Are you the only other female member?" Ashby asked as nonchalantly as she could manage.

"This place doesn't attract many girls," Lacey smiled. "It has a bit of a reputation."

As if on cue, the fight in the central ring was paused by the angry short man. It appeared one boxer had drawn an awful lot of blood from his opponent. Possibly using his teeth.

"I like it though. These guys aren't so bad. No ogling like in some of the other places." Lacey paused to take a swig of water. "And I get to punch people which, if I'm honest, I quite enjoy."

"Yeah," Ashby nodded, "I like that too. Punching people is great." She hoped the fairly obvious lie wasn't detected.

"I assume you are here to learn to box? There aren't many other options..." Lacey waved her arm at the scene around them to emphasise the lack of opportunity for Pilates.

"Definitely!" Ashby replied. "Is there anybody more my size to spar with? I feel you may have some advantage over me."

Lacey laughed at this. Not only was she a good head taller but it was clear she could comfortably lifted Ashby over that extra head.

"There is. She's not around today but tends to be here at least three times a week. A girl about your height and build. She mostly trains on the bags, she'll be delighted to finally have a partner she can spar with fairly."

"Anyone I might of heard of?" Ashby asked, straining to keep up her nonchalance.

"Her name is Leigh Delamere, works up at the race track. Nice girl but lot of anger in her. For her size, she really does a number on the bags!"

"Sounds perfect," Ashby said. It was time to get what she was after. "When is she usually here?"

"Usually it would be late on a Sunday, Tuesdays and Thursdays but she hasn't been in then this week." Lacey said with a frown. "In fact, I haven't seen her this week at all!"

"Do you know where she lives?" Ashby asked hopefully, probing further.

"I might." The defences were up and suspicion aroused. Ashby had gotten too personal too quickly and cursed herself for it.

"You could check on her if you did is all I mean." Ashby tried to cover it up but Lacey wasn't buying it.

"Yeah I could," Lacey replied coolly. "You seem really interested in her though and you wouldn't be the first asking after her this week."

Ashby figured it was time to come clean. Lacey didn't seem like someone who you could fool for long.

"Lacey, I'll be honest with you. I'm not here on a taster day."

"No shit." Lacey put her hand over her mouth in mock shock.

"I'm a reporter for the *Everyday Post*. I'm investigating the death of Kirby Grindalythe. I really need to speak to Leigh as I think she could have some crucial information. I've been trying to track her down but with no luck. Can you help me?"

Lacey paused to think on this.

"At least you've been honest... eventually. Which is surprising given the absolute rag you work for," Lacey smiled. "And you are a lot nicer than the other fella who came looking."

"I'd love to know who that was too?" Ashby asked hopefully. Lacey took a big drink of water before coming to a decision.

"I'll help you," she said, "but first you'll have to beat me."

Ashby looked horrified at this suggestion. There was no way she was going to be able to beat Lacey in a fight. She doubted she could even reach the other woman's face with her fist, let alone throw a punch at it. Lacey clearly picked up on what Ashby was thinking and laughed.

"Not in a fight, Ashby!" She laughed some more. "That wouldn't be fair. I mean in a contest with the skipping ropes! You had some good moves earlier and I like a challenge."

Ashby heaved a sigh of relief. This sounded slightly more manageable and less fatal.

"You could just tell me," Ashby pointed out.

"I could, but where's the fun in that?" Lacey replied with a wink.

Chapter 17

Lacey had a word with the angry bald man and the central ring was cleared of detritus from the previous fight. The other boxers in the gym took a break and gathered ringside, intrigued as to what was going to happen. Almost as intrigued as Ashby herself; she hadn't taken part in a skip-off in many years. She went through her old repertoire in her head. Her many years in the school skip team and the trophy she had won was still somewhere in her flat, giving her confidence that this was worth a punt. She was smaller and faster than Lacey, of that she was sure. However, Lacey was clearly more practised and had kept up with her just fine earlier. It was going to be a close run thing. Ashby had to get in the zone. It was crucial she learned where to find Leigh and who else was looking for the missing mechanic.

The competitors did some warm up stretching before the angry bald man told them to take their positions in each corner of the ring.

"The rules are simple. Miss Green has initiated the challenge so she sets the pace and will perform the first sequence." He shouted at them. "Miss de-la-Zouch, you will then copy her sequence before adding a sequence of your own. This will continue until one of you has made three mistakes or stops the rope, after which the remaining skipper is the winner. Am I understood?"

Both Ashby and Lacey nodded. It was classic stuff and well known to anyone who had ever skipped competitively.

"Remember, no body contact. However, this is a seedy boxing gym so I will allow some rope-to-rope interference," the angry man continued to scream at the contestants, unnecessarily loud based on his proximity. Ashby winced. She had only ever played it clean before, in the more highly regulated skipping leagues. This was going to be tough and she would have to expect that Lacey would play dirty.

"Now, I want a good clean skip off," he continued. "Well, minus the bit I just mentioned. You will begin on the bell. Skippers, shake ropes."

Ashby and Lacey took hold of each other's skipping rope loops and gave them the traditional shake before moving back to their competitive position - facing each other in the ring, a rope's distance apart. Lacey unravelled her rope and did a few lazy practise swings before blowing Ashby a kiss, possibly as an attempt to psyche her out? Ashby mentally prepared herself for the test ahead.

Suddenly, the bell rang and Lacey set the pace. She started with a few slow turns of the rope but soon settled at a more competitive rhythm. Ashby was forced to match speed - this was not going to be easy. Just as Ashby made it up to pace, Lacey started her sequence. A Side Swing, followed by a Double Side Swing & Jump before transitioning into a Skier.

Simple stuff, a warm-up more than anything else, though at this pace it would be a tricky enough prospect. Ashby let the rope fly past her face twice before copying the sequence. No errors, a good start and the crowd gave a murmur of approval. It was Ashby's turn to set a sequence. Like Lacey, she decided to start with some easy moves and blow off the cobwebs. Making a mistake on your own sequence was considered a very poor show and the mark of a truly rank amateur.

Ashby upped the pace slightly, just to show she meant business here, and then made her moves. A Bell, a Straddle and finished with a Scissors. Nothing to set the world alight but it got a small clap of appreciation from the watching boxers. Lacey gave a brief smile, upped her pace and ploughed straight through Ashby's sequence. Without a pause, she started on her own, a Straddle Cross, a Crossover and ending with a Wounded Duck followed by a Full Turn. This got the crowd excited and Ashby could see she was going to have to pull out some advanced moves to win. Fortunately, they did not know her competitive background. She followed Lacey's sequence and then ploughed right in with her own moves. Ashby threw down a Forward 180, followed by a Backward 180 then capped that with a Full

Twist. This trio earned a smile from Lacey and a roar from the crowd. They were enjoying the contest.

Lacey worked through Ashby's sequence, again without problem. This time, however, before setting her moves, she took the time to up the pace once more. This made Ashby nervous - it was faster than she had skipped in a decade. The rope in front of her face was a blur. Before she had time to think further, Lacey performed a Kickswing, a Caboose and then finally a Peek-a-Boo. Classic crowd pleasers and the watchers responded with throaty, toothless cheering.

Ashby steeled herself, allowing a few rotations before copying. She managed the Kickswing, and most of the Caboose until she made the first mistake of the match. She was too slow with the crossover and caught her left foot, not enough to completely disturb her rhythm but enough for the angry man to raise an arm and log the mistake. The crowd went wild - they didn't want the newcomer to beat their fellow gym member. One-nil to Lacey.

Ashby recovered and finished off the Peek-a-Boo without issue. The damage had been done though and her confidence was shaken. It took a few revolutions before she could get the rope back to competition pace. She could see Lacey grinning. Ashby was determined to wipe the smile off her face, it was time to go for it. She took a deep breath before pulling out some of the most complex moves she knew. She started with a Double Peek-a-Boo, just to make a statement, before moving to a Double-Under-With-Cross and capping the sequence with an Awesome Annie.

The crowd loved it, Ashby took a lot of satisfaction in seeing Lacey's eyes widen for the first time in the contest. It had only been for a fraction of a second, but it sent a clear message. Lacey allowed the rope to do two revolutions before starting. She had no trouble with the Double Peek-a-Boo, nor the Double-Under-With-Cross. However, the Awesome Annie proved to be a step too far. She was too slow with the alternate and the rope touched

100

her shoulder on its way round. Not enough to stop her, but it caused another arm raise from the angry man[30] and levelled the score to one-one.

The crowd began a slow clap whilst Lacey composed herself and started her next sequence. Ashby would have held her breath if she didn't need every ounce of it to keep the rope moving and keep jumping. She hadn't skipped this much since she was in school. Her arms were aching and legs burned with fatigue. Tomorrow was going to be a couch day...

Lacey, as if she had read Ashby's mind, upped the pace once more. She could see Ashby was blowing hard. Ashby could tell that Lacey would be able to beat her for fitness, she had to hope her skill was greater to close this out. However, first it was Lacey's turn.

She started with a Side-Swing-Double-Under, a Grapevine and ended on a Pretzel. By this point, the crowd were climbing the walls at the contest. Ashby had a serious challenge to follow those moves. She knew she could do them, but at this pace? There was only one way for her to find out: she needed to go for it.

She finished the Side-Swing-Double-Under and the Grapevine. She was starting the Pretzel when it happened. She had forgotten the referee's warning at the beginning. He would tolerate a level of underhand play she had not previously experienced. Whilst Ashby was moving for the leg-over, Lacey skipped closer to her. Her rope grazed Ashby's, touching it only ever so slightly. A kiss. At this speed, not enough to stop the whirling cord but enough to send it off course. It disrupted Ashby's rhythm enough that she couldn't complete the move. Her right arm caught her right leg and she never made it over. The crowd howled. She managed a heroic hop to save the revolution and stay in the match but she could see the referee had raised an arm. Two-one to Lacey. One more mistake from her would see the match over. As she got back up to speed, she saw Lacey give her a wink. The pain in Ashby's arms was becoming unbearable, her breathing ragged and heavy - she couldn't keep this pace up.

---

[30] By now, Ashby had decided to accept that he was some form of referee.

It was time for no-more-nice-Ashby. It was time to bring out the moves that had won her championships. Ashby did something unusual at this stage of the competition, she slowed the pace[31] and took a deep breath before putting down her best sequence. The nuclear option.

Ashby let rip with a Double-Cross-Back, followed by a Forward-Knot. She ended the sequence with a move she had never seen bettered before. Her personal favourite: a Front-Back Rope Release[32]. All three were risky. She took great satisfaction in seeing Lacey's eyebrows raise. The crowd by now were figuratively and literally punching each other with excitement. The moves were complex, risky and spectacular. A wrong step could hospitalise a contender or even a bystander

Lacey took a good few seconds to prepare herself. The display didn't look like it would phase her though. To Ashby's dismay, Lacey managed the Double-Cross-Back and the Forward-Knot without incident. The crowd baying, she started on the Front-Back Rope Release. The start went well for her and it looked like it was going to be a perfect set. At the last second of the release, Ashby decided to employ a little of her own psychological warfare and gave Lacey a flirty wink. It had the desired effect and caught the eye of her opponent. Lacey didn't quite drop the rope but the catch was not clean. Not enough to win it for Ashby, thanks to the slower pace Lacey recovered, but it was enough for the referee to call a point. Two-two. Sudden death. The slow clap started again. Lacey took the opportunity to bring the pace back up again. The clap increased in tempo. Ashby summoned her last reserves and followed suit.

The rope had gone beyond a blur in front of Ashby's eyes. It was almost solid in appearance. All she could see through the whipping rope was an occasional glimpse at Lacey. It was faster than Ashby had ever taken a rope before. She could see that even Lacey was sweating now, her muscles covered in a glistening sheen. The crowd had given up clapping - they

---

[31] Totally allowed on her turn, just unusual.

[32] I seriously recommend look these all up. They are very impressive.

couldn't keep up. Silence reigned the gym except for the whip of rope hitting the floor of the ring. Ashby reckoned that if the ropes touched at this speed it would tear the handles from her hands, likely losing her a layer of skin. She had to push the thought away as Lacey increased the pace further. Even the boxing athlete was starting to breath hard. Still no sign of a move from her; maybe she was going to just try and outpace her? It could work. Ashby was not going to be able to stand much more of this.

Then the move came. It was not a move that Ashby thought possible at this speed.

Lacey did a Push Up Jump.

And then, whilst she was recumbent, she did another one.

And then another one.

She sprang back to her feet, the rope still whirling and gave Ashby a smile. A smile that knew it was not going to wiped off. Then, the slightest of upward nods. A nod that said: "Top that". The crowd went bananas. Ashby wasn't sure but she later thought she had seen some faeces throwing from a particularly excited individual.

Ashby was still whirling the rope and struggling to breath. It was going to take a Herculean effort to even do one Push-Up, never mind three. The crowd calmed and silence returned. They sensed that Ashby was about to make her attempt. She felt that they believed that she could do it. She had shown herself to be a competent roper - they had every right to believe. Ashby steadied herself and took one last deep breath.

She squatted down.

She hurled the rope around her back.

She dived forward.

Chapter 18

"And then what? Did you manage it?" Wenlock was hooked. After the skip-off at the boxing gym, Ashby had called him saying she needed to talk about what she had found out. They had met up on a bench in Anearby park.

"What do you think?" she said, surprised that a crack detective such as Wenlock had failed to notice the huge bandage across her nose, sitting beneath her two black eyes.

"I see," said Wenlock, a bit embarrassed. "It looks painful. How are you feeling?"

"Like an idiot," Ashby replied. "Also, in pain. I hit the floor of the ring hard and apparently blacked out for a good five minutes. When I came to, most of the boxers had left. Fortunately, Lacey managed to stem the bleeding from my nose and get me cleaned up in the changing rooms."

Ashby shifted position on the bench they were sat on. It was a cold, grey afternoon and her bum was going numb. Bizarrely, Wenlock appeared not to be bothered by the low temperature and was wearing a disgusting paisley shirt, beige shorts and flip flops. He had brought with him what appeared to be a pack of semi-feral dogs. She hadn't had chance to ask him why yet.

"Did Lacey give you Leigh's address?" Wenlock asked. His mind was back on the case he wasn't allowed to work.

"No, she was true to her word. She wouldn't give it up to a loser. But she did tell me that she had already been to Leigh's house to check up on her and that Leigh wasn't there. She also told me who the other person asking after Leigh is."

"One of the Cheneys?" Wenlock suggested, eager to demonstrate his highly trained intuition after his earlier misdetection.

"No, DI Wraxall Piece actually." Ashby corrected him, a little smugly, knowing it would annoy him being shown up twice. "He went to the gym the day before me. Lacey refused to give him any information so he 's going back there today with a warrant. Shame we can't do the same..."

Wenlock picked up the hint. Any information leading to Delamere would put that scumsucker Piece one step ahead.

"Sorry, no chance Ashby. If I go anywhere near this case, they'll throw the book at me. It's risky enough meeting with you," he replied after stroking a pack member of the near-wolves he had brought with him.

"Thanks for coming all the same. I could use some help." Ashby said. "What are you doing now you're suspended?"

"Oh, I'm not suspended." Wenlock answered as he broke up a particularly violent scuffle between two of the larger canines.

"Undercover?" Ashby ventured, her guess largely based on the bizarre outfit.

"I'm just off the Grindalythe case." Wenlock looked a bit sheepish as he replied. "To be honest, there aren't an awful lot of open murder cases in town. We're a very quiet department so I spend most of my time looking after this lot."

"Must be nice," Ashby said wistfully. "Having the time off to spend with your... pets?"

Wenlock nodded cheerfully as he extricated one of his flip-flops from the mouth of a particularly persistent Alsatian.

"It's great. Much better than working missing persons, which is always incredibly busy for some strange reason. I guess Leigh will get added to their caseload."

"And the ghastly shirt?"

"I just like it." Wenlock shrugged. "Anyway, one thing you haven't told me yet is what was in the report that Regis gave you?"

Ashby's eyes lit up as she pulled the autopsy report from her bag.

"You're not going to believe it. I read it last night. It's why I called you!" She handed it over and Wenlock began to read. He finished page one and then started on page two.

"You probably don't need to go any further than that," she told him, thinking of her numb posterior. "The shocking bit was in the first paragraph of the first page."

"But that bit just says who's body it is." Wenlock looked sceptical. He always skipped that bit when he read these reports. It tended to be obvious.

"Look again," Ashby urged him. He did. His eyes visibly widened. Ashby couldn't wait any longer.

"It's not him," she said. "The body isn't Kirby."

Wenlock looked up from the report.

"It doesn't quite say that. It says they can't prove it is him - it's very different," he stated. "There wasn't much body to test and it had been one hell of a fire after the crash. That can really mess the results up."

"But there is a chance!" Ashby was excited. "What a way to fake your death, and I could believe it from him, he was always a bit of a showman."

"It's certainly a thought," Wenlock replied thoughtfully. "I can't see why he would though - he was about to win his greatest triumph. Why would he do fake his death before the finish?"

They both paused on this. It was a good question. They didn't yet have the full picture and they knew it.

"Maybe he had to do it then? Perhaps the Cheneys weren't looking to sabotage his car, they were just looking for him in general?"

"I suppose that is one theory," Wenlock conceded. "And we know there was some funny financial business going on from what his ex-wife said." He took a break from the conversation to untangle a lead from around the leg of the bench.

"There's no way Wraxall will know this. We're the only ones with the report. That gives us the edge and a new angle to push."

"Not 'us' Ashby. I'm out, remember!" Wenlock held up his hands in a 'slow down' gesture. Ashby didn't respond, which suckered Wenlock right back in. "So whose body is it?"

"The report doesn't say. Results inconclusive. No match to any known persons on record. Reading through the rest doesn't help much either. It tells you that the remains are human, they've been in a fire and they're definitely dead," Ashby reeled off the conclusions easily. She had read through the report several times already, so excited she had been at the idea that there was an extra layer to the story.

"I discovered one more thing, confirming something Ingleby Greenhow mentioned in passing, about how she had stopped funding the race team," Ashby added in-between stamping her feet to bring warmth to her legs. She really could not understand how Wenlock was able to just wear a shirt and shorts. "Grantham confirmed that the team was in financial difficulty at the beginning of the season. They nearly couldn't keep the team going until a mystery benefactor stepped in."

"Who?" asked Wenlock.

"I don't know," Ashby replied. "It's a mystery."

"I see," said Wenlock. "So in summary:

- Kirby Grindalythe's season nearly didn't go ahead as his estranged wife pulled the team funding. Fortunately, a mystery benefactor stepped in and saved them.

- Grindalythe was on track to win the biggest race of his career, at the expense of his rival Upton Scudamore.

- Before the race, Grindalythe wished to change his life insurance from his ex-wife to local politician Cheddon Fitzpaine.

- Cheddon Fitzpaine is in some way connected to a business owned by notorious gangsters, the Cheneys.

- The Cheneys had an opportunity to tamper with Grindalythe's car just prior to the race.

- Leigh Delamere, who may have given the Cheneys that opportunity, has not been seen for days.

- After we discovered that connection, I was taken off the case and it has been given to Wraxall Piece, who I am certain is just the pawn of Cheddon Fitzpaine.

- Wraxall Piece is also trying to find Leigh Deleamere and is trying to prevent people from speaking to Scudamore.

- The person who crashed in the Chapter 1 Classic may not be Kirby Grindalythe and we are the only ones who know this. Except for Regis but he thinks I am still the one on the case and not Wraxall.

Have I missed anything?"

"No, I think that summarises the story so far in a succinct manner," Ashby replied, impressed that Wenlock could pronounce a bullet point. "Maybe just a mention that we haven't yet looked into the jilted husbands of Kirby's many lovers or whether there were any irregular betting patterns on the race."

"Good point. It's certainly starting to form a picture." Wenlock could feel his detective brain firing in to action. He had been sceptical at first but there was definitely a case here to be solved. Or a lot of coincidences - both were still possible.

"If you're not too busy, it would be great if you could help out in a surreptitious way?" Ashby tried her luck, she could see the 'keep out' policy was not going to last long for Wenlock. His by-the-book attitude was starting to give way to his love for investigation. He paused to consider her request and to untangle the dog leads.

"Fine, I can look into the betting patterns. I was on my way to the bookies anyway," he gave in. "I think you'd be best placed to look at the jilted husbands given how much you seem to know about the subject."

"And finding Delamere?" Ashby asked, thinking this was a little more crucial than opening other avenues of investigation.

"Leave that to me," Wenlock said. "I have a few tricks up my sleeve still." Ashby doubted that. The sleeves of his shirt were not very long.

"And the inconclusive test results?" To Ashby, it was the burning question.

"Hold on to them," Wenlock suggested. "Not much more we can do but presume that it is still Grindalythe and see where our leads take us."

It sounded like a plan. After gathering up one of Wenlock's Dobermans who had shucked his leash, they went their separate ways in pursuit of the truth and a rare win on the horses.

Chapter 19

Wenlock sauntered from the park to Anearby Bookmakers. He tied up his pack[33] outside and walked in as casually as he could which was pretty casual as he was a regular. There wasn't much to the bookies: an aisle flanked by two rows of small, newspaper lined, booths leading up to a counter. The counter had security bars to prevent anyone from getting their money back from the safe behind. It was quiet in the shop. In fact, it was empty save for the bookie herself and an old man that Wenlock didn't recognise sitting at a booth. The booth's wirnkled resident was marking a betting slip and Wenlock's entry did not disturb him.

"Oh, hello Much," the roundish, cheerful lady behind the counter called out. "Come to settle up your account?"

"Erm, not today thanks Mrs Wells, here on business actually." Wenlock replied, a little sheepishly as he walked up to her.

"Please, Much call me Bluith. I've been asking you to do so for years!" She give him a beaming smile. "We see each other enough to be friends, almost!"

Wenlock was less sure about this idea; it wasn't generally a good friendship in which one friend owed the other a fairly substantial gambling debt. He decided to press on with the investigation rather than giving away too much of his back-story.

"Mrs Wells, Bluith, I need some help..."

"No more credit Much. My husband has strictly forbidden it," Bluith stated, a little haughtily. Wenlock paused to rub his temples before continuing. He also thought it a bit strange as he knew Mr Bluith was a baker and Wenlock

---

[33] Of dogs. Not a rucksack or similar.

also knew that Mrs Bluith owned the shop rather than her husband. He filed the information away for further investigation, specifically at the weekend when he might need some more credit.

"No, no, nothing like that. Police help. With a case." Wenlock leaned in as far as the bars on the counter allowed him to. He didn't know who the old man was but he didn't want word getting around that he was still investigating the Grindalythe case. He also wasn't keen on any more of his gambling related dealings being revealed to the local populace.

"Oooh, how exciting. I'll obviously help however I can!" Bluith leaned in too. Substantially less than Wenlock as she was quite short and very rotund, bits of her got in the way of the leaning operation.

"Who was the favourite in the Chapter 1 Classic?" Wenlock started with an easy one.

"Well that would be Kirby Grindalythe. He was going for the championship on his home course. Frankly, no-one could see any different than a win for him. He was on at 1 to 5!"

Exactly as Wenlock had expected. One of the reasons he had never been interested in motorsport was the absolutely awful odds and the fact there were few upsets.[34]

"Did anyone place money against Grindalythe? Substantial amounts I mean, not just a little flutter."

"Hmmm, let me think," said Bluith as she paused to think. Wenlock allowed her to. When she stopped thinking, she had a rummage through a drawer under the counter. "There was one bet I thought a bit strange."

Wenlock waited for her to finish rummaging and let her continue.

---

[34] Not that he had much success with his other gambling endevours

"Got it," she said as she pulled a crumpled betting slip from the drawer. She smoothed out the betting slip on the counter so that Wenlock could see what was written on it.

The slip, written in Bluith's neat handwriting, read as below:

UPTON SCUDAMORE TO WIN

7/1

£10,000

"Now, as you know, that's the carbon copy that I keep of the original so I can verify the bet when the person who placed said bet brings back the original so as to claim their winnings."

Wenlock nodded, as has been well established so far, he was familiar with how a bookies worked.

"Is that a normal amount for someone to bet on motor racing?" Wenlock asked. It was a lot of money, similar to a decent year's wages. However, Wenlock knew, based on Ashby's earlier explanation, that people who bet on the cars tended to have deep pockets.

"A bit steep," Bluith replied. "Certainly more than I've ever seen put on when the odds are so against the second favourite. As I said, everybody was backing Kirby."

Wenlock nodded. This was interesting. Now for the most interesting bit.

"Do you know who placed the bet?" He kept his voice level but both he and Bluith knew that this was the question he needed an answer to. Bluith's face broke from its cheerful smile into a look of despair.

"I'm sorry, DI Wenlock, I really don't. It wasn't a regular, that much I know."

"Man or women?" DI Wenlock prepared to start the classic twenty questions game to jog her memory. "Animal, vegetable or mineral?"

"I'm sorry, I really can't remember. The day before the Chapter 1 is our busiest of the year! I must have had thousands through the door." Bluith really did look distraught. It was not like her to forget something, she usually remembered every face.

Suddenly, a voice came from one of the booths.

"I know who did it."

Both Wenlock and Bluith turned to look at who exclaimed the bold statement. They both knew - there was only one other person in the shop. The old man.

"I'll tell you too. But there will be a price," the rumpled booth resident continued.

This annoyed Wenlock. This man should be happy to help the police with their enquires. Also annoying because it would be Wenlock footing the bill, as he wasn't technically on the case anymore.

He thanked Bluith for her help and walked over to the booth occupied by the old man. He was sat at one of the booth's stools, still studying the newspaper sports pages plastered on the wall. Wenlock sat at the other stool and looked him up and down. The man looked ancient and weathered. He was well over 80 or he'd had the hardest paper round imaginable. He looked old enough that the reason his paper round had been hard was that he was delivering stone tablets. He wore an old green mackintosh and seemed to be missing several teeth, judging by the grin permanently etched into his face. He was wearing a waterproof cap which didn't bode well for his reliability as it wasn't raining inside or outside the shop.

"And what is your name please, sir?" Wenlock decided to start polite.

"Acton Turville, at your service DI Wenlock." Turville turned to face Wenlock, confirming Wenlock's previous judgement on teeth number. Wenlock did not like the way he had been addressed. It very much suggested that Turville might have been at the inspectors service, but that the service would impart a high price.

"Mr Turville, it seems you are in possession of information that would help the police in their enquiries. May I make a suggestion that would benefit you greatly?"

Turville gave a shrug and a gesture that said 'go ahead'. The grin remained in place. Wenlock pressed on.

"That you provide that information. Who placed the bet?"

"I told you, DI Wenlock. That information will cost you." The grin spread further around the face, however no more teeth were revealed.

"I have a suggestion on how I could pay." Wenlock was really getting hacked off now. He didn't raise his voice but he did add a hint of menace to it. "I could pay by not charging you with obstructing the course of justice."

The grin carried on widening. Wenlock became worried that Turville's jaw was going to separate from the rest of his head. Then, a strange croaking noise came out of it. It took Wenlock a few moments to realise it was laughter.

"Go ahead. I'll just claim that I was mistaken and never saw the bet placed." Turville replied, once he had set his mouth back to a semi-normal shape. "I can tell you now though, I did see it placed and who placed it. Very clearly."

"Wasting police time then." This wasn't Wenlock's first difficult questioning.

"Try it, I'm wearing a rain hat inside on a dry day. I think any judge would say you were wasting your own time!" Turville once again emitted his croaking laugh. Wenlock realised he couldn't really argue with that point, or with this man. He was going to have to stump up.

"Very well," Wenlock conceded, reaching for his wallet. "How much?"

"Oh no, DI Wenlock, I don't want money." Turville's grin started to look even more sinister, which surprised Wenlock as it had been pretty grim looking already. "I have something else in mind."

"Go on then, spit it out." Wenlock put on a good show of bravado but was apprehensive, there was only so far he was willing to go to get the truth. His imagination started to go some unpleasant places trying to fathom what this old man might want.

"I want," Turville paused for effect, "to ride in a sledge, pulled by a pack of dogs."

Wenlock blinked.

"What?"

"You heard," Turville replied. "I want to ride in a sledge. Pulled by dogs."

"You're quite mad, aren't you?" was all Wenlock could manage to reply. Turville made the strange croaking sound again.

"Oh God, yes." He took off his hat and scratched his head, revealing a mess of tangled grey hair.

"He really is." Bluith had left her post behind the counter to join the show. She was leaning at the entrance to the booth. "Acton is in everyday but has never placed a bet. Even though I know you're loaded, aren't you Acton?"

Turville nodded vigorously in reply.

"Indeed. I used to be in charge of traffic management for the council. Great pension."

"And that job sent you mad?" Wenlock asked.

"Oh no, I was mad before I started." Turville replied before making another hooting noise. "They only employ people like me for traffic management. Who else but a raving lunatic would come up with a double-mini-roundabout!"

Wenlock couldn't argue with that. Turville wasn't finished though.

"I'm particularly fond of all the zebra crossings I put right on the exits of roundabouts. They really did snarl things up. And the cycle lane that leads down the stairs by the side of the cathedral[35]. I think that was my favourite."

Wenlock could see he needed to interrupt Turville to stop him jabbering on. Lord knows there were plenty of mad traffic management ideas out there for him to describe.

"So why the dog-sled desire?" he asked.

Turville paused for a second to consider this.

"Probably all the barking coming from outside. I don't really think much beyond the moment if I'm honest," he replied.

Wenlock felt a plan beginning to form. He knew someone with a pack of dogs[36], all he needed was a sled of some form. And maybe some snow, though he hoped that point would be negotiable as he wasn't likely to find any at this time of year.

"One thing first: how do I know you are telling the truth?"

This seemed to stump Turville. He thought for a few seconds before giving his answer.

---

[35] This really exists in a British city I shall not name. On those stairs there is a sign showing the way to a nearby city via another cycle path. Unfortunately, the sign points directly at the front door of a building with no other way around. Marvellous stuff.

[36] Him, obviously.

"Good point. You can't. However, you will be able to ask the bet placer and they will corroborate it!"

Wenlock once again could not stand in the way of Turville's logic. For a mad man, he was surprisingly rational.

"OK then. We have a deal. I have a pack of dogs outside that'll easily pull you and a small, wheeled sledge. I hope that will be good enough as I assume you are aware there isn't any snow outside?"

"Oh, yes," Turville replied. "That will be fine. But I will only tell you the name after the sled ride."

"I think I have something that would work as a wheeled sled!" Bluith joined in, caught up in the excitement. "My son has a toy car that he can sit in. Acton would fit that."

For the first time in a long while, Much Wenlock smiled inside the bookies.

Chapter 20

While it made complete sense for her to be the one to do it, Ashby was not looking forward to investigating the 'jilted husbands' angle of the story. It was not because finding who the husbands were would be difficult; Kirby Grindalythe's love life had been well documented by newspapers. In particular, by the *Everyday Post* and specifically by Ashby herself.

Ashby was not looking forward to it for two reasons:

1. The easiest way to look at back issues of the *Everyday Post* was to go their office in town. Ashby worked at this office. She didn't like going to work at the best of times but right now it had been three days since a huge motor racing event had happened and she hadn't submitted her story to the editor because she had been so busy being in it.
2. Most of the newspaper coverage of Kirby's love life had been done by the reporter who covered the motor racing segments. This was Ashby herself, and she hated re-reading her own work[37].

Nevertheless, she manfully drove to the office to do the research. Ashby's experience told her that after a career made of avoiding doing it, only hard work and diligence is the way to find the truth.

The office of the *Everyday Post* was an extremely ugly building. It had been built by the founder of the paper to remind the people of the town of the importance of the media. To reach that effect, it was far taller than it needed to be and was painted a garish yellow so as to intrude into everyone's lives.

Ashby walked straight through the lobby and managed to get in to the lift without meeting anyone. This was fairly easy as the lobby was mainly the

---

[37] Put bluntly, she was not a very good writer.

lift and a small reception desk. The lady at the reception desk didn't even look up as Ashby breezed in.

Rather than head to floor 6, where her desk frolicked amongst the herd of other sports reporters, she pushed the 'B' button that she hoped would drop the lift down to the basement archives.

Whilst the lift music hummed a jaunty jangle that sounded suspiciously like the tune to a particularly vulgar folk song, Ashby took some time to reflect on the fact that it had been many years since she had been down to this floor. The archives were not a place that sports reporters went often. Most of her research stemmed from attending races and glamorous parties. Or, more accurately, being near glamorous parties and desperately lobbying the security guards to let her in.

The jolly jingle stopped as the lift came to a halt. Outside the lift, the archives stretched before her. Racks and racks of newspapers, thousands of issues. Legend had it that the very first edition of the *Everyday Post* was in there somewhere. The newspaper had been pumping drivel into the local community every day for the past one hundred and thirty six years; a bigger waste of paper you would not find.

Ashby put these thoughts aside and walked to the brand new filing system that had just been installed. No longer was a long montage needed for researching - the miracles of technology meant that Ashby could simply look up what she needed to on the new 'searching engine' and have it in her hands seconds later.

The filing system searching engine was taller than the basement itself. It fit in the building by starting in the basement then extending up in to the floor above, hence why there was so little lobby space available. The machine had several levers: one for every letter of the alphabet and several more to input the commands required to execute a search. It was largely brass and occasionally steam escaped from the labyrinthine pipe work required to run such a technological marvel. Ashby was terrified of it and rightly so. Last year, it had eaten a mail boy who got too close whilst the engine was processing a query on missing earrings.

Ashby entered in the search term she needed, pulling the levers one at a time. As she did so, the letters she had selected popped up on individual cards behind a glass plate, set at eye level[38].

"K I R B Y   G R I N D A L Y T H E"

She pulled the final lever to enter the command. The searching engine worked its technological magic. Whirring noises emitted from the floor above and a strange clunking began somewhere below her. A whistle sounded in the depths of the archive and then finally the machine's manipulator flew in to view, looking like a fold-up washing line with claws. It raced on tracks through the stacks at breakneck speed, pulling seemingly random editions of the newspaper from the shelves around it. Eventually, it shuddered to a halt next to Ashby, a tall pile of relevant newspapers in the tray at its side. Ashby took the stack and resisted the urge to thank her mechanical helper. No sooner than she had lifted up the papers the manipulator whizzed off again, back in to the depths of the archive. Undoubtedly to perform some nefarious deed.

Ashby took the papers, sat at a desk with a reading light, and began to look over her old work. Headlines from years ago raced at her from the printed pages. The top of the pile was the most recent, a mid-week piece she had done about the build up to the Chapter 1 Classic. A brief mention of Kirby's most recent fling with a famous actress - no jealous partners involved, Ashby recalled.

She went back through this year's racing season, making careful notes on when she had mentioned a lover or partner in the story, who they were and what she remembered of them. The year gave way to the mid-season break, when the motor racing pages move away from the action itself and onto the off-track antics of the drivers and the preparation work done by the teams.

---

[38] Not Ashby's eyelevel as she was quite short. Damn the patriarchy.

She noted more names and also some spectacularly inaccurate punditry speculation on the season ahead from some of her favoured sources. Ashby made a note not to call them back for next season.

The hours in the archive flew by as Ashby routed further through the pile and back through her own memory. If nothing else, the exercise was proving useful to pick up some of her overused phrases and shoddy grammar. Her list of names to investigate took up three pages in her notebook. Damn Kirby and his libido, she thought to herself.

The more Ashby wrote, the less she was turning up. A typical selection of her list read:

- Ryme Intrinseca - foreign actress, single at time of affair
- Iwerne Minster - divorced at time of affair
- Mawgon Porth - model, widowed

It seemed that, whilst he had shown little regard for the sanctity of his own marriage, Kirby had been surprisingly respectful to that of others.

Ashby came to an article she had written a year ago, a mid-season piece describing one of Kirby's many victories. The photo next to it was of Kirby, smiling and tousled haired, his racing scarf and overalls still on. In one arm, an open bottle of champagne, his other arm was around a woman who Ashby vaguely recognised, a woman who was certainly not Ingleby Greenhow. The woman in the picture was a little older than Kirby and very attractive - definitely Kirby's type, Ashby thought to herself. The woman was leaning in to Kirby's chest in a way that certainly suggested that they knew each other better than just as friends.

She checked the caption of the picture, a caption her photographer would have written.

*Race winner **Kirby Grindalythe** celebrates victory with fan **Cherry Burton***

Ashby read the article she herself had written to accompany the picture. No mention of Cherry Burton. Ashby wracked her brains to think who Cherry might be. The photo must have been added to the article after Ashby had submitted it and she tended not to reread her old articles[39]. She made a note of the name of the photographer and decided to plough on through the pile of old papers.

Eventually, the articles began to reference Kirby less, his glory seasons in the spotlight giving way to his early career, overshadowed by the rivalry between Scudamore and Cranswick that had been the story of the time.

Ashby came to an article from six years ago. Splashed across it was a black and white photo that caught her attention immediately. It was a picture of a youthful Kirby after his first podium finish, messy haired and grinning as always post race. To his left stood Hutton Cranswick with a first place medal around his neck, smiling as one might after a victory. Standing to the left of Cranswick was another familiar face. This time, it was Cranswick's arm wrapped around her and Cranswick the photo's final subject was leaning in toward - once again, a little too closely to suggest a friendship. Ashby read the caption below:

Hutton Cranswick bags another victory and a first podium for newcomer **Kirby Grindalythe.** They celebrate with **Cherry Burton.**

If what the picture suggested was true, it made for an interesting link between the two men. How could she have not spotted it before? It was her job to know these drivers inside out after all. She raced through the article, devouring every word. The more of it she read, the more impressed she was. It was some of her best work and so early in her career too!

There, in the article and plainly obvious, it spelt out who Cherry was:

"Hutton deservedly celebrated his lead in the championship with style, embraced by fiancé Cherry Burton. A surprising match for the daughter of our esteemed local Bishop!"

---

[39]Her writing is truly average and revisiting that gave her no pleasure.

How could Ashby have forgotten something like that? It was strange; she had no recollection of having ever known it. A creeping sense of dread swept across her. There was probably a reason she didn't know this. It also lead to a reason why the writing was so good.

She checked the name at the top of the page.

She hadn't written it.

It had been her predecessor's last article.

Chapter 21

At Anearby park, Wenlock was putting the finishing touches on his makeshift dogsled. As he worked, he questioned how his life had lead to this. After a period of deliberation, and tying a series of particularly tricky knots, he decided it was probably some form of punishment for an unspecified past misdeed. Nothing really bad, maybe pushing a priest over or insurance fraud.

Wenlock banished thoughts of karma from his mind and hooked the dogs up to the kart, no mean feat with his unruly pack.

"Come on then, get in the kart," he instructed Acton Turville, who had busied himself by extracting an old newspaper from a bin and fashioning it in to an origami swan.

Acton stuck up his fingers in a V at Wenlock[40], shuffled over to the kart and got in. The wind blew the origami swan away as he folded his various coats on top of himself. Wenlock stepped back to admire his handiwork.

He didn't find a lot to admire. The cart Bluith had brought had been converted from an old tricycle into something reminiscent of a shopping trolley by the addition of a large wicker basket where the seat would be. To this cart, Wenlock had wrapped a rope with a large knot at one end. Along the rope, he had tied several other ropes, each rope leading to a dog. The ropes were then attached to the dogs via their harnesses, as Wenlock wasn't a fan of collars.

"How do I steer?" Acton asked Wenlock.

---

[40] Not like a 'peace' sign - the naughty way.

"I don't know really," Wenlock admitted. "If I'm honest, all I've done is tie my dogs to a bastardised tricycle. I don't think you'll get far enough to need to turn."

Bizarrely, Acton seemed satisfied by this completely unhelpful response and nodded as if it had in fact been useful information.

"How do I make them go?" Acton continued his training into the arcane art of makeshift dog sledding.

Wenlock had thought of this. It probably wasn't his best idea but time was short.

"I'll tell you, but first you have to tell me who you saw placing the bet." Wenlock was desperate to know before Turville set off; he was worried that there was a very real chance Acton might be killed by this particularly stupid activity.

"Get stuffed, Copper." Acton started to get out of the kart. Wenlock held up a hand to stop him. He had another idea.

"How about you tell Bluith, and then when I set the kart off she can tell me? Is that OK with you Bluith?"

Bluith nodded and smiled. She hadn't stopped smiling since they left the bookies. Wenlock knew Bluith pretty well but had never seen her so happy.

"Oh yes, secret's safe with me Acton!"

Turville considered this, nodded and waved Bluith over. She leaned down so her ear was at the level of his scraggly head as he sat in the kart. Acton told her the name, she gasped and gave a little nod before straightening up and backing away.

"Right, now you can tell me what he told you and we don't have to go through with this dogsled nonsense," Wenlock ordered Bluith, tired of the whole ridiculous situation.

"Not a chance! A bookies' word is solemn and sacred." Bluith stuck her chin out at Wenlock, who frowned and swore under his breath. It looked like he was going to have to actually continue down this mad path. He pulled a wrapped piece of steak from under his coat and picked up a very long stick he had found earlier on the 'walkies'. The second the steak made an appearance, the full pack of hounds sat up instantly. A cacophony of barks announced their keen interest in the newly appeared meat.

"Do you always carry that?" Turville asked.

"Only when I'm walking the dogs," Wenlock replied.

Wenlock unwrapped the steak and skewered it on the end of the stick. Then, he very carefully passed the stick to Acton.

"Just wave the steak/stick in the direction you want to go and shout 'din-dins'," Wenlock instructed.

Whilst it had been helpful to tell Acton, Wenlock's actions had an immediate effect on the dogs who jumped into action at the sound of 'din-dins' and ran at the steak.

As previously described, steak and stick were being held by an extremely surprised Acton Turville who was sat in the kart. With the kart attached to the dogs, as the dogs ran toward the dangling steak, the kart went forward. The kart went forward very, very quickly and that was the last Wenlock saw of Acton Turville for a good long while. However, his screams of excitement mixed with fear could still be heard in the background.

With Turville off on his promised dogsled ride, Wenlock turned his attention to Bluith.

"So, who was the mystery punter?" he demanded short-temperedly.

"Shouldn't you make sure he's OK first?" Bluith asked. She had watched Acton shoot off in to the distance at a pace that could be best described as 'heart-stopping' and the smile had rather drained from her face.

"I'm sure he'll be fine," Wenlock replied casually. "I've already walked them once today so they should settle down after an hour or so."

"Well, that's alright then." Bluith nodded, cheering up again. She leaned in to Wenlock in a conspiratorial fashion. "Acton said he saw Newton Ferrers place the bet."

After imparting this information, she shot back and put her hand to her mouth. She evidently thought the information she had passed on was of the most scandalous nature. Unfortunately, it had not had the desired effect on Wenlock who hadn't the foggiest idea who that person was. He relayed his lack of knowledge to Bluith.

"Oh, sorry. He also said to mention that Ferrers is Mayor Fitzpaine's assistant," Bluith repeated her mock-shock-hand-over-mouth gesture. This time Wenlock joined her, in a completely none-mock fashion.

"I know!" Bluith giggled with gossip's delight. "Acton said that he recognised him from when he used to work at the council."

Wenlock had to admit that this was something as juicy as the steak currently motivating his wayward dog pack to drag Turville around the park. He would have to take the information with a pinch of salt, Acton could hardly be relied upon as a witness. On the other hand, there was no way of Acton knowing that Fitzpaine was already on Wenlock's list and thus inventing the link as a credible red herring.

"Are you going to bring him in Inspector?" Bluith asked, mainly to break the silence/drown out the noise of Acton Turville being dragged around the local area by a pack of steak-crazed dogs.

"I think I will, Mrs Wells, I think I will."

It was at this moment that the distinctive shape of Ashby's Civet screamed in to view at the edge of the park. She parked it at the road side with the lolling grace of a half-cut hippo before slamming the door and running toward where Wenlock and Bluith were stood.

"Friend of yours?" Bluith asked politely.

"More of a colleague really," Wenlock replied. An awkward silence followed for a little while as Ashby ran to meet them. They were quite a long way into the park.

After a long 3 minutes, Ashby arrived. She paused for breath before speaking.

"How did you find me?" Wenlock interrupted.

"Not... important. Come... quick... no time... to explain."[41] Ashby had started to speak but was rather out of breath. She put her hands on her knees to recover. Wenlock noticed she had two newspaper clippings in her hand. He thought quickly and acted decisively.

"Mrs Wells, would you mind recovering my dogs when they get tired please?" he asked Bluith, who nodded in a fashion that Wenlock took as consent.

"Thank you. Ashby, let's walk back to your car and you can explain to me what you've found out."

***

On the walk back across the park, Ashby managed to get her breath back and explain her findings at the archive. She showed him the pictures, beginning with the one of Grindalythe with Cherry Burton.

"You can't tell me that she is just a fan. Look at how they both lean in to each other!" she proclaimed, stabbing at the picture with an inky finger.

"They do look close. I would agree, it doesn't look like a photo with a fan."

---

[41] If you're curious and like a sense of completeness: Ashby had driven to the bookies, expecting to find Wenlock still there. She found a sign on the door written by Mrs Wells saying that the shop was shut as she was at the park watching a man get tied to a makeshift dogsled.

"And look," Ashby continued. "They definitely knew each other as here they are together with Hutton Cranswick."

Wenlock took a good look at the second picture.

"I think I remember this - it was a rumour at the time. Bishop Burton's daughter was rumoured to be 'stepping out' with Hutton Cranswick. Did you not know about it?"

"It was before I moved to town," Ashby explained. "I'll be honest, I rather blagged my way in to the job. I knew nothing about racing when I arrived. I learnt as I went."

Wenlock thought this sounded odd but decided not to pry. It did explain a lot about the general quality of the *Everyday Post*.

"Perhaps after Cranswick died, Kirby Grindalythe and Cherry Burton became friends?" Wenlock ventured.

"I'd bet it was more than that," Ashby replied.

"Surely you would have known about it if it was?"

This one did stump Ashby for a moment.

"True. I covered most of Kirby's 'romantic adventures' in one way or another. He was rarely discreet. I can honestly say I never saw any connection between the two of them."

"Even when they appear together in a picture on a story you've written?" Wenlock asked, quite surprised by this.

"I don't tend to look at the paper once it's published," Ashby confessed. She took one look at Wenlock's incredulous face and decided further rationale was required to convince him. "The *Everyday Post* is a bit of a shit-rag, if I'm honest. Even I don't buy it."

This seemed to convince Wenlock.

"Perhaps he managed to keep some things quiet. Not always something you want in the press, the idea you are having an affair with your old rival's ex-beau, whilst you are still married to someone else. Why did this get you so excited then?"

"It got me thinking," Ashby started to quicken her speech, she was clearly excited. "I knew so much about Kirby, I spent hours writing about him. How did he manage to keep an affair like this quiet, and why?"

"A fair point. We ought to pay her a visit."

"I agree," Ashby had been busy between her time at the archives and her frankly illegal race across town. "And here's where it gets good. There's no sign of a Cherry Burton in the phone book or elsewhere in the archives of the *Post*. It was strange; if she had married and changed her name or died I would have expected it to be in the 'announcements' section, especially given who her dad is."

"Perhaps she left town, went somewhere the *Post* doesn't cover?" Wenlock posited.

"It's possible," Ashby shrugged. "But I doubt that anyone could disappear so cleanly. The *Post* tracks people well, especially the offspring of minor celebrities. I think our best bet is to pay a visit to the Bishop, see what happened to his daughter."

"I agree," agreed Wenlock in an agreeable manner. It was his turn to share what he had learnt.

"I've just found another connection with Fitzpaine. It seems his assistant placed an uncharacteristically large bet on Scudamore winning the Chapter 1 Classic."

"Fitzpaine again!" Ashby exclaimed. "We have to get to him. This can't all be a coincidence."

"It won't be easy to prove. The witness was far from reliable," said Wenlock, thinking of Turville and wondering where he and the sled had got to. They reached the Civet and got in. Ashby started the engine and they set off on the road.

"Then we need to get to Ferrers. Make him admit what's going on. I've met him before. He's Fitzpaine's right hand man. If Fitzpaine is up to something, Ferrers must be in on it."

"We have some more leads to pursue." Wenlock gave a wide smile. This was turning in to a real case.

Then he remembered he wasn't supposed to be on the case.

Then he remembered everything he was doing was in unpaid overtime.

He stopped smiling quite so widely.

Chapter 22

Wenlock suggested they play Paper, Scissors, Rock to decide which lead they followed up next. Ashby pointed out that she was driving, so they were doing what she wanted.

It took an hour to drive from the park to Anearby Cathedral, workplace of Bishop Burton, the presumed father of Cherry Burton. Wenlock gazed with new knowledge upon some of the unnecessary traffic calming measures and ineffective contraflow management systems that slowed their progress on the 4 mile jaunt. He reflected on how mad Acton Turville really was to create such a hellish municipal infrastructure . Then he remembered that the man had voluntarily strapped himself into a makeshift dogsled. He was marvelling at a particularly fiendish speed bump that forced drivers into a cycle lane and cyclists into a tree when he realised Ashby had been talking to him.

"Are you listening?" she demanded. Not paying as much attention to the road as Wenlock would have liked.

"No, sorry I got lost in my thoughts. What did you say?" Wenlock replied apologetically.

"I said that I think that Kirby and Hutton died on the same corner of the same track, and if they were both romantically linked to Cherry Burton that is just too much of a coincidence for me." Ashby laid out her theory succinctly.

"It's a stretch," said Wenlock. "I struggle to think that someone would successfully fake an accident to kill Hutton Cranswick and then repeat it in exactly the same way to kill Grindalythe."

Ashby took a roundabout slightly too fast, causing Wenlock to grab the dashboard for stability. When he had righted himself, Ashby replied.

"Who investigated Cranswick's death? I remember it was given to the police to look in to at the time, but the answer came back quickly that there was no foul play. Cranswick went too fast round the corner, a simple accident."

Wenlock thought on this for a moment. He cast his mind back to four years ago. He was still in the murder unit at the time, but he hadn't even been involved in that case. He found the answer, deep in his memory.

"Wraxall Piece! That's who led the investigation. I remember now! He was working in the murder unit with me at the time. It wasn't long after that case he got his promotion and moved to Major Crimes!" Wenlock thumped the dashboard and grinned with glee. Ashby looked at him disapprovingly.

"That's walnut you know!" she reproached him for his dashboard-directed violence. Wenlock was fairly sure it was fake but didn't have the heart to tell her.

"I bet the bastard covered it up and that's what got him to the top. He always was a globulous shit," Wenlock postulated smugly.

***

After a small detour to the petrol station to fill up the thirsty Civet, Ashby parked and they walked to the ornate front doors of Anearby cathedral. The doors were open and they walked in. The cathedral was a magnificent structure inside. Wenlock felt a small rise of shame that he had lived in town most of his life and never paid it a visit[42]. The whole place was empty aside from a kindly looking old lady sat knitting by the entrance. She was wearing a shawl and a name badge that read "*My name is Shirley Warren,*

---

[42] I'm not going to describe it. If you've been in a cathedral before, you know what they look like: Towering vaulted ceilings, stained glass windows. In the apse was the Bishop's massive organ...

ask me about the Cathedral". It seemed a sensible place to start looking for the Bishop.

"Excuse me," Ashby politely caught the lady's attention. Shirley Warren stopped knitting, adjusted her outsized purple-rimmed spectacles and gave a welcoming smile.

"Hello, dears. Are you here for a tour of the cathedral?" she asked, making a reasonable assumption.

"No, we're here to see Bishop Burton. Can you tell us where we can find him?" Ashby got to the point straight away. She didn't need to hear about the magnificent 16th century carvings in the quire stalls.

"Hmm. He's probably in here somewhere - I saw him earlier." The old lady rubbed her forehead. "But I am an old woman and my memory gets foggy. I don't think I can remember where he is."

"If you could think hard ma'am, it would really help us out. I am a reporter and the man with me is a police officer. We'd like to ask the Bishop some questions." Ashby leant down to the old lady's eye level, a polite smile across her face.

"Oh that's nice, dear. Have you heard about our collection? We're raising funds for a new roof," said Shirley Warren, indicating to a large, glass money box beside her. Wenlock could see it was quite full and mainly with large denomination notes.

"I hadn't heard about the collection. However, I would very much like to speak to Bishop Burton. Are you sure you can't remember where he is?" Ashby continued to try her luck at extracting the bishop's whereabouts. Wenlock's years of experience with informants gave him a strong feeling on how this conversation would play out.

"Ohh, I am old and my mind is failing me. I had an idea where he might be, but it is fading fast now," the sweet dear said, a little over-dramatically, Wenlock thought.

134

"This is a very big building; it will take us a long time to find him if you aren't going to help us." Ashby's voice was starting to strain. Wenlock thought he could see a vein appearing on her forehead. He decided it was time to step in before Ashby brained the little old lady with her own knitting needles.

"I'm feeling charitable today, ma'am. Have a little for the roof collection." Wenlock dropped some coins in to the glass box. They didn't make much noise as their fall was cushioned by the aforementioned pile of bank notes already residing inside.

"Why, thank you, dear. That is most kind of you." The old lady's smile got even sweeter. Something Wenlock hadn't thought possible. "You know, I think my memory is getting a little better. The Bishop is definitely in the Cathedral as I haven't seen him leave."

"Can you tell us where in the cathedral he would normally be found?" Ashby tried again, having calmed down a little following their small success.

"Oh dear, oh dear. My mind is not what it once was." Shirley furrowed her brow once more.

Wenlock sighed and pulled out his wallet. Selecting a rather dog-eared note, he stuffed it in the collection box. The old lady was delighted, the smile returning once more to her wrinkled face.

"Crikey, isn't it strange what jogs your memory." she said, patting Ashby on the arm in a friendly manner. "You'd usually find the Bishop somewhere near the back of the cathedral."

"I've just given a fairly large donation to the roof fund. Surely that is worth something slightly more specific?" Wenlock's patience broke, he was sorely missing the ability to haul the old bat in on obstruction charges.

135

"It's a big roof dear," came the reply. Shirley was one tough customer. Wenlock selected another note from the wallet and stuffed it into the bulging collection box.

"Yes, I remember now!" The committed Christian jumped to life. "The Bishop is definitely near the back. He's in the Sacristy!"

Ashby gave Wenlock a blank look. A blank look which Wenlock returned. It seemed Ashby had not visited the cathedral before either.

"Can you tell us where the Sacristy is please?" Ashby asked hesitantly.

"It shows you on these leaflets." Again, the sweetest smile spread under her ridiculous spectacles. Wenlock suspected she had been enjoying herself.

"Can we have a leaflet then, please?" Ashby persisted, the strain returning to her voice.

"Of course, dear. The leaflets are 50p each."

"Shirley, you can't be serious?" Wenlock snapped.

"I am serious, and that's Mrs Warren to you, thank you very much."

Chapter 23

With the aid of the overpriced leaflet, Ashby and Wenlock found the entrance to the Sacristy. The leaflet informed them that the Sacristy was a room where a priest prepares for a service, and where vestments and articles of worship are kept.

Wenlock knocked on the ancient wooden door and, after a few strange shuffling noises from inside the room, it opened to reveal a man Wenlock recognised to be the Bishop. He was an elderly gent, clean shaven, with a small pair of dark glasses and a bald pate. Wenlock was slightly disappointed to note that he wasn't dressed in his full Bishoply regalia and had instead opted for a slightly more comfortable shirt and trouser combination. He did, however, still have his clerical collar on.

"Hello, can I help you?" asked the Bishop.

"Hello, I'm Detective Inspector Wenlock and this is Miss de-la-Zouch. Do you mind if we ask you a few questions?" Wenlock made the introductions. Ashby gave a small wave.

"Why, yes, of course," said the Bishop. "Anything to help a fellow civil servant. As did not the angel Gabriel say: 'All thee do is call me, I'll be anything thou needst.'?"

Wenlock had to admit that he had no idea if the angel Gabriel did or did not say that.

"Not to matter. Please, do come in to the Sacristy." The Bishop smiled and stood aside, letting them through the door. "It also doubles as my office," he added in an unnecessarily conspiratorial manner.

The Sacristry was a fairly large example. It had dark wood panelling on the walls and some rather frightening looking portraits of previous bishops glaring down from on high. On one wall was a large glass cabinet that contained the Bishops vestments as well as a manner of shiny baubles, trinkets and priceless treasures. On the opposite side of the room was a gargantuan wooden desk, behind which stood a tall wooden chair that blocked out most of the room's only window. In front of the desk were two chairs that the Bishop motioned for Ashby and Wenlock to sit in. The Bishop himself sat in the great wooden edifice on the other side of the imposing desk. It rather dwarfed him and made it look like they were having a conversation with a wizened child.

"Now, what is it you would like to ask me about? If it's missing people you want, I'm sorry to say I haven't seen any." The Bishop spread his hands apologetically.

"Bishop Burton, we'd like to ask you some questions about your daughter, Cherry," said Ashby as she produced the newspaper clippings from her handbag.

"We'd like to know what the relationship between her and the man in this photo was." Wenlock took up the line of questioning. After a rather comical sequence, in which Ashby had to crawl a small way on to the outsized desk so she could pass the photo to the Bishop, he managed to take hold of the clipping. He peered at the picture over the top of his glasses for a short while before replying.

"That would be young Mr Cranswick in the photo. He and Cherry were engaged to be married, until his tragic death." The Bishop sat back in his chair. "A terrible shock to us all. Cherry brought him round to our abode for dinner many times and I was terribly fond of him. As the prophet William-Joel does say in the book of *The Stranger*: 'Only the good die young'."

"Now Bishop, please can you tell us the relationship between your daughter and this man," Ashby asked as she once again went through the rather awkward process of clambering across the vast desk to hand over the second clipping.

"I can indeed," replied the Bishop. "That is Kirby Grindalythe, the poor young fellow who tragically died this weekend."

Wenlock and Ashby both nodded with encouragement. They didn't need him identifying - it said his name in the caption. After a short pause, the Bishop continued.

"Yes, I believe he and Cherry also had a relationship. He was not brought round for dinner however, I merely heard of his association with my daughter via my wife. I believe Cherry had confided in my wife that the relationship was not exactly a popular one with other parties." The Bishop took a disapproving tone when delivering the last piece of information.

"How so?" Ashby could see this was going the right direction.

"Well, at the time, the man who was being brought around to our house for dinner by Cherry was not this young man at all. It was an older gentleman to whom she was engaged. This is after Hutton Cranswick had his accident, you understand. I think if Cherry's fiancé had known of Cherry's relationship with Mr Grindalythe he would have been most displeased."

The Bishop paused to push his glasses back up on to his nose before delivering another sage and wise saying.

"After all, did the martyr Phillip not say in the book of *Genesis*: ' There are too many men, too many people, whom are making too many problems and there art not much love to go around.'?"

Once again, Ashby and Wenlock had to admit they did not know if Philip said that. What they did know was that this had become a very promising line of inquiry.

"Do you believe Cherry's fiancé, the older gentleman, ever found out about the affair?" Wenlock probed.

"I do not." The Bishop gave the lightest of shrugs. "As I mentioned, I did not truly know of the affair myself, only second hand knowledge. One might say, as did St Marvin, 'I heard it through the vine of the grape'."

"And who was the older gentleman Cherry was engaged to after Cranswick?" Ashby asked.

"That would be the man who went on to make my daughter the happiest woman in the world by taking her hand in holy union last year. I have their picture together right here."

The Bishop turned around a photo frame that had been sat on his desk facing him. It was a picture of Cherry in a wedding dress, smiling with a bouquet in hand. The groom, stood next to her, was a tall, handsome man, several years her senior. Both Ashby and Wenlock recognised him instantly. An inscription ran across the bottom of the photo frame in an annoying cursive font.

'To commemorate the marriage of Cheddon and Cheriton Fitzpaine'

It explained why Ashby had not been able to trace the wedding in the *Everday Post* archives. She had the wrong name to search with. Cherry was short for Cheriton.

" I think Cheddon had his eyes set on Cherry for rather a long time. They must have met at one of the parties I held, back when Cheddon was first starting his career," the Bishop continued. "She never seemed too interested until after poor Hutton died."

"How long after Mr Cranswick's death did Mr Fitzpaine appear on the scene?" Ashby asked.

"Oh, not long. She was terribly depressed for months after the accident. It seemed over that time she reconnected with Cheddon and he comforted her somewhat. She did say she was very happy to have a man in a less risky career."

Until she craved the excitement once more, Wenlock thought to himself. It was starting to fit together now. More and more ways that the case lead back to Fitzpaine.

***

They thanked the Bishop for his time and left the Cathedral. On their way out, Mrs Warren attempted to sell them some candles, which they politely but firmly refused. This wasn't good enough to let them leave, so Ashby also ended up contributing to the roof fund in return for a tacky fridge magnet.

"Incredible," Wenlock said as he sat in the passenger seat of the Civet.

"Indeed," Ashby replied.

"The nerve of that bloody woman," Wenlock fumed.

"Oh, I thought you meant the fact that Cranswick, Grindalythe and Fitzpaine are all linked by the same lady and that it's starting to seem not much of a stretch that Fitzpaine conspired to have Hutton killed in order to get a chance with Cherry Burton. Then, after they started dating, Cherry goes back to her old ways and begins an illicit affair with Kirby. Fitzpaine finds out somehow and conspires with his mob connections to have Grindalythe killed, whilst also making a tidy profit for himself by betting on the person who is sure to win with Kirby out of the picture," Ashby summarised.

"Oh, yes. That too. As well as some form of insurance angle that we haven't really bottomed out," Wenlock added.

"Unless, of course, as the autopsy report suggests, Kirby isn't really dead and in fact faked it all to prevent Fitzpaine from actually killing him as a result of his affair with Cherry Burton," Ashby continued as she reversed the Civet out of the Cathedral car park and on to the road.

"Less likely but still possible," Wenlock conceded.

"We have to get to Fitzpaine," Ashby concluded.

"We can't. He's untouchable," Wenlock protested. "If I go anywhere near him, I'll lose my job, and frankly I'd be worried for your safety if you try it alone. He might have killed twice already!"

The car went quiet for a moment as each of them thought this through. It was Wenlock who broke the silence.

"We could publish the story in the *Post*?" he ventured. Ashby shook her head.

"We haven't got enough, it's all circumstantial and there's too much we just don't know. If we publish now, he can cover it all up and bat it away."

They had another long think as Ashby navigated an ineffable one way system.

"We need an inside source. Someone who can confirm all this. Someone who will blow the whistle on Fitzpaine, willingly or not," said Wenlock. It was classic policing, get someone at the low level, stick something on them and offer to trade up for a bigger fish.

"If that's the plan, there are two options I can think of. Either we somehow lever the truth out of the Cheneys," Ashby offered, whilst stopping to let a girl guide cross at a poorly placed zebra crossing.

"Which isn't going to happen." Wenlock could see how well it would go for the two of them to try and corner a trio of dangerous gangsters with no back up.

"Agreed. Which leaves someone in the Mayor's team, and we know that at least one of his team was in on part of the plot."

"Newton Ferrers who placed the bet on Scudamore. Potentially on Fitzpaine's behalf."

"Exactly," Ashby nodded in agreement. "And I'm glad you followed me on that logic as I've been driving toward the Mayor's office. We need to make an appointment."

"Whoa!" Wenlock put his hands up in shock, not least as Ashby nearly collided with a cyclist whose cycle lane had suddenly disappeared. "We can't go anywhere near the office. I've already outlined the reasons for that!"

"Have you ever met Ferrers before? Would he know you by sight?" Ashby asked.

Wenlock indicated he had not.

"And he wasn't at the golf course, I can tell you that. He doesn't know me but I have seen pictures of him," Ashby continued.

"But what about Fitzpaine - surely he'll be at his office?" Wenlock was nervous about this plan. He could start to see his pension pot floating away into the far distance.

"On a Thursday afternoon?" Ashby scoffed. "I hardly think so! The political set use that time to hob-nob at the country club."

"I take it you have an idea then." Wenlock could see where this was going.

Ashby grinned and put on a pair of sunglasses.

"I do indeed."

Chapter 24

"Peter & Mary Tavey?"

The names rang out through the drab but busy waiting room. Two people stood up from their chairs where they had sat patiently for their names to be called. The two people were not called Peter or Mary or Tavey. Their names were Much Wenlock & Ashby de-la-Zouch.

"This way please." The man who had called out for Peter & Mary directed them down a corridor and into an office, at which point he left them. The office was small, unassuming and the walls were painted a ghastly shade of off-yellow. There were no windows; a single electric light illuminated the room in a manner clearly designed to prevent people lingering. The office also contained a metal filing cabinet, one desk and three chairs. In the chair behind the desk was a man reading through some paperwork. He was stick thin, almost completely bald and wearing an extremely small pair of spectacles. When Wenlock and Ashby entered, the man put the piece of paper down and stood up. Wenlock was quite surprised to suddenly find himself looking upwards as the man, who had previously been sitting, was extraordinarily tall.

"Hello," said the man, extending a skeletal hand toward Wenlock. "I am Newton Ferrers, the Mayor's assistant. You must be 'Peter'." He said the name like it was difficult for his tongue.

"Pleasure," Wenlock said, shaking Ferrers' outstretched hand.

"And this must be your..." Ferrers paused for a moment as he went to shake Ashby's hand. "Wife? Mary." Again, trouble with the pronunciation.

"Niece." Ashby corrected him, rapidly. Wenlock gave her a bit of an offended look at this suggestion but went with it. There was quite an age gap between her and Wenlock, making the husband/wife cover not particularly believable. Also, he doubted that they could fake man-and-wife given the almost complete lack of chemistry between them.

"Excellent. Please, have a seat." Ferrers motioned to two chairs in front of the desk before folding back down again. "How can the mayor's office help you today, 'Peter' and 'Mary'?"

Wenlock didn't like how Ferrers was using the names. He had told Ashby they were too odd and would stand out too much. She said that was exactly why they should use them, who would use such ridiculous names as 'Peter' and 'Mary' as pseudonyms? It was a form of hiding in plain sight.

"Mr Ferrers, we'd like to talk to you today about gambling." Ashby got stuck in with the lines they had agreed in drive from the cathedral. "We feel that high stakes gambling is dangerous and we would like the mayor to propose a limit on it."

"I see. Do go on." Ferrers leaned in and adjusted his glasses. He was either actually interested in the proposal or was very good at faking interest. Wenlock suspected the latter.

"We think that not having a limit on gambling is very dangerous as it allows reckless bets to made. This can be harmful to individuals who may not know when to stop," Wenlock continued the rehearsed patter.

Ashby adopted a bit of a sanctimonious tone, almost accusatory as she delivered the killer question.

"Do you gamble, Mr Ferrers?"

There was no movement on Ferrers face at this which Wenlock found disappointing.

"I have the occasional flutter." Ferrers responded with a small, thin lipped smile. "I assume you don't have a problem with a few pounds frittered here and there?"

Ashby shook her head and replied.

"Absolutely not. We aren't looking to destroy the industry, we just want to protect the vulnerable."

"We would propose a limit of £10,000," Wenlock added. He studied Ferrers face, this time he thought he saw something. An almost imperceptible twitch above the right eye.

"I take it that wouldn't interrupt your activities, Mr Ferrers?" Ashby asked, in a jokey manner.

At this, the mask slipped. Ferrer's eyes narrowed and he sat back in his chair. He drummed his long fingers on the arms of the chair for a few seconds.

"Enough of the charade," he eventually replied, the mild mannered civil servant act dropped. "What do you want?"

Wenlock took the betting slip out of his coat pocket and put it on the desk.

"Did you place this, Mr Ferrers?" he asked. Ferrers looked down his nose at the slip, as if it were a stain on his shoe.

"I may have. What if I did?" he replied.

"It seems like more than 'a few pounds'," Ashby joined in.

"It's an awful lot of money. I wouldn't like to suggest anything impolite but I'd imagine it's more than a year's salary for a civil servant like yourself," Wenlock continued for her.

"What are you insinuating?" Ferrers responded through gritted teeth.

"Did you place the bet on behalf of someone else?" Ashby asked him.

"I don't have to tell you anything." he hissed at them.

"No, but it would be a good idea to tell me," said Wenlock, pulling out his police badge and laying it on the desk next to the betting slip. Ferrers leaned over and read the name on the badge.

"I should have known." Ferrers threw his head back and laughed. "'Peter' and 'Mary' Tavey. Ridiculous names. You must be that damned reporter then, de-la-Zouch?" he motioned his head at Ashby, who gave him a big smile and a little wave.

"We've put most of together now. We know what happened. You would do well to tell us your side of it." Wenlock started to pile on the pressure. Ferrers shifted in his seat, adjusted his spectacles and then leaned in very close to Wenlock's face.

"You know nothing," he said, very quietly. His nose inches from Wenlock's.

"We know that Fitzpaine's been having illicit meetings with the Cheneys." It was Ashby's turn. "We know that Fitzpaine's wife was having an affair with Grindalythe. We know that the Cheneys were hanging around the pits on the day of the crash."

"And we know that you placed this bet. A suspiciously large bet on Grindalythe's main rival. The man who, if Grindalythe were to crash, was certain to win." Wenlock spoke quietly. There was no need to shout with Ferrers still so close to his face.

"But only if Grindalythe crashed," Ashby added. At this, Ferrers backed off and sat back down again, fingers drumming a tattoo on the chair arm once more.

"You actually know quite a bit then," Ferrers said, deflated. His previous vitriol deserting him. Wenlock smiled internally - they had him where they wanted him.

"If you tell us what we want to know now, it'll work in your favour later." Wenlock rolled out his familiar patter for turning witnesses.

147

"And I can quote you as an anonymous source in my story instead of a full name and shame," Ashby added.

"How generous," Ferrers sneered. He took off his spectacles and wiped his face with his hands. "Fine, I placed the bet. It was my money."

Wenlock looked at Ashby. Ashby looked shocked which was how Wenlock felt.

"So not placed on behalf of, say, an extremely wealthy employer of yours?"

"No. It was me alone. As you correctly state, it is almost a year of my salary, and I lost it. More worryingly is where I got the money, as I didn't save it up." Ferrers looked tired as he said this, the bravado now completely drained from him. He slumped back in the chair, a broken man.

"Who did you get it from?" Ashby pounced.

"I need a guarantee of protection," Ferrers stated.

"As a witness, you will be fully protected," Wenlock assured him.

"I borrowed the money from the Cheneys. They have something of a loan sharking operation. As you know, the result didn't come through and I lost said money. Now, certain Cheney family members have given me a very short length of time with which to repay them, or they will break my legs."

Wenlock paused to absorb this. Then, he asked the obvious question.

"What made you think this bet was a good idea?"

Ferrers shifted once more in his chair and put the spectacles back on.

"Full protection, yes? That includes immunity from prosecution?" he asked, pointing at Wenlock.

"Within reason, yes," Wenlock replied. Ferrers did some more drumming whilst deciding if this was enough. Eventually he sighed and continued.

"I overheard the Mayor talking on the phone a few days before the race. I don't know who he was talking to and I couldn't hear their side of the conversation, but I could hear what he was saying to them."

"Go on." Ashby was on the edge of her seat now.

"The Mayor said that the result of the Chapter 1 was going to be a shock. He said he was sure of it. He said he had made arrangements to see that Grindalythe wouldn't be a problem anymore."

"And you're sure of this?" Wenlock asked. It was pretty damning stuff.

"Absolutely! Enough to put £10,000, that I didn't have, on it!" Ferrers spat back. "And if Cheddon Fitzpaine says he has sorted something, it means it is sorted. I've been his assistant for the last eight years, I should know. Also, I know who he was on the phone to."

Ashby and Wenlock were hooked. They leaned over the desk.

"It was Middleton Cheney. I put the call through to Fitzpaine." Ferrers sat back in his seat, a bizarrely triumphal look on his face.

At this moment, a phone on the desk rang. Ferrers looked at Wenlock who motioned for him to answer it[43].

Ferrers picked up the receiver. He nodded a few times and gave some noises that sounded like agreement. He didn't look very happy. Then, he took the receiver from his ear and held it up in Wenlock's direction.

"It's for you." He said. Wenlock frowned at Ashby and then took the phone from Ferrers' outstretched hand. He put it up to his ear.

"Hello? DI Wenlock speaking," he said down the line.

"Not for much bloody longer it isn't," came the reply. It was the DCI. "Get back down to the station, double bloody pronto and bring that bloody

---

[43] Only a monster can tolerate the noise of a ringing phone for any length of time.

reporter with you." The line went dead. Wenlock handed the phone back to Ferrers who put it back on the cradle.

"I think someone recognised you in the waiting room." Ferrers gave as an explanation. The colour had mostly left his face now. Whatever the DCI had said to him had clearly shaken him up.

"I take it you heard that," Wenlock said to Ashby, who nodded.

"We can still protect you," he said to Ferrers. "I just need one more thing."

Ferrers, looking every inch the broken man, gave a wave that Wenlock took to mean 'go on'.

"Can you give me the Mayor's itinerary? I have an idea."

Chapter 25

"Wenlock, I'm going to need an extraordinarily good reason not to take your badge off you, cancel your pension and then crush your bollocks in a vice."

The DCI was not very happy. Ashby could tell this by the way his face had turned an unholy shade of puce and his rather magnificent moustache was bristling orthogonally away from his face.

In addition, he was shouting quite loudly and threatening to castrate one of his employees in a particularly brutal manner.

"I gave you some extremely clear instructions, Wenlock." the DCI continued. "I don't know how I could have made them clearer, save for tattooing them on your hands or carving them in to your thick skull."

They had arrived at the station and been shown directly into the DCI's office by the Desk Sergeant. The DCI had been reading a paper, he allowed them to sit down before he looked up and began his diatribe.

The longer he had ranted for, the louder and further out of his chair he had got. Ashby had been glad that so far it had been largely directed at Wenlock; she wasn't sure how well she would react. It was certainly going a long way to explaining Wenlock's occasional foul-mouthed outburst.

"And believe me when I say this, if I had known you would go on to disobey these clear instructions, I would have tattooed them on. With a very rusty and fecally contaminated knitting needle. The reason you give for this had better be so damnably good it would seduce a nun. It better be so good it would swear a leopard off meat. It better be good enough that I don't order you shot on the spot!" the DCI carried on, punctuating the last few lines of outrage by hammering his desk. He then abruptly stopped and sat back down.

"And you must be Miss de-la-Zouch," the DCI said, in a much more normal tone. "Big fan of your work, really. I adore the motor racing section in the *Everyday Post*, only reason I buy it. Rest of it is just shitraggery really."

"Thank you," Ashby said, politely and hoping she had escaped from the dragons breath.

"However, you've really gone a little beyond your area here. I mostly blame DI Wenlock, as you might have noticed, but I am also fairly narked off at you too," he added, in a reasonable and even tone.

"Sorry," Ashby found herself muttering.

The DCI appeared to be finished with Ashby as he returned his gaze to Wenlock. Wenlock remained silent. Ashby guessed that he had seen all this before, and more than once.

"Well, pray tell, DI Wenlock. What was so important for you to ignore a direct order I gave to back off the case and allow DI Piece to investigate in your place?"

Wenlock paused for a moment longer - Ashby thought it might be for dramatic effect. Then, he launched in to it. A full explanation of all that they had discovered, the picture it painted and how it had all linked back to Fitzpaine. The DCI sat patiently through it all, not saying a word. Finally, Wenlock wrapped it all up.

"I expect DI Piece, the witless scum-sucker, didn't manage to unearth anything. That is why I disobeyed your order sir." It was Wenlock's turn to be out of his seat. Ashby had never seen him so animated. "I am sorry to have done that, but we really need justice to win out on this one. A man has been murdered, potentially two men. The rich and the powerful can't just be allowed to get away with this. It's not what I joined up for. It's not what we joined up for! To let smarmy gits like Fitzpaine get away with murder makes me feel sick. The corruption has gone on too long, and if we find out the Chief is in on it then so be it. We'll arrest him too. I couldn't take it anymore. I had to do my job, even without overtime."

Ashby was impressed. It had been an impassioned speech. It would have been better with a stirring string quartet but those sorts of things don't tend to be hanging around offices. She felt like clapping but managed to stop herself. The DCI went very quiet. He was clearly thinking deeply. He put his hand over his mouth and stared directly into Wenlock's eyes for nearly a full minute. Then, very slowly, he took his hand away from his mouth, picked up the phone on his desk and spoke.

"Get me the Chief."

There was a pause. Ashby could hear the operator's voice on the other end of the phone but couldn't make out what they were saying.

"Get me the Chief, please."

Some further unintelligible squawking followed from the phone, a pause and then:

"Sir, can you come down here please. It's important." The DCI put the phone down. Ashby heard a chair scrape in a room upstairs and then the sound of boots on wood. Then, boots coming down stairs. Eventually, the boots made it to the office door, they let themselves in and walked to the DCI's chair. The DCI stood up and let the Chief sit down. The DCI leaned on a window frame behind the desk.

"What's this all about then Budleigh?" asked the Chief to the DCI. He looked remarkably similar to the DCI except his moustache was even more magnificent and his belly a little rounder.

"I've got something you need to hear Woodbury," the DCI said, addressing the Chief. Then he turned to Wenlock. "Tell the Chief what you just told me. You can leave out the speech at the end - I don't see that as necessary."

Wenlock shifted uncomfortably in his seat. After a short pause to gather himself, he dutifully began the story again. Wenlock repeated it exactly as he had to the DCI. He stopped just before he called DI Piece a 'witless scum-sucker'.

153

This time it was the Chief's turn to be quiet. He leaned back in the DCI's chair, one hand over his mouth. Slowly, he removed it.

"That is quite a tale, DI Wenlock. It has some fairly meaty allegations. Do you have any actual proof of Fitzpaine's involvement? It's all fairly circumstantial."

Wenlock winced a little at this.

"I just need to interview him. We have enough. All I need is to get in a room with him, one on one."

The Chief started nodding.

"I see. I know what you are thinking. You think Cheddon Fitzpaine and I are pals, that I'm covering for him somehow," the Chief started.

Wenlock winced even more at this. He had certainly implied it in his story.

"Well we're not. I don't like him, not one bit. I just have to be civil with him as it's part of my job. After all, he is the mayor and I am the Chief of Police."

Ashby let out a little of the breath she didn't realise she had been holding.

"He is a powerful man, well protected in this town, even from me. At the moment, I don't know if you truly have enough to bring him in," the Chief continued. He seemed genuinely apologetic.

Ashby could see that Wenlock had a little smile in the corner of his mouth.

"I have a plan sir. A way to corner him . It's a simple idea, but I believe it will be effective. We need to get him somewhere where he can't deny that he is up to no good. Catch him red handed."

The Chief raised an intrigued eyebrow..

"Even better news is that I have Fitzpaine's calendar." Wenlock was fully smiling now. "I know exactly when we can get to him."

154

The Chief raised his other eyebrow.

"Best of all, our opportunity is tonight!" Wenlock ended triumphantly.

Chapter 26

"This is an incredible coincidence." Ashby commented. Wenlock nodded in agreement.

"I mean, the fact that he happened to be doing this tonight. We might have had to wait days, perhaps even weeks!" Ashby continued. Wenlock nodded in agreement once again before resuming his progress through a large sandwich. They were sat in the front of Wenlock's Muskrat; the night was dark and cold. It was well past Wenlock's tea time, hence the sandwich.

"If it hadn't been tonight, we would have completely missed the opportunity. I doubt we would have been able to convince anyone and I expect you would have been fired," Ashby was undeterred by the silence.

Wenlock shrugged, nodded and went back to the sandwich. It was tuna-mayonnaise, a particular favourite of his. He also had some tea in a thermos flask and a bag of cheese & onion crisps. The only thing he planned to share with the rest of the car was the smell.

"Not to mention just narrative pacing in general," Ashby marched on. Wenlock wiped the sandwich remnants from his mouth before replying.

"In my line of work, this happens surprisingly often," he stated in a matter-of-fact tone. "I try not to think about it too much."

"Do you think we'll have to wait much longer?" the DCI's voice wafted in from the back seat. "It's a bit squashed back here."

"I hope not, sir. Fitzpaine's diary said that he would be here. It's blocked out from 7pm until now." Wenlock replied. "If you wouldn't mind, sir, could you put out the pipe? I'm struggling to see out the windscreen."

The DCI made some grumbling noises about covering the tuna smell but duly complied. Wenlock thanked him politely, glad that the fog impairing his vision was beginning to lift.

"I take it you recognise where we are?" Ashby asked to the back seat area.

"It's Unit 472A, Bowmore street. Also known as the Cheney cake factory," came the voice of the Chief who was in the back of the Muskrat with the DCI. "I used to raid it all the time, back when the outfit was run by Old Man Cheney. Barely caught them at anything though- they've always been slick."

"This is where we tailed Fitzpaine to a few days ago. He went in the door over there." Ashby pointed up the road to the door in the factory wall that featured extensively in Chapter 8 & Chapter 9. The darkness made the area oppressive. Where previously it had been merely quiet, now with the gloom it was ominous. There was a solitary electric light above the door in question and a token handful of street lights on the road - not enough to keep away the fear that it was not them doing the watching.

Wenlock had parked the Muskrat in the same position as during the previous visit. They had been waiting for Fitzpaine to emerge for over an hour and it was getting a bit smelly in the car, particularly after Wenlock's sandwich and the DCI's incessant pipe smoking.

"If all you've said turns out to be true Wenlock, you have performed a sterling bit of police work. A true example to the rest of the force," the Chief said, perhaps trying to atone for handing Wenlock his suspension from the case earlier in the week, Wenlock thought to himself.

"Yes, sir. You wouldn't have got such intuition, graft and dogged determination from that stink-rat Wraxall Piece." Wenlock almost spat out the name of his nemesis on the force to punctuate his point.

"Erm, do you mind Wenlock?" came Piece's objection. He was in the back of the Muskrat as well, wedged between the DCI and the Chief.

"I do not mind," Wenlock turned to look at the back seat. "Why did he have to come?" he asked the DCI. The DCI looked over to the Chief.

"You know full well this is still DI Piece's case," the Chief replied. "Until Fitzpaine walks out that door and a firm link can be made between him and the death of Grindalythe, we are still merely humouring you." Wenlock noticed the edge in his voice. It seemed his conciliatory tone of moments ago had been a mere pleasantry. Wenlock turned back to face the factory door and sulked for a moment. He still believed that Piece was involved in a cover up, even if it was looking like the Chief and the DCI were not.

Wenlock was handed his chance to find out. The door to the factory swung open. Out of it stepped Fitzpaine. Before leaving the murky doorway, he turned to shake the hand of a hidden figure who remained inside. Then, he checked both directions down the road, an attempt to see if he was being observed? Clearly in vain as he did not see the Muskrat full of police officers[44].

As he appeared, commotion broke out in the car. Almost in unison the DCI & the Chief exclaimed their surprise. Ashby shouted something that sounded to Wenlock a bit like 'Get him'. DI Piece also made a noise but Wenlock didn't want to tune in to his weasel frequency.

Fitzpaine, appearing not to hear the outburst from the collected watchers, started to make his way down the pavement back to his parked car. The sleek, silver Ocelot was in-between the door and where Wenlock had parked. The mayor froze when he heard the mighty 2 cylinder engine of the Muskrat fire up. Wenlock turned on the full beam of the headlights, partially for effect, and drove slowly toward the mayor.

Fitzpaine watched in bewilderment as the Muskrat full of people pulled up next to him. Wenlock wound down the window.

"Nice evening for a stroll, Mr Mayor," he said in a cheerful tone.

---

[44] And one journalist who had noticed more smells than just Wenlock's sandwich and the DCI's pipe.

"Wenlock!" seethed Fitzpaine. "Did my warning at the golf course not sink in? The DCI will have your badge for this."

On cue, from the backseat of the Muskrat the DCI wound down his window.

"Probably not, Mr Mayor." he said, with a cheerful inflection. "We have a few questions for you."

"Good lord!" Fitzpaine exclaimed. "When the Chief finds out that you've joined in with Wenlock's madness, you'll be out on the street with him!"

At this point, the Chief himself got out of the car. He leaned on the roof to talk to Fitzpaine.

"I don't think I'll be firing my brother, Mr Mayor."

"Woodbury! By God, are you in on this lunacy?" Fitzpaine was truly shocked now. The usual smarmy anger was melting under the sparse illumination of the thinly spread streetlights.

"I'm afraid so, Cheddon. We just want you to answer some questions, straighten a few things out for us," the Chief continued in a reasonable tone, an impassive smile fixed on his face to convey the full force of his reasonableness.

"I'll have the lot of you fired," Fitzpaine snarled. Wenlock could see the anger rising in the usually well-composed politician. They needed to get him down the station and quick to make him crack.

"Perhaps." The Chief remained calm. He had lit a pipe now. The DCI, seeing that this was once again permissible, almost dropped his matches whilst trying to join in. "Perhaps, but we still need to ask these questions. Would you mind coming with us? If it all turns out to be naught, we'll keep it just between us."

Fitzpaine looked like he was going to refuse. Wenlock could almost see the calculations taking place as the beleaguered mayor worked out what would play best for him. He wouldn't want to force the police into getting a

159

warrant, then the story would go everywhere. If he were to answer the questions, smooth it over, it could all go away and leave him scandal free. Wenlock watched closely as this all shot through Fitzpaine's mind. The shoulders sagged, Fitzpaine shrugged.

"Fine, I'm sure we can sort this out. Whatever you've been told is merely a misunderstanding. We'll all go home and have a jolly laugh about it after." Fitzpaine had changed tack, no longer the indignant man of power. He turned his act to the charming politician.

"I'm sure we will," the Chief smiled. Probably smiled, it was hard to tell under his luxuriant moustache.

"I'll meet you at the station then?" Fitzpaine asked, motioning to his silver Ocelot which still looked rather marvellous even under the poor street lighting of the rundown industrial area.

"I think it best if you ride with us actually," the Chief said evenly. Wenlock supposed he didn't like the idea of the Mayor getting too far ahead of them; there was no way for the Muskrat to keep up. Especially laden as it was with the local constabulary's command structure.

Fitzpaine bent down and looked in the Muskrat.

"There's not a lot of room for me in there Woodbury... Oh, hello, DI Piece," he said as he made out the other occupants of the car. "Ah, and Ms de-la-Zouch. Good evening to you too."

Piece gave the Mayor a hesitant wave. Ashby gave him a two-fingered V-sign[45].

"Would you allow someone to drive your car back to the station?" the Chief offered as a way of making space in the Muskrat.

---

[45] As before, not in the way that means 'peace'.

"I absolutely would not." Fitzpaine replied, somehow without a hint of malice. The Chief scratched his magnificent facial hair for a moment while he made a decision.

"Right then. DI Piece, you're walking," he ordered, pointing at the unfortunate detective. The DCI got out og the Muskrat and Piece dutifully followed him. Fitzpaine took Piece's place in the middle-back seat and the DCI got back in again.

When all were crammed in once more, Wenlock pulled away from the kerb and headed back in the direction of the station. Although he tried to keep a shred of dignity, he did give a wave to Piece as he started his trudge back in to town. Piece kept his dignity by not responding in kind.

Chapter 27

Very few words were said on the way back to the police station. Fitzpaine tried to start a few conversations but the police officers around him remained silent. Ashby, though she desperately wanted to begin the interrogation, remained silent also.

Their arrival at the home of local justice went unnoticed as, at the insistence of Fitzpaine, they entered through a back door. Wenlock was disappointed that they went to the Chief's office for the discussion rather than an interrogation cell, however he understood. The ice, on which they skated, was thin.

In the office, Fitzpaine immediately settled himself in to the Chief's large leather chair. At the Chief's instructions, Wenlock and Ashby sat opposite the Mayor across the Chief's large mahogany desk. Ashby marvelled at the office's exquisite interior. It was situated on the top floor of the station and boasted a high, nicotine stained ceiling. To her left, Fitzpaine's right, a large window afforded impressive views of the car park and a public toilet. Night still shrouded both locales in mystery but Ashby could see the local drug vendors brazenly plying their trade by the more adequate street lighting provided by a central location. The DCI and the Chief himself brought chairs from other rooms and sat at the edge of the office. The DCI and Chief lit their pipes again. When everyone was sitting comfortably, the Chief began.

"DI Wenlock, commence when you are ready."

Before Wenlock got chance to start, Fitzpaine interjected.

"Point of order, if this is a police interview, should the journalist be here?" he said, motioning toward Ashby.

"DI Wenlock has brought her along on the case as a special advisor," the Chief began. "In addition, this is not a police interview, Cheddon. This is a discussion held between a group of adults. We're not accusing you of anything, we just want some explanations. I will allow her to remain, unless you'd like this to be an official police interview?" he added, pointedly.

Fitzpaine indicated he would not. This seemed to satisfy the Chief and he repeated his instruction for DI Wenlock to commence, this time with more force. Wenlock guessed that the Chief's blood sugar was getting low and wasted no time.

"Mayor Fitzpaine, please can you confirm some facts for me?"

"I'll certainly try." Fitzpaine beamed back. The earlier rage almost completely evaporated. Fitzpaine had put on a guise of total reasonableness.

"Are you married to Cheriton Fitzpaine, more commonly known as Cherry and formally known as Cherry Burton?" Wenlock began.

"I am indeed." Fitzpaine gave a bemused smile. "I hope they'll all be this easy!" he said as an aside to Ashby. Wenlock could see what the Mayor was trying to do, bring Ashby in on to his side, make Wenlock seem like the idiot. Fortunately, Ashby was having none of it.

"I can promise they won't be," she shot back at him.

Very briefly, Fitzpaine's amiable persona dropped and Wenlock could see the anger lurking behind. Wenlock pressed on.

"And can you confirm that your wife was previously engaged to Hutton Cranswick?"

A further bemused smile from Fitzpaine.

" I say, Inspector, this is an odd line of questioning."

"Just answer the question," Ashby bit back at him. Wenlock suspected she was rather enjoying this.

"Yes, she was," Fitzpaine complied with the demand, making a show of spreading his hands as if to say 'at-your-service'.

"Would it be fair to say that you pursued her prior to her engagement to Cranswick?" Wenlock asked, keeping an even and reasonable tone.

Fitzpaine did not take kindly to this question.

"Look, you've brought me in here and not told me anything of why and now you are asking ridiculous questions about my wife. What is going on?" The amiability was dropping like a poorly hung curtain. "Woodbury, what is going on here?" Fitzpaine appealed directly to the Chief.

"Just answer the questions, Cheddon," was all he got as a reply. The Chief had his arms firmly folded and an expression on his face that suggested no quarter would be given.

"If it helps, Mr Mayor, we already know the answer. We just need you to confirm it," Ashby added, her tone dripping with faux-sweetness. Fitzpaine squirmed in the Chief's large leather chair before replying.

"It is true. I've known Cherry for a long time. Bishop Burton introduced me to her at one of his fund raisers about eight years ago. I tried, unsuccessfully, to 'woo' her many times. Then she became engaged to Cranswick. Naturally, I stopped after that and we remained friends," Fitzpaine recounted. Wenlock saw him soften slightly as he spoke of his wife. He wasn't sure whether it was real or affected.

"Until Cranswick died in the Chapter 1 Classic of four years ago," Ashby prompted. "After which you rekindled your interest. Quite quickly too I hear."

Fitzpaine looked shocked at this.

"She came to me; she was a friend. I comforted her. One thing eventually led to another but I would not manipulate a friend in such a way. There was a completely reasonable amount of time in between." Fitzpaine looked wounded at the suggestion, however Wenlock struggled to believe his sincerity.

"You were engaged to her less than a year after Cranswick's death. Doesn't sound like a reasonable amount of time to me," Ashby surmised what the rest of the room had been thinking.

"I admit it might seem quick to outsiders," Fitzpaine conceded. "But we had been friends for so long, it felt natural to us. Like we belonged together, and why wait?" he asked rhetorically.

"Did you have an affair with her whilst Cranswick was still alive?" Wenlock asked. It was his turn to be brusque. Fitzpaine recoiled at the question.

"Absolutely not. I was nothing but honourable. Cherry was devoted to Cranswick and he to her!" he answered, the volume of his voice elevated slightly. Wenlock again saw the anger rise only to be controlled.

"So to get a chance at Cherry, you needed Cranswick to step aside in some way?" Ashby popped the leading question. Fitzpaine wasn't an easy target, his eyes narrowed.

"What are you suggesting?" he directed back at Ashby, his guard up. Wenlock chose not to answer that one and he gave Ashby a look to restrain her. There was more of a story to weave yet.

"What is your relationship with the Cheneys?" Wenlock asked instead. Fitzpaine blinked at the sudden change in topic.

"I am aware of them," Fitzpaine gave a cautious response.

"Are you aware of their activities?" Wenlock continued.

"They own a factory in the industrial estate." Fitzpaine kept his tone even. "They make remarkably good cakes."

"They are also major players in local organised crime," the Chief added from the back of the room. "Something we have discussed together in the past."

"Perhaps," Fitzpaine replied coolly. "I would suggest that is more your area of expertise than mine."

"Have you met with the Cheneys?" Wenlock continued the questioning.

"As they are a major employer in the town, I have met with them on occasion. It's necessary for us to discuss town business, union disputes and such the like," Fitzpaine responded in a matter-of-fact manner.

"Quite regularly, according to your diary." Ashby pushed the diary Wenlock had taken from Ferrers across the table to Fitzpaine, who looked at the organiser like it was a dead badger.

"I don't keep the diary. That is handled by my assistant, Newton Ferrers."

"Who diligently writes your appointments in it," Ashby finished for him. "Including those at the cake factory. The kind of appointment we picked you up from today."

"How very thorough of him. I shall have to give him a pay rise," Fitzpaine commented sarcastically.

"You should," Wenlock interjected. "He needs the money. He's got quite the debt to repay to your friends at the cake factory."

Fitzpaine looked confused at this.

"What on earth do you mean?"

"Mr Ferrers overheard a conversation you made on the phone suggesting that you had fixed the outcome of the Chapter 1 Classic so that Upton Scudamore would win. He placed rather a large wager on it, with money he didn't have," Wenlock continued. "And we know the phone call you had was with Middleton Cheney."

"Is that what this is about? You think I fixed the Classic?" Fitzpaine snorted with derision. "That's preposterous. I did nothing of the sort. I can't be held responsible for a man mishearing a phone conversation he eavesdropped on!"

"We think you might have fixed the Classic," Wenlock added quietly.

"In the worst possible way," Ashby added.

Fitzpaine took this like a slap in the face.

Chapter 28

"Did you, or did you not, approach Ingleby Greenhow on the subject of Kirby Grindalythe's life insurance?" Wenlock changed tack abruptly again, causing Fitzpaine to snap out of his verbal-face-slap-shock.

Fitzpaine shook his head in disbelief before composing himself and answering.

"I did, yes." There was a tone of resignation in his voice. Wenlock suspected that Fitzpaine was beginning to get worried. He suspected that Fitzpaine was beginning to suspect that Wenlock suspected him of doing things worthy of suspicion. The frequent protestations of misunderstanding the questions were becoming less frequent.

"And did you succeed in having Kirby Grindalythe's substantial life insurance payout in the event of an accident changed from Ingleby to yourself?" Ashby asked.

"Yes, I did," Fitzpaine answered. There was a gasp from one of the other occupants of the room. Had Fitzpaine broken? Wenlock wondered, was there a confession on the way?

Probably not, he decided. If they were going to nail Fitzpaine, it would only be through confronting him with an overwhelming surplus of proof. Fitzpaine wasn't going to give up; he had to be beaten.

"Aren't you going to ask me why?" This time, it was Fitzpaine's turn to ask an unexpected question.

"We don't need to ask. We already know, Fitzpaine," Wenlock started. It was wrap up time. One of the key skills of a great detective is knowing when to do a great monologue. When to collect the strands of mystery, built throughout the case, and craft them in to an unassailable truth that no guilty party could deny. That time was now.

"You switched the insurance policies because you knew they were going to pay out, and soon." Unfortunately for Wenlock, Ashby had also sensed the moment and pounced first. Wenlock later reasoned it was because she was younger and her reactions were quicker.

"You conspired with the Cheneys to fix the Chapter 1 Classic by tampering with Grindalythe's car. We know that one of the Cheneys managed to sneak in to the garage, luring Grantham away using Leigh Delamere's fabricated technical troubles as bait."

"Leigh Delamere who has since gone missing," Wenlock managed to interject. If someone was stealing his thunder, he wasn't going to let it be a true monologue.

"Thank you, DI Wenlock," Ashby ploughed on. "And you sent your tame policeman, Wraxall Piece, to track her down. DI Piece also put Scudamore under guard so he couldn't reveal her whereabouts - or lack of whereabouts."

Fitzpaine opened his mouth to interrupt. Ashby was having none of it and continued.

"That's just the 'how' and the insurance money is only half of the 'why'! We know that you had another motive for wanting Grindalythe gone."

At this point, Fitzpaine had given up trying to protest and had his head in his hands. Wenlock could see he was a beaten man.

"Because your new wife, who had a taste for the dangerous, was having an affair with him. You killed Grindalythe for the money *and* to get him out of the way as a romantic rival. The same motivation and, presumably, the same method as you did four years ago with Hutton Cranswick." Ashby delivered the killer blow, sat back in her chair and folded her arms. Silence reigned for several seconds. The room was quiet enough to hear a surreptitious drug deal go down in the square outside.

"Do you agree with Ms de-la-Zouch's summation, DI Wenlock?" the Chief asked from the back of the room. Wenlock paused for effect before he replied.

"I do, sir."

"Well, then. What have you to say for yourself, Fitzpaine?" the Chief addressed the beleaguered Mayor. Wenlock noticed it wasn't first name terms between them anymore.

Fitzpaine still hadn't moved from having his head in his hands. Slowly, those hands began to stir, massaging his scalp, as if he had a terrible headache that he could press out of his skull.

"I'd like to make a phone call, please," he managed, eventually. Wenlock looked at the Chief. The Chief nodded - he could hardly refuse a man his phone call. Wenlock gestured to the phone on the Chief's desk. Fitzpaine picked up the handset. It felt like an eternity watching him slowly turn the rotary dial to each number. Everyone in the room could hear the tone ring, then an inaudible voice at the other end announced that the phone had been answered.

"Hello. This is Cheddon Fitzpaine," Fitzpaine said down the line. "Yes, I am. I need you to come down here and straighten something out for me. Yes, right now. It's very important. I think you know I can pay for it. The police station. I'll have them send you right up to where we are. Thank you."

He put the phone down.

"I hope he's a good solicitor," Ashby taunted Fitzpaine.

"He isn't," Fitzpaine replied drily.

Chapter 29

Fitzpaine indicated he would say no more until his visitor arrived. The DCI was left in the Chief's office to watch over Fitzpaine and so the Chief, Wenlock and Ashby took a tea break in the station communal kitchen.

"It's pretty strong stuff," said the Chief, shuffling uncomfortably on the plastic chair. Wenlock didn't see the Chief down here much.

"It is," Wenlock agreed dutifully.

"Thanks for making it," the Chief added.

"No problem," Wenlock replied. A little unsure what the Chief meant now.

"The tea," the Chief clarified. "It's strong. The accusations against the Mayor as well, I suppose. Almost unbelievable."

"Certainly hard to believe," Ashby added. "Even I'm struggling and I work for the *Everyday Post*. We print all kinds of daft shit in there."

"But we have investigated thoroughly," Wenlock added hurriedly. "I wouldn't believe it myself if it wasn't for all the evidence."

"Hmm." The Chief made noises of agreement whilst sipping his strong tea. "Amazing Fitzpaine would risk it all for money and a woman."

"Not just any woman, sir. She has been the object of his desires for a long time now, and he had already gone to so much effort to get rid of Cranswick," Wenlock pointed out.

"It's also a lot of money," Ashby supplemented the motive. "Far more than most would make in a lifetime!"

"Hmm." The Chief made more agreement noises. "I do wonder how he got Ms Greenhow to switch the insurance."

"Possibly intimidation," Wenlock ventured. "He is a powerful man. Or possibly other means. I don't think Ms Greenhow cared too much for the money."

"She is already pretty minted," Ashby agreed. "Her great-grandfather invented soup."

Their conversation was curtailed by a noise from outside the police station that sounded like a pack of baying wolves.

"Crikey," said the Chief. "What the devil was that?"

"It sounded like a pack of baying wolves, sir," Wenlock answered.

"I agree that's what it sounds like, but surely it can't be. Wenlock, go and have a look," the Chief instructed. Wenlock reluctantly obeyed. He left the break room, went down the corridor and hesitantly approached the front door of the station.

Behind the door, the howling grew louder. It was definitely dogs, or worse. Wenlock edged closer, his trepidation greatened with each step. As the noise reached fever pitch something knocked. Three, slow, booming knocks.

Wenlock froze. The noise of the angry animals outside abated, then he heard the patter of animal feet on the ground, as if they were running away. Three more, slow, booming knocks. A voice came from the other side of the door.

"Erm, hello? Is there anyone in there? Mr Fitzpaine sent for me."

Wenlock instantly relaxed. Whatever the strange noises outside had been, they had not been emanating from the owner of the voice. Frankly, if the owner of that voice could survive whatever had happened out there, Wenlock would be fine. He walked the final few steps and swung the door wide open.

"Hello," said the figure on the other side. He was a small, bespectacled man wearing a rather hastily assembled blue suit and carrying a rather smart brown leather briefcase. "I'm Burnham Norton, I've been send for by Mr Fitzpaine."

"What were the strange noises?" Wenlock asked, he scanned the car park in either direction but could see no sign of the beasts that had stood his hair on end with their cries.

"Oh yes. That was dogsled that brought me here. Hard to get a taxi at this time of night. Only mode of transport I could find. I was nervous too but the tramp doing the driving seemed to get me here alright."

Wenlock pieced it together.

"Turville! He's got my dogs and has started a taxi service!?"

"Then you know more than I," Norton replied. "I couldn't get any sense out of the driver. I think he might have been mad."

Wenlock thought he might be going a little mad himself. Fortunately, he pulled himself together.

"I can explain later. You'd better come in. Follow me."

***

Everyone gathered once more in the Chief's office. Fitzpaine was still behind the oak desk, Ashby and Wenlock faced him with the Chief and the DCI lurking in the background. A plastic chair was fetched from the break room for Norton and he had been sat next to Fitzpaine. Wenlock thought that the poor chap looked utterly bewildered by what was going on, which was fair as he had been dragged out of bed late at night and hurried across town by an unlicensed dogsled taxi into the Chief of Police's office.

"Very well. Where were we, DI Wenlock?" the Chief kicked things off by delegating the kick off once again.

Wenlock made a great show of looking at his notebook. This was pointless, as it was completely blank, but it seemed like a good way to start.

"We had surmised that Mr Fitzpaine had conspired with the Cheneys to kill Kirby Grindalythe by tampering with his car. This had been done for the reasons listed forthwith:

1. To collect on Grindalythe's substantial life insurance. Fitzpaine is the sole benfactor having obtained that right from Grindalythe's ambivalent ex-wife.
2. To eliminate Grindalythe as a love rival as he was engaged in an affair with Fitzpaine's wife.
3. All of this was performed in a copycat manner to how Fitzpaine murdered his previous rival, Hutton Cranswick, four years ago."

"I do wish you wouldn't list things in that format Wenlock, it gives me a headache," the DCI piped up.

The focus returned to Fitzpaine who seemed unphased by the accusations. No more was his head held in his hands. Ashby remained uncharacteristically quiet. Burnham Norton was looking at Wenlock intently, clearly listening carefully to every word.

"It was at this point that Mr Fitzpaine requested to call his solicitor, who has now arrived." Wenlock finished, gesturing to Norton and everyone in the room looked at him. At this point, Norton sat bolt upright and his eyes widened. Wenlock would say it was with shock.

"Oh gosh, I'm not Mr Fitzpaine's solicitor," he blurted quickly.

This was unexpected. Everyone looked a bit shocked except, Wenlock noted, Fitzpaine who for the first time in hours was smiling.

"Well who are you then?" the Chief was the first to react. Fitzpaine's smile widened.

"I'm a loss adjuster," Norton replied.

Chapter 30

"You're a what?" It was Wenlock who woke up first. This was unexpected.

"I'm a loss adjuster," Norton replied earnestly. "An insurance professional whose job is to investigate insurance claims on behalf of the insurer once they reach a certain size..."

"We know what a loss adjuster is, Mr Norton," the Chief interrupted. "What DI Wenlock means is what relevance do you have to all... this?" The Chief waved his arm in the direction of the assembled personage. Norton looked quite bewildered at the question and particularly at how annoyed everyone had seemed to become at his profession. Fortunately for the beleaguered insurance professional, Fitzpaine stepped in.

"Mr Norton is a loss adjuster for Welwick, Skirlaugh & Skeffling. They are the insurance company who underwrote Kirby Grindalythe's life insurance," Fitzpaine explained, in a slightly patronising manner. Norton nodded along to the explanation.

"Is this correct, Mr Norton?" the Chief asked.

"Yes, yes it is," Norton nodded enthusiastically. "I was the loss adjuster assigned to the case of Mr Grindalythe's crash in the Chapter 1 Classic."

"Budleigh, ring Skirlaugh at the insurers and check out his credentials will you?" the Chief instructed his brother, who nodded and left the room.

"I take it you paid out on the life insurance?" Wenlock took up the questioning of Norton.

"Yes, I found that Mr Grindalythe's crash fulfilled the terms of the insurance policy and we paid out £500,000 to Mr Fitzpaine as directed by the policy documentation," Norton answered politely. "I wrote quite an extensive report on the subject." He opened up the briefcase he had been clutching to his chest during the questioning and brought out a large stack of papers held together by a blue, leather ringbinder. He waved it out to Ashby and Wenlock for them to take it. Ashby seemed to lurch to life and slowly took the report from him. She opened it on her lap as the others continued talking.

"That testimony proves nothing Cheddon," scoffed the Chief. "If you had orchestrated the crash then you must have done it in such a way as to fool the insurance agency!"

Fitzpaine smiled at this and made to answer, however Norton beat him to it.

"That is quite impossible, sir! My investigation was extremely thorough. I can assure you that crash was not intentional" Wenlock could see Norton become agitated at the Chief's suggestion. He clearly didn't like his integrity being questioned.

"How can you be so sure?" Wenlock asked him. As he did, he noticed that Ashby had remained quiet since starting to read the report; this made him nervous. Wenlock turned to look at Ashby and saw that she had gone a little pale and shrunk back into her chair.

"I am an experienced crash investigator, DI Wenlock. It is not an insubstantial pay out for Welwick, Skirlaugh & Skeffling and I am their most senior loss adjustor. Not to mention the publicity of such an investigation," Norton started.

Wenlock could see this was going to be a long answer and so got comfortable.

"I studied the scene of the crash in great detail. By measuring the tyre marks on the road, I could determine the length of time spent braking by Mr Grindalythe and, by plotting the trajectory of the debris, I could ascertain the speed at which Mr Grindalythe's Fforde Panther hit the tree. Which was very fast, I can tell you!" Norton continued.

"136 mph," Ashby added. She had been reading the report. Wenlock did not like the look on her face.

"Indeed! I cross-checked that with the telemetry that had been recorded by the car's onboard computational engine and found it to be an accurate estimate." Norton was stopped at this point by Wenlock.

"Telemetry?"

"Yes. It was simple for me to take a look at the speeds..." Norton began, wary of being accused of being patronising again.

"Actually, this time I don't know what that is," Wenlock confessed.

"Telemetry is an automated communications process by which measurements and other data are collected at remote or inaccessible points and transmitted to receiving equipment for monitoring," Norton explained. "It's all very new - they only started to use it this season. It makes investigating this sort of thing far more straight forward."

It was Wenlock's turn to go pale.

"It was simple for me to take a look at the speeds Grindalythe had previously achieved round that particular bend along with the bank angles of the wheels and the down force the car provided each time." Norton ploughed on, he was clearly enjoying himself now he was discussing something familiar. "What I found was that the last time Grindalythe took that corner..."

Ashby interrupted this time.

"He entered at a slightly different angle to the racing line that the previous tyre marks left by his and all other cars indicated," she said slowly, carefully and unhappily. Ashby continued reading from the report in her lap. "'The wheels weren't able to grip effectively for that speed and angle. The car span off the track and into the surrounding trees.'"

"That's right, Miss!" Norton almost clapped his hands, happy that somebody had finally read his report. "An unfortunate accident, caused by driver error!"

The room went silent as this sunk in.

"It is a very dangerous sport," Norton added, slightly unhelpfully. The room stayed quiet.

Fortunately, the DCI arrived back in the room to break the silence.

"I just got through to Skirlaugh, Norton checks out. Senior investigator at the firm," he reported. His report was greeted by further silence.

"What did I miss?" he asked legitimately.

***

"Could the car have been tampered with in some way to cause that kind of error?" Wenlock asked Norton once the DCI had been brought up to speed. Wenlock wasn't quite ready to give up yet.

"I do not believe so," Norton answered. "This was an error in the positioning of the car. There isn't the technology available today to remotely control cars in such a way."

"He got that answer from Grantham and an independent consulting Professor," Ashby added slowly, still without looking up from the paperwork in her lap. "It's here in the report."

"How can I be sure you're not making this up and aren't just a part of the ruse?" It was the turn of the Chief.

"I'm an insurance agent, Chief Salterton. I have no imagination." Norton replied. "It's rather a prerequisite of the job."

Wenlock had to admit, he had them there.

The awkward silence set in once more, no more questions came from the interrogators. It was Fitzpaine who eventually shattered the peace.

"That appears to settle it. I assume you'd like me to explain away some of your other accusations? Might as well whilst I'm here," he added with mock graciousness.

The Chief waved a weary hand to say 'go on'.

"Kirby and my wife are not and have never been 'lovers', that is a fiction you created," Fitzpaine began. "They were just good friends and had been for a long time. As you undoubtedly found in your investigations, Kirby was not one to philander in any relationship other than his own."

"But the Bishop said..." Ashby began to interject but Fitzpaine stopped her.

"The esteemed Bishop is a gossip and an idiot. Even his incessant quotations are fake," Fitzpaine revealed with a wolfish grin. "I believe the Chief will back me up on that."

Wenlock turned to look at the Chief who gave a resigned nod.

"Bishop Burton has been known to make up a few tall tales," the DCI chipped in. "He once accused the cathedral choir of stealing his supply of communion wafers, trimming them to be slightly smaller wafers and using the cut-off wafer to perform backstreet Eucharist rituals."

"Well... were they?" Wenlock felt he had to ask.

"No," the DCI replied firmly. "We measured the wafers and they were the same size as always. He just likes to make trouble."

"We keep it fairly quiet. He's near retirement and we'd rather there wasn't a huge fuss just yet," the Chief explained. "You know how much the ecclesiastical elections stir people up - bluntly we don't have the budget for new riot control gear yet."

With all satisfied at the unreliability of the Bishop's testimony, Fitzpaine continued."As to why Kirby only violated the sancitiy of his own marriage, the answer is that he couldn't stand his wife, Ingleby. He would always say they had nothing in common. Personally, I never understood why they didn't divorce, probably because a visit to Greenhow Manor to ask her would take too bloody long. He only went when he was truly desperate. A divorce would require multiple trips."

Wenlock considered this. It had been a pain in the backside trying to talk to Greenhow, what with all the butler based rigmarole...

Fitzpaine ploughed on with his explanations, interrupting Wenlock's thought of penguin suits.

"As you surely have found, Kirby was struggling for finance this season. His sponsorship levels without the Greenhow money were not enough and he did not have the time to find more. My wife, as an old friend of his and someone confident in his abilities, persuaded me to loan Kirby the money he needed to compete." Fitzpaine leaned back in his chair and formed a bridge with his fingers, settling back into politician mode. "Kirby is a local celebrity and a symbol of the town through his success, I felt it would be a prudent to make a quiet investment to keep that status alive. I also stood to make a tidy sum should he have won."

Fitzpaine stood up from his seat and walked round the desk. He chose an edge on which to rest against then leaned down, looking right into Wenlock and Ashby's faces.

"Kirby would have been able to pay me back with some of the winnings of the championship. As a precaution, he also switched his life insurance policy so it was set to pay to me in case anything happened. It is a dangerous sport after all," Fitzpaine continued. "Kirby also put some money on Scudamore on the off chance that Upton somehow won the championship instead. Kirby could be a bit of a rogue but he was an honourable man when it came to his debts."

"And the phone call about 'fixing' the race?" Wenlock was still questioning but his heart wasn't in it anymore. He could see the way the wind had blown. Ashby had finished the report and was cradling it in her arms, staying quiet. Fitzpaine stood up straight again, towering over the pair of them.

"The phone call was indeed to Middleton Cheney. One of the reasons I have been meeting with them so regularly is that, unfortunately, I did not have all the capital Kirby required for the loan," Fitzpaine answered. "I needed a little extra help so I went to them. They wanted assurances they would get a return on their investment. I can promise you that both Kirby and I were not keen to renege on that bargain and end our days in a store cupboard or a cake mixer. Hence the many intricate fall backs and redundancies like the life insurance."

"Why didn't you just tell us all this back at the golf course?" Ashby asked, quite angrily Wenlock noted.

Fitzpaine put his hand across his brow as if in exasperation.

"I assumed the two of you would do a thorough investigation of the technical circumstances, as I strongly suggested to you at the time. You should have come to the same conclusions as Norton and it would have cleared the manner of death quickly. No further investigation would have been required into my business, this whole episode could have stayed out of the police investigation and thus public attention... Something I trust it still will?"

The Chief and DCI gave hurried assurances. Even Burnham Norton nodded fiercely. Wenlock felt the Chief glowering at the back of his head and gave a grudging consent noise of his own. However, he spotted that Ashby had stayed fairly quiet, fortunately Fitzpaine's attention had been mostly turned to the police in the room and he appeared not to notice.

There was further pause as Wenlock and company considered what they had been presented. It appears they had been very wrong.

"I take it I can leave?" Fitzpaine asked, his personable manner returned.

"Yes, I think so," the Chief answered, his manner alarmingly cool. "I think you and Mr Norton can both leave. Thank you for your time. Miss de-la-Zouch you may also leave. We have some internal police matters to discuss."

Wenlock didn't like the sound of that. Norton left as quickly as he could. Ashby got up slowly, still holding the report and eventually left the room. Fitzpaine followed in far less of a hurry.

"See you on the green next week, Woodbury," Fitzpaine said to the Chief. "Perhaps with this nonsense dealt with you can go back to looking for all those missing people?" With a cheery wave to the remaining police officers he departed the room and closed the door behind him.

The Chief, who clearly had not enjoyed Fitzpaine's parting shot at his competence, walked round the large desk and took up the seat Fitzpaine had previously occupied. The DCI took Ashby's old seat.

"Well then, DI Wenlock. We have a lot to talk about," the Chief began.

Chapter 31

Wenlock was exactly where you would expect one to be after an evening such as that - at Anearby pub. He had found a comfortable stool at the bar and allowed himself the luxury of a sprawl across the dark wooden altar to alcohol. Few would argue that he did not deserve a spot of antisocial spread-eagling.

The pub was emptying due to the late hour, spilling its many revellers out onto the local kebab shops and public transportation infrasturcture. The few hardcore remained. Specifically, Wenlock and the barman. In the 56 minutes that Wenlock had frequented the establishment, he had managed to sink five passable pints of bitter and a martini bought for him as a proposal by gent who later left disappointed.

As he sprawled, Wenlock mused. Was this his lowest point? Hard to say. He had been a divorced, loner detective for quite a while now - it was a position that led to its fair share of stinking moments. It was only on this contemplation that he realised he was no longer a divorced, loner detective. He'd been fired, making him merely a divorced loner.

Upon this realisation, he held up his hand to signal for more drink. The barman, ever the opportunist, took advantage of the vague signal and supplied the supine ex-investigator with a glass of long gone off lager. Wenlock didn't care. Cocking his head to one side, he slowly drizzled the beverage into his welcoming booze aperture.

The chat with the Chief had been mercifully short and fairly free of foul language. The Chief had outlined that there would need to be an inquiry followed up by a disciplinary hearing - at the conclusion of which Wenlock would no longer be in his employ. Wenlock's hard won pension would evaporate and his picture would be placed on the DCI's dartboard until someone else made a bigger cock-up.

Wenlock had protested that surely none of this could be known until the inquiry concluded and the disciplinary hearing completed. The Chief had nodded sagely, took this thought on board and then patiently explained exactly what the findings were going to be. He even had the DCI take notes to ensure the report would be verbatim.

Wenlock was interrupted from his reverie by a most unwelcome noise. The voice of that malodorous shitrat, Wraxall Piece.

"Hello, Much. Thought I might find you here." The corrupt, stinking weasel droned. Wenlock stopped his complicated beer delivery system to respond.

"Come to gloat?" he slurred, mostly comprehensibly.

"Not really," Piece replied. "I wanted to congratulate you."

This crossed several wires in Wenlock's already addled mind.

"Sarcastically? In a gloat-esque manner?"

"Not at all," Wenlock noticed Piece was glancing around the bar in a furtive manner. His rat-like eyes penetrating every dark nook and cranny of the boozer. "I actually think you were on to something."

"So did I. That was the bloody problem," Wenlock shot back, slowly but angrily. However, Piece wasn't put off.

"Look, going toe-to-toe with Mayor is not a winning play. I should know. How do you think I kept this job for so long?"

"By being a useless stooge?" Wenlock ventured, knowing full well it had been a rhetorical question. Piece merely smiled, clearly used to taking this sort of abuse.

"Something like that. Say, did you ever talk to Grantham about the telemetry?"

Wenlock attempted to shake his head. However, as it was still attached to the bar it ended up as more of a roll.

"Nope, Ashby spoke to him. I'd never heard of the stuff. I wouldn't have even known to ask him about it had I been there."

Piece stopped acting in an unobtrusively furtive manner and now was being very overt in his suspicious behaviour. He looked over his shoulder to confirm the barman was out of earshot then leaned in close to Wenlock's reclined form.

"You should ask where the telemetry comes from," Wraxall whispered. "And you should have shower," he added, not incorrectly.

Wenlock tried to ask further questions but Piece was out the door before he could complain that it had been a long day and usually his hygiene standards were exemplary.

Great, thought Wenlock, more unpaid work.

Chapter 32

"You look awful," Ashby stated, correctly.

"Thanks," Wenlock replied, "Concentrate on the road."

"Why are we doing this again?" Ashby asked, not unreasonably.

Wenlock sighed, rubbed his eyes and repeated the explanation he had given when he showed up at her flat, half-cut, in the early hours of the morning.

"Wraxall Piece told me to ask Grantham about the telemetry. I should let it go but he might actually have uttered something useful for the first time in his miserable life. You're driving because I am hungover and had to give the Muskrat back. I walked to yours."

"I see." Ashby hadn't been amused by the unannounced appearance of the bedraggled, smelly, and heartily pickled ex-detective incessantly buzzing her intercom at 2 am. Mostly because she had never told him where she lived. After she forced a few pints of water down him and he had a 3 hour kip on the sofa, they wound up back in Ashby's Civet and driving to the racetrack.

"You know I am sorry about the whole telemetry thing, right?" she asked, hoping he wasn't too angry that her sloppy racing knowledge had cost him his job.

"Bluntly, I'm fuming," Wenlock replied, surprisingly calmly. "However, who else was I going to call about this? The police? Also, you know where to find Grantham. Now, shut up and concentrate on the road. I'm having a nap."

He was being rude, but Ashby couldn't blame him all that much. She did as he suggested and they were at the racetrack before the dribble running down the sleeping Wenlock's stubble reached his shirt collar.

***

Grantham had just about started his day when the dishevelled duo[46] pitched up at his garage.

"Hello, Miss de-la-Zouch. Pleasure to see you again," he started cheerfully. "And you've brought another visitor. Hello, sir."

"Hello, Grantham. Good to see you again. This is DI Wenlock," she said, indicating to the mess of a man stood beside her.

"Just Wenlock actually," he replied. "Don't want to add 'impersonating a police officer' to my charge sheet."

"However you please, Mr Wenlock." Grantham stuck out his hand to allow Wenlock to shake it. Wenlock gave a good look at the greasy appendage but decided against it.

"I've hurt my finger," he gave as a lame excuse. Grantham didn't seem to mind and shuffled over to the kettle in the corner of the garage.

"I'm just putting on a cuppa. Can I get you both one?" he called over his shoulder. Wenlock looked to Ashby who frantically, but silently, indicated not to accept.

"No thanks, we just had one," Ashby replied for them both. Her toilet trips had not been the same since the last one.

"Right you are." Grantham began operating his overly complicated all-in-one-mug-tea-kettle system. "What can I do for you folks today?"

---

[46] Wenlock looked the worst but Ashby hadn't come off great from the night either.

"We want to ask you about telemetry," Wenlock started. "I understand you had a conversation with an insurance firm regarding the telemetry from the Chapter 1 Classic. Can you tell us what you told them?"

Grantham finished his tea making and indicated for his visitors to take a seat on some stacks of tyres. They hesitantly complied.

"I surely can. I told them that the telemetry from the race day was available and that they were welcome to take a look at it." He was still smiling as he said this, but Ashby could see this was going to be a painful conversation for the loyal mechanic.

"Can we take a look at it Grantham?" Ashby asked. "We're interested to know what it says for ourselves."

Grantham nodded and walked to a corner of the garage. In said corner was a grey, metallic filing cabinet, a surprising piece of order in the greasy, mechanical chaos. He opened the top drawer of the cabinet and began flicking through the dividers until he found what he was looking for. He reached in and withdrew a long sheet of thin, light blue paper that was folded to a size that a human could manage to hold. Handling it with care and only holding it by the corners, he walked the paper back across the garage and into Ashby's hands. His efforts had not been in vain and it was transferred to her with minimal grease attached.

The paper was about the width of a tabloid newspaper and covered with neat, ordered, typed rows of numbers. It was impossible to tell how long the sheet was due to the folding but Ashby would guess at least 14 feet. The numbers seemed to have no discernible pattern or meaning that Ashby could make out on first inspection. Occasionally there were letters and symbols mixed in but none of it made any sense to her. She showed Wenlock, who took a glance and gave up. He was barely upright at this point and the stuffy garage was making him feel ill.

"I think we're going to need a bit of help understanding this, Grantham," Ashby said. "What does any of this mean?"

He seemed to perk up at the question. It was something in his skill set.

"Aye, it's complicated looking stuff. I was sceptical when we first introduced it but it has really made a difference to our work on the car." Grantham walked across to sit next to Ashby. Wenlock obliged by vacating his tyre seat.

"See now, this column shows the time since the race started, the next one gives speed data. This one is wheel alignment versus chassis and this one is ..."

"Grantham. How was this data used to show that Grindalythe's crash was an accident?" Wenlock interrupted. He couldn't hang on much longer before needing a coffee and/or a vomit.

Grantham, though taken a back at the bluntness, was clearly used to being told to get to the point. He nodded then started running the long sheet through his hands until he reached the last foot of paper.

"Starts here Mr Wenlock, this time is that of just before... the incident." Grantham paused before pointing to the time column. "What you can read from this is that Mr Grindalythe accelerated here. I can read across where this was on the track from the race clock. This bit tells me the speed - too fast for that corner by about 3 mph."

"Only 3?" Ashby asked. Grantham nodded vigorously.

"Oh yes, doesn't need to be much on that corner. This is our home track, we are both very clued up on how much the car can manage," Grantham paused before correcting himself. "We both were..."

"That chimes exactly with what the investigator reported," Ashby said to Wenlock.

"It should do," Grantham agreed. "It's what I told him and it's what the copy he took with him said too."

"What the hell could Wraxall have meant then?" Wenlock asked, mostly to himself. "Why did he tell us to look at this?"

Ashby shrugged and stared at the data again, willing it to give up its secrets.

"Maybe he really was just wasting your time?" She ventured. Wenlock considered it, but it was too strange a thing, even for Piece.

"How does the telemetry work, Grantham?" Wenlock let out a sigh, he didn't really want to know but maybe it would yield a clue.

"Well, Mr Wenlock - are you familiar with a tachometer?" Grantham started. Wenlock was about to admit he was not when Ashby interrupted with a rude word.

"Excuse me?" Wenlock replied.

"Sorry," Ashby apologised. "I just spotted this at the end of the data sheet." She held up the very last lines of the paper for Wenlock to inspect. The rows of numbers ended and there was some actual, readable, words printed at the bottom:

© CHENEY DATA INDUSTRIES

UNIT 472A

BOWMORE STREET

ANEARBY

Wenlock repeated Ashby's rude word and subsequent apology. They looked at each other in silent shock for a second.

"Er, can I ask what's going on?" Grantham asked.

"You can Grantham," Ashby finally replied. "This address is somewhere we have been in the past few days, twice actually. We were under the impression it was a cake factory."

"Those Cheneys, eh?" Wenlock said, with a grin. "They've got their fingers in many pies."

*

Chapter 33

"Piss off," said the security guard in no uncertain terms.

"But we're health inspectors! You have to let us in!" One of the health inspectors protested.

"No you're not," sighed the guard with mock weariness. "You're just two people in white coats pretending to be health inspectors."

Wenlock had to admit, the security guard had a point. This was exactly the situation. He had warned Ashby it wouldn't work but she had convinced him otherwise. Having driven across town in Ashby's Civet and procured themselves some white coats from a work wear store, they were stood in the main reception area for Unit 472A - the Cheneys' cake factory. They had walked in to be met by a receptionist who immediately called for the security guard.

"Can you prove we're not?" Ashby was persisting. "If we're health inspectors and you don't let us in, we'll revoke your baking license! Is that a risk worth taking?"

"I know you're not health inspectors because you put your white coats on *before* entering the factory. If you put them on *before* entering the factory they get dirty and bring in contamination," the guard explained, surprisingly patiently. "White coats are worn only in the clean areas."

"Also," he added, pointing at Ashby, "you're a woman wearing a false moustache."

Both points were going to be difficult to disprove. His logic seemed sound on point one, and Ashby had insisted on wearing a false moustache. Wenlock had tried to explain there was no reason why there couldn't be a female health inspector but she wasn't to be swayed. She'd gathered her hair

192

under a flat cap and decided to wear a large pair of sunglasses to complete the look. None of it was particularly convincing.

Whilst Ashby argued the toss with the security guard[47], Wenlock surveyed the lobby they were in. The entrance to the factory was on a different wall to the door they had staked out earlier. They had assumed that door would be locked, hence the more 'subtle' approach. Behind Wenlock was a large set of glass double doors from which he and Ashby had entered. There was a row of chairs up against the walls to either side, presumably as an area where visitors with legitimate business could wait for the attention of the receptionist who was sat behind a toughened glass panel in a separate office. The walls were yellow and there was a large but rather sad looking potted plant in one corner. There were some framed, old advertisements on the wall showing a ruddy faced baker flogging various, flour-based fancies.

In front of Wenlock and Ashby was another set of double doors that presumably led into the factory itself. Between the duo and their goal was the security guard. The guard, while not huge, was a bit more than Wenlock felt he could handle in his current delicate state, even with Ashby as back up.

Eventually, Ashby's moustache fell off so they had to concede defeat and leave. Once outside, they reverted to Wenlock's back up plan of walking the factory perimeter and looking for any open windows.

"I think it might have worked if we'd made some I.D. badges," Ashby sulked. Wenlock thought it best not to respond and began his survey of the factory walls. The front of the red-brick factory from which they had emerged had several windows, presumably for offices, but none on the ground floor. More specifically, none on the ground floor that hadn't been boarded up from the inside, entirely ruling them out as entry points. Their perimeter search followed the front wall and went round the corner, taking them to the opposite side of the factory from the door they had observed Fitzpaine's comings and goings. This side of the factory also yielded little

---

[47] And the glue on her false moustache slowly melted.

joy. There was a loading bay, however it was firmly shut with no visible means of opening it from the outside. The loading bay door was only just wide enough to let a lorry in and out so they discounted trying to slip through when a delivery came. The idea of hiding in a lorry also crossed their minds but was ruled out on the fact that Wenlock's blood sugar was getting low and he didn't want to hang about waiting for one to show up.

This side of the factory was similar to the front in that all windows that had existed on the ground floor were boarded up or bricked over. Certainly no way to quietly slip in. They walked for what seemed like an age to arrive at the factory rear, once again the same story. No other entrance, all windows boarded up.

"If it wasn't for all that smoke belching out of the chimney, you would think the place was shut," Ashby remarked. Wenlock had to agree - it was a bit strange. Eventually they came to the final side of the factory, the one they already knew well. They walked to the black door that they had staked out earlier and gave it a try but, as predicted, it was locked. Neither of them knew how to pick it.

"I usually spend my time arresting people for doing that," Wenlock replied to Ashby's assumption that he might have that skill.

They were stumped and so walked back to the Civet dejected.

"There must be another way," Ashby started. "Maybe if we hire a van and set up at the delivery area?"

"Maybe." Wenlock wasn't really listening. "Why would all their windows be boarded up? They're clearly operating. Surely they must just have to have the lights on all the time inside, running up their electricity bills."

"Maybe they don't want people looking in?" Ashby ventured. "Stealing their cake-making techniques?"

"Perhaps. That would make sense for the ground floor, but not the floors above," Wenlock replied. "It seems a lot of trouble to go to for a cake factory. They're certainly hiding something in there."

Ashby got back in the car, Wenlock stayed outside for a minute longer, trying to think of another way to get them inside. He was about to get back in when his eyes fell on a piece of dog muck in the gutter running along the road. A plan formed as he sat in the Civet's faux-leather passenger seat.

"We need to call a taxi."

Chapter 34

Today had been a pretty good day, the security guard mused. He had told some 'health inspectors' to 'piss off'. Nothing else had happened and his shift was ending in twenty minutes. All-in-all, a very good day.

He had retreated back to the comfort of his post in the security office and was idly flicking through a newspaper when he got another call from reception.

"Hi, yeah, the 'health inspectors' are back. Can you come down?" the receptionist said over the phone. The security guard, impressed the receptionist could pronounce an inverted comma, sighed, put down the paper, hitched up his belt and left the comfort of his office. These idiots just won't pack it in, he thought to himself. He didn't try to imagine what they wanted - he didn't want to know. That was well out his job description. He just needed them to piss off for good.

As described by the receptionist, the 'health inspectors' were indeed back in the lobby. The lady looked apologetic, the man looked like he had a splitting headache and only hours left to live.

"Hi, us from earlier." Began the women, she even gave a little wave. "I realise we got off on the wrong foot and all but... do you think my colleague could use the toilet? He's rather desperate."

The absolute bloody nerve! What the hell were they thinking? Trying to worm their way in to the building again no doubt, thought the guard. Not on his watch - certainly not with only ten minutes till the end of his shift.

"No. Piss off," he replied. A man of few words maybe, but no-one could gather mixed messages from them.

"I need to vomit," said the man. The guard believed him, the gentleman looked like death, but this did not mean he would grant access. In fact, it made him less likely to, as the nearest toilet was one used by the guard himself.

"I feel quite like vomiting too," said the female 'inspector', now moustache free. "Are you sure you can't let us in?"

"No. Use the plant pot, then piss off," was the guard's response. He felt happy with it. He felt it carried the correct gravitas to hammer home the fact that they were not coming in and he really didn't care for their predicament.

It was at this moment that the double door to the outside world burst open. This was an unwelcome surprise to the guard. He was not unprepared in the event that there were reinforcements to these intruders, however the reinforcements were not what he expected.

The doors were burst open by a pack of dogs. The dogs were attached by rope to some kind of makeshift go-cart. 'Steering' the go-kart was what looked to be a grubby, green mackintosh with a scaggily, grey beard and a battered waterproof cap.

In the split second that the kart/sled arrangement burst in to the reception, its driver[48] let slip the reigns by which he had tenuous control over the pack.

"Havoc!" the mackintosh cried, and let slip were his dogs of war.

The pack of hounds tore around the room. A duo of Doberman upended the neat rows of chairs. A trio of terriers knocked over and peed on the potted plant. A splinter group of spaniels ran around the guards legs in a frantic circle, occasionally nipping at his heels. The instigator of the scene sat on his vehicle in the middle of the lobby, cackling like a maniac - an act that seemed only to spur the dogs into further acts of carnage.

---

[48] Pilot? Operator? Chauffer?

The guard was in for a busy last ten minutes of his shift. One thing he had not spotted in the maelstrom (and at this point was far from his mind in all honesty) was what had happened to the 'health inspectors'.

***

The 'health inspectors' had managed to use the pooch-based disarray to slip passed the guard, through the double doors and in to the factory. They found themselves in a short corridor,A door to their left clearly led to the small office that contained the receptionist and to their right was the toilet they had used as a ruse to get back in to the lobby area. They heard a commotion at the far end of the corridor as a squad of security guards burst out of what was presumably the security office to support their beleaguered colleague. Ashby and Wenlock managed to dive in to the toilet just in time to avoid being spotted.

When the noise in the corridor died, down they made their move further in to the facility. They were still wearing their coats and Ashby had managed to pilfer a clipboard to make them look vaguely official.

They walked along the corridor trying to look as if they belonged and knew exactly where they wanted to be, in case they were surprised from one of the many doors leading off. They passed the open door to the security office from which they could hear a guard shouting down a telephone[49].

The corridor took a left turn and then, after 10 yards, a right. So far it was deserted. They were now in a corridor that appeared to run along the edge of the building. There were boarded up windows running along the entire left-hand-side. The whole length was lit by a harsh electric light that reflected off walls which were the same shade of yellow as the reception. The right-hand-side was far more interesting. The right wall of the corridor was a long series of windows that looked out on to the factory floor.

---

[49] "Who let the dogs out? Who? Who? Who? Who? It doesn't matter who, just get them out of the bloody reception!"

"It looks like a cake factory to me," Ashby whispered as they slowly made their way along the corridor. Wenlock nodded in agreement. He could see large machines passing Victoria sponge bases along conveyor belts, tubes squirting icing on to battenburgs and large vats mixing who-knows-what. He was no expert but he could tell this was very much a cake making operation and had no relevance to telemetry creation.

"Walk slowly. Let's have a closer look," he muttered. As he did so, a set of double doors that led to the factory floor swung open. Two hair-netted men in white coats walked out of the doors and turned left - straight into Ashby and Wenlock's path. Wenlock looked at Ashby, slightly panicked, but she was already in full flow.

"... and that's how we can increase the biscuit margin, less butter and more sugar," she jabbered. Wenlock nodded his head, attempting to look interested in her nonsense. As the men came close, she gave them a nod as if of recognition and they returned it. Wenlock had to stop himself from breathing a sigh of relief. He'd never really been one for the undercover work.

The hairnetted duo passed them and so Ashby and Wenlock followed the corridor to its end at the far side of the factory floor.

"Well," Ashby said. It was a statement and a question. "I didn't see anything."

Wenlock shrugged in response. It all looked right; machines were making cakes. There was a group of people on a production line in the far corner, doing tasks too delicate for the machines, and some inspectors keeping an eye on things but really nothing to report.

"Maybe Piece was winding me up," Wenlock offered. "He is a shit."

"Maybe," Ashby replied. It was her turn to be deep in thought. "This should be the wall with the door in it. You know, the Fitzpaine entrance."

Wenlock nodded. That felt right.

"Well, where is it then?"

Ashby was correct. The door wasn't in this corridor at all.

"You've got a point there," Wenlock added. "How long were we walking around the outside of the factory for?"

"Longer than we have been walking on the inside," Ashby said in agreement.

"There's something not right here," Wenlock replied. They appeared to be at the end of the corridor. There was another door next to them that led on to the factory floor but that was it. The corridor itself stopped dead.

Or did it?

Wenlock took a step back.

"There used to be a door here," he said, a bit cryptically. "Look."

He pointed at the wall in front of them. It had been well plastered but there was a faint outline of a door shaped hole. A ghost of portals past.

"There's more to the factory," Ashby said excitedly.

Wenlock nodded in agreement. But how to get to it?

Chapter 35

Wenlock and Ashby went back to the window to look at the factory floor again. Specifically at the wall on which the plastered-over door sat.

Now they knew what they were looking for, it didn't take long to spot. At the other side of the factory floor, there was a door in the wall in question. It looked unassuming, like a utility cupboard. No sign hung on or above it.

They could have believed it was a utility cupboard except for one detail. There seemed to be a man guarding it. At first, it seemed like an employee on a break, but the longer they looked, the more obvious it was. The man wasn't dressed like the security guard from the reception - he was wearing a white coat and hairnet like all the employees in the factory floor area. However, he never left the area around that door.

"We just need a way to shift him," Wenlock pointed out, fairly obviously. Ashby agreed but was equally thin on ideas. They had played many of their best cards already, their disguises were weak and they were struggling to think up a legitimate reason to go through a door with no idea what was on the other side. Finally, her vomit trick was neither appropriate nor hygienic.

Divine providence, however, had other ideas. A commotion occurred amongst the workers on the cake assembly line as they spotted an intruder in their midst. A Dalmatian had burst in to their midst and was tearing around the factory floor. Mr 'Piss Off' from earlier was in hot pursuit, looking hot, bothered and bedraggled. Ashby moved fast.

"Follow me," she hissed. Wenlock complied. She ran down to the double doors and barged her way on to the factory floor.

"Don't just stand there, help him!" she yelled at the 'employee' guarding the 'utility cupboard' whilst pointing at the Dalmatian who had already made it to the Battenberg assembly machine.

The door guard looked a bit shocked but sprang gamely into action, joining Mr 'Piss Off' in the frantic Dalmatian chase. The Dalmation was now weaving in and out of the legs of the production line team, none of whom looked to have the slightest inclination to stop him. Door guard and 'Piss Off' followed close behind, bowling-hair netted factory workers across the conveyor belt.

In the chaos, Ashby and Wenlock slipped through the 'utility cupboard' door unnoticed.

It became instantly clear that a utility cupboard it was not. It was in fact another long corridor, similar to the last one but now on the opposite wall of the factory. Exactly like the previous, it had a row of windows running down one wall but all of them were boarded up. The lighting in this corridor was far lower, dimmed to make sure none escaped to the outside world.

On the other side of the corridor to the windows was a series of dirty grey-blue doors. Fortunately, these appeared to have words painted on them in black. Wenlock closed the door through which they had entered and joined Ashby in reading the painted words.

"'MEN'," Ashby read out loud. "Bollocks, after all that have we just found the toilets?"

Wenlock shrugged. He had spotted a set of toilets on the factory floor and in addition to those near reception. It seemed like an overabundance of facilities. The words on the doors had been painted on roughly, without much care. It was in stark contrast to the far more professional looking areas they had passed through. The whole corridor was dirty, but not unused. The floor was covered in foot prints and scuff marks leading from the doors to and from the factory floor. He came to the next door and, unsurprisingly it had 'WOMEN' daubed across it.

Ashby was first to the next door.

"'BATHROOM'," she read out. "'Men', 'Women' *and* 'Bathroom'? This is weird."

Wenlock nodded to agree, it made little sense. He daren't speak more than necessary - it was so quiet in this part of the building. They could hear the machinery working next door in its unending cake-based quest but none of the voices and dog-based commotion that was certainly still unfolding.

They carried on past a door marked 'LAUNDRY' before the corridor took a left turn. Still empty of people, it offered more doors for them to explore. One thing Wenlock noticed was that although the machinery noises from the cake factory floor were growing more muffled as they got further away, they were being replaced by other mechanical sounds. As they cautiously made their way down the next corridor, he read the names painted on these doors. A particularly large room, judging by the spacing between neighbouring doors, was marked 'TEXTILES'. Ashby put her ear to this door, clearly having had a similar thought to Wenlock regarding the source of noise.

"Sounds like sewing machines," she said. "Lots of them."

Strange, but not what they were looking for. This corridor clearly stretched across the width of the building, It ended with a right-hand turn to another, seemingly final, corridor. The left-hand wall was completely blank, no windows at all and only one door. Wenlock recognised which one it must be.

"The entrance we watched Fitzpaine use," he said to Ashby, pointing up the hallway. Ashby, however, had been paying attention to the corridor's other wall.

"Look," she hissed, her turn to point. "That door: 'DATA INDUSTRIES'. Just like the others: blue-grey with black paint labelling whatever was inside.

They both put an ear against the door this time, straining to hear anything that might give them a clue as to what was on the other side. It was mostly quiet, a rhythmic knocking noise that sounded vaguely mechanical and some uneven shuffling that might have been a person. No voices. No clues.

Ashby put her hand on the door knob, she gave it a small turn and it moved. It wasn't locked.

"We've come too far not to," Ashby stated, anticipating hesitancy from Wenlock. However, this time Wenlock wasn't going to argue with her. They had no idea what they were going to find but he'd be damned if they weren't going to take a look. He gave a little internal prayer that it wasn't a room full of vicious gangsters or worse, crocodiles[50] and then nodded to Ashby.

Ashby took a deep breath to steady her nerves, twisted the door knob fully and swung the door open in a smooth motion, thinking to catch anyone behind the door by surprise.

She succeeded. The room's two occupants were very surprised indeed.

---

[50] It was very unlikely to be, but Wenlock really hated crocodiles. More the idea really; he hadn't come in to contact with many. I mean, they have 80 replaceable teeth and are able to close their massive jaws with a pressure of 5000 psi in less than half a second when the mood takes them. Potentially devastating in enclosed spaces so you can see where his fear came from.

Chapter 36

Wenlock surveyed what Ashby had just revealed. A relatively small room, about eight feet wide and 10 feet long with worktops running up both walls. No windows, ceiling the same height as corridor outside and only the door they had entered through. The walls were bare breezeblock and fairly sloppily erected. The whole room was illuminated by a bulb hanging from the ceiling, no lampshade, giving a rather cell-like appearance to proceedings.

The room had two occupants, one on each side. Until they had been interrupted, the occupants had been assembling small mechanical devices of some sort. The internal mechanisms of which, cogs, wheels and wires, were strewn across the worktops. One occupant was a man, wearing an oil stained coat that had once been white. He was well in to his mid-fifties, balding and and very thin with jam-jar glasses perched on his forehead and some kind of magnification device in his hand. He looked familiar but Wenlock couldn't place him immediately. At this point, the male occupant was merely gawping at the intruders.

The second occupant was a women in her early thirties who reacted far quicker.

"Come in, but whatever you do, don't shut that door," she hissed urgently. Ashby and Wenlock complied, Ashby kept her foot in the door to stop it closing behind them. As she did, she and Wenlock noticed that the door through which they had entered had no knob or handle on the inside.

The female occupant was wearing a white coat too, but much newer and far less stained. Her blonde hair, which had recently been cut very short in a haphazard way, looked matted and dirty.

"Leigh? Leigh Delamere?" Ashby recognised the lady instantly. "It's Ashby de-la-Zouch - I met you a few times when interviewing Scudamore."

"Is there anyone else in the corridor?" Leigh cut Ashby off.

Ashby took another look to check and shook her head.

"Good. Yes, I remember you. Who's he?" Leigh said brusquely whilst pointing at Wenlock.

"Much Wenlock, ex-detective and hound-based taxi firm co-owner," Wenlock introduced himself[51]. "We haven't printed business cards yet."

Leigh gave Ashby a look that very much suggested bafflement.

"We've had a strange week," Ashby offered by way of explanation. "What are you doing here? Who's he?" she indicated toward the room's so-far unnamed occupant who had stayed quiet and gawped through the entire exchange thus far.

"He's Woodford Halse, and we're both here very much against our will," Leigh explained.

As Leigh said the man's name, Wenlock's brain offered up the information of where he recognised Woodford Halse from. He was an open missing person case file, from several years ago. His picture had been in the papers and on posters throughout the town.

"Woodford Halse, the missing engineer?" Wenlock asked. Woodford gave a weak smile and a wave in return before returning to gawping.

"That's him. He's been here much longer than me and is in a bit of a state. He doesn't say much," Leigh answered for the lost-looking Woodford. "I haven't got time to explain more, we need to leave before they come back."

---

[51] He and Acton had come to a business arrangement before they pulled off the dog based distraction in the factory reception room.

"They?" Ashby asked - not unreasonably.

"I said later!" Leigh snapped back. "How did you get in here? Can we get out the same way?"

Wenlock shook his head.

"No chance. We came in through the front of the factory with a dog-based distraction. Not a trick we can use twice sadly," he explained.

"What is it with him and dogs?" Leigh asked Ashby who gave an exasperated shrug in return.

"There is another door out. It's just up the corridor from this room." Wenlock offered, trying to shake Leigh's opinion of him to something other than a weird mutt-obsessive. "It leads straight outside. Only problem is that it's locked."

Leigh thought for a few seconds before responding.

"We can work with that," she began to gather tools that were strewn across the worktops. She couldn't carry them all so she handed a reciprocating saw and the large gas cylinder that powered the tool to Wenlock.

"Ashby, check the coast is clear," Leigh instructed. Ashby snuck another look through the gap in the door, before opening it wider to check both ways. She nodded and so Leigh gave her orders to the room.

"OK, we have to move quick. Straight to this door, no messing about. Ashby, look after Woodford. When we get to the door, I'll try to knock the lock through with these." She indicated the small hammer and chisel she had picked from the bench. "If these aren't enough, dog-boy will need to pass me the reciprocating saw and I'll cut the deadbolt, OK?"

Although Wenlock wasn't enjoying his new nickname, he nodded.

"Sorry about the dog-boy stuff, I'm under pressure and have forgotten your name," Leigh added.

Wenlock nodded again; it was forgivable given the circumstances.

"Still clear out there, Ashby?" Leigh asked. Ashby checked and nodded again. Leigh took a deep breath.

"Now or never then. Let's go, quickly but quietly."

Ashby opened the door fully to let the team out before going back in to grab Woodford by the wrist. He complied as she dragged him out, albeit not as quick as Ashby would have liked.

As she escorted the spaced-out engineer, Leigh and Wenlock went straight up the corridor to the door. Leigh took one look at the lock and threw the hammer and chisel to the floor.

"It's going to have to be the saw," she said. Wenlock handed it over. "Keep an eye out."

She slid the blade of the saw in the gap between the door and the frame, just above the handle.

"Open the valve on the cylinder, quarter turn," Leigh instructed. Wenlock complied, turning the valve the requested amount. The saw started up with a tinny whine which pierced through the otherwise quiet corridors. In his imagination, Wenlock could hear it echoing all the way back to the factory floor.

The whine got much worse as Leigh started cutting. The deadbolt shrieked as the saw attempted to slice through it.

Leigh gritted her teeth and pushed down hard on the saw. She was making progress but the noise was so loud that it was definitely going to be heard somewhere in the building.

Ashby had brought Woodford over to the door Leigh was working on and then ran back to the corner of the corridor, peering round to look out for anyone coming from that direction. Woodford gave Wenlock a faintly bemused smile as Wenlock watched Leigh's slow progress.

Leigh had been cutting for an agonising thirty seconds when Ashby rushed back to her, she tapped Leigh on the shoulder and frantically gestured for her to turn the saw off. Leigh complied.

"Men," she said. "With guns - coming this way. They're moving slowly, checking the other doors are all closed, but they'll be here any minute."

"Shit, I need another couple of minutes at least," Leigh replied. "Are you armed?"

Wenlock and Ashby shook their heads, as did Woodford.

"Better do some praying then," she responded before getting back to work on the lock.

Wenlock's brain raced. They had no weapons; he had seen nothing in the workshop that could help them in a gun fight. Their only hope was getting through that door before the guards saw them and started shooting.

He had an idea of how to speed up their lock-breaking progress, but he'd only get one shot. He motioned for Ashby to grab hold of Woodford's wrist and prepared himself. He would have to do it at the last possible moment. He would have milliseconds to pull it off, between the guards rounding the corner and them realising what was happening.

Leigh managed thirty more seconds of agonising lock cutting before the men rounded the corner. Neither were in security guard uniforms. One wore a black leather jacket, the other a cream woolly jumper. As Ashby had reported, they were carrying guns - specifically revolvers. This was all Wenlock had time to register before making his move.

He dragged Leigh away from the door with one hand and stepped backward at the same time. As he did, it dislodged the saw and so he was able to hear a shout from the armed men. He didn't know what was said - he wasn't stopping. With Leigh out of the way he threw his full weight including that of the gas cylinder, against the door.

It gave; Leigh had cut through enough deadbolt. Wenlock stumbled into the street, temporarily blinded by the daylight after the dim corridor. Ashby followed him through, dragging Woodford behind. Leigh jumped through after them. As she did, Wenlock heard the dual crack of the pistols from inside and saw a lump of doorframe splinter as a round impacted. He didn't need to give any instructions, Ashby was sprinting full speed now to where she had parked her Civet, Woodford in tow. Wenlock gave chase, hoping Leigh was following him. He needn't have worried; as he rounded a street corner he took a moment's pause and dared a look back at the factory door, the younger woman overtook him. From the corner, he could see the guards had reached the factory door and stopped, unsure about giving chase. Leather jacket ran back inside - presumably for reinforcements. With a decision clearly made, the other walked quickly and purposefully to where Wenlock was hiding, revolver raised, presumably unsure if his quarry was armed. Wenlock didn't wait for the guard to arrive. He sprinted after Ashby as fast he could - the Civet was parked at the end of the next street.

He made it to the car as the guard rounded the corner. The Civet was a sporty 2+2, Ashby had managed to manoeuvre Woodford and Leigh into the backseats and take the wheel as Wenlock threw himself into the passenger side. As he did, the guard opened fire. His first shot went well wide but the second thumped in to the Civet's rear bodywork.

"Drive!" Wenlock roared, not that Ashby needed telling. She revved hard and slammed the gearstick into first as a third shot grazed the car's thin roof. As they pulled away, Wenlock risked a look in the wing mirror and could see the guard running after them, firing still. A round slammed into the boot and another into the rear bumper eliciting a stream of swearwords from Leigh. After these two shots, no more followed as the revolver was empty. Wenlock breathed a sigh of intense relief as they pulled far away from the be-jumpered figure. Ashby, for once, concentrated on the road.

Chapter 37

Ashby blitzed through the industrial estate, avoiding flat-capped workers carrying large panes of glass and strategically placed cardboard box piles. The car stayed silent to let her concentrate, Leigh watching through the rear windscreen for any sign of pursuit.

"Anything?" Ashby asked as she reached the ring-road, pulling an illegal undertake at the roundabout to allow her to join the labyrinthine mess that was the bypass.

"No sign," Leigh replied, shaking her head. "Either you lost them or they didn't bother to give chase."

Although this was ostensibly good news, Wenlock had a nagging sense of dread that it was not as fortuitous as it appeared. However, his train of thought was derailed by a question from Ashby.

"Where to?" she asked.

"The police station," he answered. "It should still be safe there." Ashby nodded and got on with the task of breaking as many traffic laws as she could manage in a four mile drive. Wenlock turned to the passengers in the back seats.

"And perhaps you can tell us what the hell is going on?" Wenlock asked the cramped pair. Woodford gave a slightly dozy smile in response; Leigh slumped into her seat and let out a huge sigh.

"Near the end of the Chapter 1 Classic, I was grabbed from my garage by some men. I don't know who they were but I know who they were working for," she began. "They put a bag over my head and pushed me into the back of a van. I guess they must have taken me straight to that place."

Leigh took another deep breath to compose herself. Wenlock, though full of questions, held his tongue.

"They took the bag off my head once we were inside the building, stripped me down, blasted me with a cold water hose and then hacked most of my hair off," she continued. "I won't go through all the details, but after a day or two they locked me in the room you found me in. Woodford was already in there."

At the mention of his name, Woodford stopped looking out of the window at the traffic and looked as though he was about to say something. Leigh and Wenlock waited but nothing came out of his mouth. He shook his head and went back to watching the reactions of the angry motorist victims of Ashby's manic progress across town. Leigh continued her story.

"They told me to assemble telemetry units. That's what Woodford had been doing in there, day after day. I'm not sure how long for. He really doesn't talk much."

"He's been missing for two years," Wenlock remembered.

"Damn," was all Leigh said in response. She gave Woodford a friendly stroke on the arm. He patted her hand in response.

"The men just said to me: 'Watch what he does and copy him.'," Leigh said. "I learnt how to assemble the units that way. If I made similar progress in a day, I was OK. If not..."

Leigh didn't finish the sentence and Wenlock thought it best not to ask.

"Then you turned up," Leigh finished with a smile. More of relief than true happiness. "I've lost track of time a bit - how long was I in there for?"

"Best part of a week probably," Wenlock answered. "I must admit, I've lost track too."

Leigh didn't look very happy to hear this.

"It felt much longer," she muttered.

"I can only imagine," Wenlock sympathised. "Do you think the men were working for the Cheneys?"

Leigh nodded.

"I take it the building you found me in was one of theirs?" she asked.

"Yes. A cake factory. The address was printed in a copyright notice at the bottom of the telemetry printout," Wenlock replied. This made Leigh snort with laughter.

"You've got to be kidding me? Surely they weren't that stupid?" she asked, somewhat rhetorically. Wenlock shrugged.

"I never saw the programming - that had all been done before I got there. Nor any print outs," Leigh explained. "I guess I wasn't there long enough... It was good thinking by someone to leave a little clue." At this, they both looked at Woodford who was still smiling amiably and gazing at the houses whipping by the window.

"So why did they take you?" Ashby broke the silence from the driver's seat.

"I didn't do what they wanted," Leigh replied. "Middleton Cheney visited me just before the race and told me to sabotage Upton's car. I refused."

Eyes wide, Wenlock turned to look at Ashby. Ashby looked back at Wenlock with a similar expression[52].

"They wanted you to sabotage Scudamore's car?" Wenlock was first to speak again. "Not to help sabotage Grindalythe's?"

Leigh looked puzzled at this.

"Of course," Leigh responded. "I'm Scudamore's mechanic, not Grindalythe's. It would be pointless asking me to try and sabotage

---

[52] Momentarily, then her eyes went straight back on the road.

Grindalythe's car. Anyone who knows anything about racing knows that Grantham won't let anyone near his precious Panther."

"But you asked Grantham to help you with something on the day of the race, right?" Ashby asked as she pulled the cramped Civet into the police station car park.

"Yes, he helped me diagnose a problem with the engine I couldn't figure out. Overbraiding that bloody solenoid," Leigh nodded. "I was an idiot not to spot it but my mind wasn't really on the job that day. What with being threatened by gangsters and all."

"Did they tell you why they wanted Scudamore's car sabotaged?" Wenlock asked.

"It wasn't really a collaborative relationship," Leigh responded sarcastically. "Very much a: 'Just do this or else'."

"To protect their investment," Ashby answered for Leigh. "Scudamore was the only person who was likely to even get close to Grindalythe on the day."

Wenlock let this sink in. It made sense. The Cheneys wanted Grindalythe to win so that Fitzpaine could pay back the loan they provided him, likely with a healthy bonus on top. They were covering all their bases.

"What are you talking about?" It was Leigh's turn to ask questions. Wenlock told her it was a long story and that he would explain later.

"Well," said Ashby after Wenlock had made that rash promise. "We're here. Now what?"

She was correct. She had driven them safely[53] to the police station car park, as instructed. All eyes were on Wenlock for him to deliver the next step of his plan.

---

[53] relatively

214

Chapter 38

"That's your plan?" Ashby asked, incredulously.

"I'll admit it's not complicated but it should work," Wenlock replied.

"I don't see why it wouldn't," Leigh offered.

"You don't know our current relationship with the police," Ashby responded, shaking her head. "I don't think they'll believe us."

"Why not? I thought he was an ex-policeman?" Leigh asked, jerking a thumb toward Wenlock.

"My unemployment came about rather recently and has cast me in an unfavourable light with the local hierarchy, vis-a-vis 'jumping to conclusions' and 'wasting time with fictions'," Wenlock explained, sheepishly.

"And I'm equally well liked," Ashby chipped in. "For similar reasons."

"I'm very much looking forward to your explanation of the events of the last few days to understand what the hell you are talking about," Leigh replied. "But my legs have gone numb in the back seat here, so shall we just get on with it and worry about if they believe us or not when that happens?"

Ashby reluctantly agreed, after all they had a bit more hard evidence this time. They unfolded themselves from the cramped Civet.

"After you," Ashby indicated the path to the police station door to Wenlock. "This is your idea."

Wenlock surveyed the police station front. It hadn't changed a bit in his absence[54]. The crumbling stonework was as soot blackened as he remembered. The stairs up to the front door were still dangerously uneven and the sash window frames still rotting gently.

Wenlock steeled himself for the welcome reserved only for a disgraced ex-officer.

***

What he got was a bored, gum-chewing Desk Sergeant manning the front desk.

"Hello, DI Wenlock," she said, once she deigned to look up from her newspaper. "I thought you retired?"

"Not really," Wenlock replied, slightly irked already. "I was fired. Last night."

"Oh, I see," replied the Desk Sergeant, without a hint of rancour, sympathy or even interest. "What are you doing here then?"

"I need to see the Chief. Immediately."

The Sergeant frowned at this.

"If I were fired, I wouldn't come to work the next day," the Sergeant offered as unwelcome advice.

"Thanks for your opinion. I'll remember it for next time." Wenlock responded. "Is he in his office? Can I go and see him?"

The Sergeant didn't even need time to think. She was already back to reading her newspaper as she replied.

"Sure, knock yourself out."

***

---

[54] of about 18 hours.

Wenlock led the way to the Chief's office on the top floor, followed by Ashby, Leigh and Woodford - who had decided to wave through any open door or window they passed.

Once they arrived, Wenlock steeled himself before the wood panelled double doors to the Chief's sanctum. The office where, less than 24 hours earlier, they'd questioned Fitzpaine and Wenlock had lost his job. The return to the station and it's banal normality had caused the adrenalin from the chase at the factory to finally leave Wenlock's system. As a result, the hangover was returning with a mighty vengeance, coupled with his lack of sleep. Ashby had to give him a nudge before he plucked up the courage and energy to knock.

"I think I've made my open door policy very clear," came a shout from the other side of the door. "I don't have one, now go away."

"He's in then," Leigh whispered. Wenlock nodded, procrastinating.

"Go on then!" Ashby urged. "Too late to back out now."

Wenlock took another deep breath then opened the door to the office. The Chief was at his desk reading a report, a pair of small glasses perched on his nose above his marvellous moustache. He looked up at the intruders.

"Wenlock? Ms de-la-Zouch? What the bloody hell? I thought I was very clear..." he spluttered. Wenlock held up a hand to interrupt before the Chief could continue.

"I can explain," he said. "Just give us a chance."

"I gave you a pretty bloody good chance yesterday," the Chief responded quickly. "I think the DCI was clear as to what would happen if you returned."

"I don't remember all the details but I know it was pineapple based," Wenlock responded, trying not to think about the grotesque threats made to him the previous evening. "But I'm here all the same. That's how important this is!"

The Chief gave this some thought and then noticed the other two who had entered behind Ashby and Wenlock.

"Fine," he said, putting down his report and spectacles. "You have five minutes before I call Budleigh... and then another ten minutes whilst he fetches a pineapple."

Chapter 39

"Yes please, straight away... No, no need for that, his explanation for being here is actually pretty good," the Chief said into the phone before putting it down.

Ashby and Wenlock recounted the events since Wenlock's firing, leaving out the part with Wraxall Piece at the pub - Wenlock still didn't know how he fit in. The Chief had listened patiently and decided to call the DCI to the office, sans-pineapple. The DCI entered the room moments after the Chief put down the phone. As he walked in, the first face his eyes rested on was that of Woodford Halse, at which his jaw promptly dropped.

"Good grief," said the DCI.

"Indeed," said the Chief.

"Woodford Halse," said the DCI, pointing at Woodford Halse.

"Indeed," said the Chief.

"I've had men looking for you for two years, Mr Halse," the DCI addressed the scruffy ex-missing person, who smiled faintly at the surprised policeman.

Suddenly furious, the DCI turned to Wenlock.

"Did you kidnap this man?" he demanded.

"Actually, Mr Wenlock found him," Leigh jumped in. "As well as myself, captive in a factory owned by the Cheney siblings."

The DCI's jaw dropped a little further. It dropped so far that some teeth could actually be seen peaking out below his moustache.

"Good grief," he repeated.

"Indeed," repeated the Chief. "Take a perch Budleigh. We'll get you up to speed."

***

"Just down the hall from the door we staked out?" the DCI asked, once he had been fully informed of recent events. "Fitzpaine must have at least been aware, if not complicit. We know he had been there several times."

"Perhaps," shrugged Leigh. "I didn't see him so I can't be sure. Maybe Woodford has?"

Sadly, Woodford was still not talking. During the conversation so far, he had mostly busied himself with doodling on a burglary report that had been sitting on the Chief's desk.

"However, it could be a while before he says anything," Leigh finished.

"Who did you see whilst you were there?" Wenlock asked, keen to know who they could implicate.

"Those guards you saw were the main people, and..." Leigh started but stopped suddenly. A horrified look crossed her face.

"Who, what?" Ashby reacted first.

"The others," Leigh said in a small voice. "All the others who were there."

"Who? Who are the others Leigh?" the Chief asked. His voice calm, even and professional.

"I was only in the telemetry unit room during the day - or what I thought was the day. At night I was locked in a dormitory," Leigh finally answered, almost whispering. "There were at least eight other women in there."

Silence from the office's other occupants as this sunk in.

"And, presumably, they kept Woodford in a similar dormitory," Leigh's voice became even quieter as she spoke. Her train of thinking not leading in a pleasant direction. "With the escape, I just didn't think about them I was so busy..."

Wenlock and Ashby exchanged a glance, both were thinking the same thing. The doors marked 'MEN' & 'WOMEN' hadn't been toilets.

"We have to go back," Leigh started up again. Her tone urgent. "We have to go back, what will they have done to the others?"

The DCI reacted first, by swearing.

"I'll round up who I can," he said before leaving the office immediately. The Chief picked up his desk phone and gave out a series of calm instructions to someone on the other end.

"All available cars to Unit 472A, Bowmore Street. Instruct them to surround it immediately but as discreetly as possible. Cordon the roads in the vicinity. No-one is to enter until we get there. Occupants are armed and considered to be trigger happy."

"What can we do?" Leigh asked as soon as the Chief put the phone down.

"You can stay here and look after Mr Halse. The pair of you have been through enough. Stay in this office and I will send an officer up to protect you until we return," the Chief replied, standing up and heading to the exit of the office as he did. "Wenlock, you have knowledge of the factory. You're temporarily re-instated and coming with me."

"And me?" asked Ashby as Wenlock got up to follow the Chief. He replied with a stern expression.

"Officially, I am telling you to stay here with Ms Delamere and Mr Halse." After this, his face broke to a kinder grin. "However, if I have learned anything over the past few days, it's that trying to tell you what to do, Miss de-la-Zouch, is a waste of time."

Ashby found it much quicker to drive across town with a police escort[55]. The cars turned off their sirens as they entered the industrial estate, not wanting to alert the factory to their presence. The four full police cars, accompanying van and tagalong Civet drove as quietly as they could and as close as they dared to Unit 472A.

They stopped on a street out of sight of the factory that had already been cordoned off by officers. Ashby parked up and joined Wenlock, the Chief and the DCI who were talking to the uniformed officer in charge of the cordon.

"No movement, sir." the officer said. "We've intercepted a lorry bringing a delivery but no-one has left the factory."

"Did you search the lorry?" the DCI asked.

"Flour, nothing unusual," the office replied. "We've held on to the driver just in case."

"Very good," the Chief responded. "The cordon surrounding the factory is to remain in place. I'll be leading the team going inside."

The gathered officers looked puzzled at this unusual approach so the Chief explained himself.

"I've been trying to nail this lot since before most of you were born. I'll be damned if anyone else is going to do it."

The DCI waved over a pair of officers who had unloaded a crate from the back of the police van. They carried the crate across and opened it. Wenlock groaned when he saw what was stacked inside in neat little rows.

"Sorry, Much. I know you're not a fan of these but you'll have to take one," the DCI said politely but firmly as he started handing out revolvers from the crate to the surrounding officers.

---

[55] Except for the double-mini-roundabout. Those things are an abomination.

222

"You know I'm useless with the bloody things," Wenlock complained as the DCI waved the handle of one at him.

"Take it, Wenlock," the Chief instructed. "They've already shot at you once today. They're clearly not in the mood for negotiating."

"You know that more officers are injured by their own firearms than by criminals, right?" Wenlock grumbled.

"Whilst that might be correct, it's only true for forces that are constantly armed and not when arms are used in specific applications," the Chief responded. "And you know it. Take the gun and let's hope we don't have to use them."

Wenlock could see it was an argument he wasn't winning and grudgingly took the revolver from the DCI's outstretched hand.

"Can I have one?" Ashby asked, trying her luck. She received a withering look from the gathered officers.

"Miss de-la-Zouch, this is as far as you go. We can't have a civilian joining in the raid," the Chief said.

"And no disguises," Wenlock followed up the Chief's comments, anticipating Ashby's thought process. "We're trained on how to deal with this sort of thing and we don't want you to get hurt."

"The insurance paperwork would be a nightmare," the DCI added.

The officers turned their attention away from her as they planned the raid using a hastily drawn sketch Wenlock had made in muck on a police car bonnet. They knew they needed to maintain the element of surprise. The last thing anyone wanted was a hostage situation. Ashby pretended to sulk whilst racking her brains for ways to sneakily join them.

Chapter 40

Mr 'Piss Off' was now seriously pissed off. After he and the rest of the security guards had cleared the dogs out of the factory, the general manager had rounded them all up, said that the shifts were being extended and that nobody was going home. No-one had caught the mad, macintosh wearing, mutt-bringer and the manager was worried that he would be back with more dogs. Thorough searches of the factory had been ordered. One of the guards asked about the strange banging noises he had heard coming from outside the factory but the manager explained it was a car back-firing, purely a coincidence and unrelated to the hound incident. Someone pointed out it had back-fired six times in a row which earned him the cancellation of his overtime payment and so the rest had shut up. With all the excitement, the fake health inspectors had been completely forgotten about.

The consequence of all this was that Mr 'Piss Off' was now back in the security office reading his newspaper, four hours after his shift had been due to end. He was puzzling over a fiendish cryptic crossword question[56] when he got a call through from the shift manager telling him that the flour delivery had arrived late and he was to supervise it being unpacked from the lorry. Mr 'Piss Off' hitched up his belt and made his way to the loading area, still chewing on the crossword question.

The flour lorry had been waved through the delivery door and in to the unpacking area of the factory floor. Mr 'Piss Off' had the unenviable job of opening the lorry first to make sure it contained flour and not thieves. He had found this strange when he first joined the staff here. No other factory he had worked at had been so protective of its operations. On the other hand, the pay was good and, aside from the strangeness today, it was a quiet

---

[56] Number 4 across: 8 letters, starting with 'S' and ending with 'E': "A knight who forces things open.".

gig. He, like everyone in town, had a good idea of who owned the factory, and who would be stupid enough to rob it?

He nodded to the driver of the lorry who stayed in his cab, as was the procedure, then walked to the rear of the vehicle. He pulled the lever that released the roller door on the lorry trailer, threw the door upward and looked inside. The trailer was crammed with blue uniformed police officers, all armed with revolvers. One of the revolvers was pointed at him.

"Surprise," said the male fake health inspector from earlier.

"4 across," Mr 'Piss Off' replied as he put his hands in the air.

The police officers streamed from the lorry, flooding the factory floor. They waved the revolvers and instructed the workforce to follow the security guard's example. Wisely, they complied.

When Wenlock had finished handcuffing Mr 'Piss Off', he caught the Chief's attention and pointed to the door he and Ashby had snuck through earlier. It was currently ajar.

"Over there. It was guarded when we came through earlier. By someone not in a uniform."

"I saw someone slip through there as we were rounding people up," the DCI chipped in.

"We need to be quick then," replied the Chief. "Lead the way Wenlock."

Wenlock complied, sprinting across the factory floor, followed closely by the team of officers assigned to search the hidden part of the building.

He opened the door quickly to catch anyone on the other side by surprise. He peered into the gloom of the boarded up corridor. At the far end stood a figure. Before Wenlock could react the figure raised a gun of their own and made to fire.

Wenlock froze.

Fortunately, the officer behind him was more alert. She barged past Wenlock and fired first, the figure crumpled over.

"That was close, eh?" the gum-chewing Desk Sergeant remarked to Wenlock. He managed a weak nod in reply.

"Come on," she urged him on with a nudge. "Not done yet. Which way?"

Officers started to stream past them, kicking open the doors labelled MEN, WOMEN and BATHROOM. They moved quickly into the rooms, finding them all empty. Wenlock looked in the one marked MEN. Leigh had been correct - they were dormitories. Each wall lined with around ten bunk beds, all empty but clearly occupied recently. Wenlock hoped they weren't too late.

"Carry on along the corridor. There's plenty more," he instructed. The Desk Sergeant set off in front; Wenlock followed close behind. They came to the slumped figure at the end of the corridor and Wenlock saw it had been the man in factory worker clothes who had been guarding the hidden door. This was good news. He hadn't gone far enough to alert the other guards, wherever they were.

The Desk Sergeant rounded the left hand corner and they came to the room marked TEXTILES.

"Behind here?" she asked. Wenlock shrugged in response.

"We didn't go through earlier."

"Let's find out then," she replied, slightly more gung-ho than Wenlock cared for. She signalled for two officers to join her and then opened the door quickly. Inside, Wenlock saw it was essentially a small textiles factory. Several rows of tables, all facing forward and all equipped with a sewing machine. Like the telemetery room where he had found Leigh earlier, the walls were bare breezeblock and the door had no handle on the inside. Unlike the telemetry room, this one was empty. It had been clearly in use recently. Half finished trousers hung from the sewing machines. Whoever had been here had left, or been forced to leave, in a hurry.

With the room secured, Wenlock and the Desk Sergeant went to continue moving through the corridor when they were joined by the Chief and the DCI.

"Found anyone?" the Chief asked. Wenlock shook his head.

"Round the corner is the telemetry room and the door we left by. That's as far as we got earlier today. I don't know what's beyond there," Wenlock replied.

"Let's hope it's the missing people," the DCI voiced what they were all thinking. The Chief nodded and motioned for the Desk Sergeant to lead the way. The DCI had once told Wenlock that the sergeant was the most experienced marksperson on the force, but a little bit trigger happy. Useful in these situations but also a good reason to mostly keep her desk bound.

The Desk Sergeant peaked around the corner, saw there was no-one and motioned for the others to follow her. The telemetry room door was shut and the door by which Wenlock had escaped earlier had been hastily boarded over. Wenlock knew it would be as they had scouted it before coming up with the flour lorry plan.

The Desk Sergeant opened the door to the telemetry room, confirming their suspicions that it was empty. From now on, they were in unknown territory.

Chapter 41

Ashby was furious. Wenlock had spotted all her attempts to sneak in to the back of the flour van, no matter how well she glued on the false moustache.

Now she was at the outer cordon, waiting for news on the raid and stewing. She voiced her frustrations to the officers left behind but few sympathised with her plight. Most seemed pretty happy not to be sneaking in to a gangster-owned factory potentially full of armed men and hostages. None of them would let her get any nearer to the action. All she could do for now was wait.

A small crowd had gathered at the road block, people wanting to get to their jobs or make deliveries. The police were tight-lipped on why they couldn't go through. 'Ongoing operation' was the line given to all who enquired. One member of the crowd spotted Ashby sulking on her car bonnet and sidled over.

"How did you get on earlier?" a scraggily beard mouthed from underneath a dirty, green, waterproof cap.

Ashby jumped in shock at the talking mackintosh before realising who it was.

"Hi, Acton. Yes, thanks for the distraction. It's opened rather the can of worms," she replied.

"Glad to be of service," he said. "Most fun I've had in a while."

"Did you get the dogs back?" Ashby asked.

"Oh yes. They're tied up round the corner having a drink. Really made a mess of the place. Great fun." Acton took a handful of pilfered cake from his jacket pocket and started munching on it. He offered some to Ashby who politely, but firmly, declined.

"So, what's all this about then?" Acton waved a cakey hand at the roadblock.

Ashby looked round and saw that the police weren't in ear shot. Acton had been a big help and it seemed the least she could do was let him in on what was going on.

"Much and I found people held captive in the factory, the police have gone back in to see if there are more," she whispered.

Acton nodded and continued to munch on his fistful of cake.

"Sounds exciting," he eventually replied.

"It does, yes. I'm pretty narked at being stuck out here to be honest." Ashby voiced her frustrations once more.

"Doesn't seem fair," Acton agreed. "Want me to do the dog trick again?"

Ashby thought about it but realised that disrupting the roadblock set up to prevent the escape of criminals just so she could be part of the action might be a tad selfish so shook her head.

"Did you try sneaking past?" Acton asked, still happily munching his pilfered Battenberg.

Ashby listed her attempts. Wenlock had instructed the officers to keep her a close eye on her and they had, for once, proved very competent at this.

Acton listened patiently, finishing one pocket of cake and moving on to the next before offering a final suggestion.

"Have you tried the sewer?"

Ashby gave him a funny look.

"In general? Or specifically?

"To get in." Acton waved his hands toward the factory. "Sewers lead you everywhere in this area. Big enough to walk through, they have to take all the industrial waste."

Ashby did not know this.

"Back when I was on the council, I tried to put a few traffic tunnels in to the system, you know just to create some pinch points, but there were so many sewers even I had to stop," Acton continued.

"How do I get in?" Ashby saw her opportunity, her best chance to see at least part of the raid unfold.

"Any manhole cover round here should work." Acton replied. "I think I saw one near where I left the dog pack. I can show you if you like?"

Ashby nodded. The police were busy now turning people back from the roadblock and were no longer paying attention to her. She jumped down from the car bonnet, reinvigorated.

Acton lead her round the corner to the manhole in question. Ashby noticed there was no obvious way to lift the metal cover guarding the entrance.

"Despair not," the wily mad man told her. "I always carry a key."

Ashby thought to voice how strange this was before remembering that the man ran a dog taxi service. Instead, she thought it best to just go with the flow as the dishevelled pile of Turville got to work on removing the manhole cover.

In a matter of minutes, and causing only a few bruised fingers, the cover was off and the smell of sewer wafted up Ashby's nostrils, causing her to gag a little. As Acton had said, there was plenty of room down there and the water at the bottom looked to be only ankle high.

"Need any help getting in?" Acton asked. Ashby replied she would not and set about gently lowering herself down. The sewer was tall enough for her to stand in with almost another half a foot of headroom above her.

With Ashby now on the sewer floor, Acton was just a floating head above her, haloed by the daylight from the manhole. An unlikely saviour.

He called down to her, "You might want this."

He dug in his pocket for a second before dropping down a cake covered torch. Ashby caught it and turned it on. It didn't exactly illuminate the tunnel but it was enough to see what she was stepping in[57].

"The factory is that way," he said, pointing in what was hopefully the right direction. "Have fun."

Ashby thanked him and set off down the tunnel.

---

[57] Something she instantly regretted.

Chapter 42

Wenlock, the Desk Sergeant, the Chief, the DCI and four more armed police officers crept cautiously along the dimly lit corridor. No more doors greeted them on the right-hand wall. Eventually, the corridor took a right turn, signifying the back of the factory. The Desk Sergeant peeked round once again and declared it safe. After the corner was a staircase leading upward; bare wood, suggesting it had been recently erected. Next to the staircase, set in the floor, was a 2 foot diameter drain cover. The cover was not sat correctly in its hole. It looked like it had been placed in a hurry, perhaps after someone had climbed through it.

Wenlock groaned, he didn't like where this was going. The DCI shushed him. The Chief had clearly spotted the same thing as Wenlock and silently waved his instructions to the assembled officers. He, the Desk Sergeant and the other two officers would go up the stairs. The DCI, Wenlock and two officers were to open the manhole and follow where it led. Wenlock protested silently but furiously that he was a bit claustrophobic and wasn't in the right shoes for a sewer chase. The DCI agreed and suggested that they went in the upstairs party. Several quick games of paper-scissors-rock decided the unfair outcome: Wenlock and the Desk Sergeant would go through the manhole, the Chief, the DCI and the other four officers would investigate the stairs.

In a huff, Wenlock and the Desk Sergeant removed the manhole cover and peered into the gloom below as the upstairs party crept upwards. Their suspicions had been correct; the hole had a ladder propped inside leading down around 8 feet into the murk.

The Desk Sergeant pulled out a torch and cheerfully offered to go first. Wenlock nodded. He would have kissed her with gratitude if it wasn't considered sexual harassment in the workplace.

The Desk Sergeant had clambered down the ladder and reached the bottom before Wenlock had got off the first rung. He looked down as she stepped off the ladder. He could see her torch swinging left and right to pierce the gloom.

"Sewers," he said, "why did it have to be sewers?"

The Desk Sergeant hissed back that she didn't know and could Wenlock please hurry up as she had seen something move and wanted to chase it. Wenlock complied, scrabbling down the ladder as fast as he dared. On reaching the bottom and submerging his shoes in 4 inches of sludgy factory waste, he saw tunnel properly. The ladder was at a dead end, giving them only one direction to go. He could just about stand up but it was too narrow for any more than one person at a time. The walls were redbrick and it was very dark. He prayed the sludge was factory waste and not human. On seeing back-up arrive, even if in the form of Wenlock, the Desk Sergeant bounded off down the tunnel. Her torch the only source of light. Wenlock kept up as best he could.

After following the sewer for a minute, they came to a T-junction where their tunnel met another. The Desk Sergeant switched off her torch. Wenlock was about to ask why when she put a finger to her lips to shush him. Then he realised, he could see her. There was another source of light coming from the right hand of the T. The light flickered and bounced off the walls, getting dimmer by the second. Someone with a torch was running away from them. Now they had stopped moving they could hear hushed but urgent voices in the distance and splashing, suggesting movement of feet through shallow 'water'. The Desk Sergeant crept round the corner, torch still off. Wenlock followed and now he could see figures moving in the distance, framed in the tunnel by the light from their torches. They weren't far ahead. The Desk Sergeant left her torch off and increased her pace to catch them, presumably to get in revolver range. Wenlock reluctantly followed, splashing in the darkness. They were moving much faster than the party ahead. As Wenlock got closer, he could make out it was far more than just one or two people. As Wenlock realised this, the Desk Sergeant held up her hand for him to stop. She turned and nodded. They were only 40 yards away now, close enough to challenge. Wenlock nodded in reply that he was ready, which was only a small lie.

"Stop, Police!" the Desk Sergeant shouted as she turned on her torch, illuminating the figure at the rear of the fugitive conga. The figure did stop but swung their torch to illuminate the officers, temporarily blinding them.

Then all hell broke loose.

The torch-wielding rear-guard fired a gun. Fortunately, it ricocheted off the tunnel wall and bounced off in to the distance. The noise was ear-splitting and caused Wenlock and the Desk Sergeant to duck before the Desk Sergeant returned with a shot of her own - blinded by the torch she also missed. The figures ahead ran. The gun shots had nearly deafened Wenlock but he could make out screaming noises coming through from those reluctant to run and holding the others up. His ears rang incessantly. The torches let Wenlock see more of what was ahead of the figures as they ran: a junction again. The majority of the torches disappeared off to the left, at least one off to the right. There wasn't much time for decision making. The Desk Sergeant went left and Wenlock went right at pace.

This turned out to be a mistake as the right hand turn was sloped, very steeply. Wenlock barrelled round the corner and immediately lost his footing in the gloom. He fell several yards down the slope surrounded by a torrent of sewage sludge before the tunnel levelled out again and he came to a stop.

Lying on his stomach he managed to lift his head. He saw the end of the sewer: an outlet. Light from the outside world streamed in through a large circular opening. The sludge he had previously been surrounded by rushing out, suggesting a long drop from the outlet to ground below.

Framed in the tunnel opening was the outline of a man. It seemed one of the factory fugitives had made the same mistake at the junction. Wenlock started to get back to his feet.

"Slowly, please, DI Wenlock," said the figure.

"Fitzpaine?" Wenlock recognised the voice even if he couldn't make out the man's features, blinded as he was by the light from the outlet.

"Yes, the Cheneys called me in after the mess you made earlier today by finding our little backroom operation. Wanted my help to smooth it all over. Lord knows what they expected me to do," he replied, surprisingly nonchalantly for a man cornered by a police officer. "Such a shame, we had a good thing going on at the factory! People who annoyed the Cheyneys, or me, would dissapear and then suddenly become free labour. Quite brilliant. We made an awful lot of money. What a mess you've made of a wonderful system."

Wenlock reached his knees, breathing heavily and slightly winded from both the fall and all the recent running around. His heart thumped in his chest far louder than he cared for.

"Hands up, then. It's over," Wenlock instructed wearily. If it wasn't for being caked in effluence and his seemingly impending coronary, he would have been quite enjoying this moment.

"Perhaps for you," Fitzpaine replied. It was at that moment Wenlock realised he was no longer holding his gun, Fitzpaine was. He gave a groan before putting his hands above his head.

"I could let you go, and you could pretend you never saw me?" Fitzpaine suggested. "This could be the start of a beautiful friendship. We could cut you in. Have you thought about taking over the missing persons cases? It would make running this operation even easier."

"That isn't going to happen," Wenlock replied. This was it; he wanted to live of course - but not under Fitzpaine's thumb. He couldn't do it, not after all he had seen.

Fitzpaine's brow furrowed and Wenlock watched as the thoughts worked their way through his head, playing out how each scenario worked best for him. Wenlock felt the sludgy water rush past his knees and out past Fitzpaine into the world. Something small and hard got stuck against his right foot. He prayed a bit. His heart beat faster, far faster than he thought possible. Suddenly, a look of serenity arrived on the politician's face as his mind was made up.

"Very well," Fitzpaine raised the revolver, aiming it directly at Wenlock. He pulled back the hammer and squeezed the trigger.

A disappointing click barely registered above the sound of rushing water. Fitzepaine looked at the revolver in confusion before trying again. Wenlock slowly got to his feet.

"I really don't like guns," Wenlock said, by way of explanation. "So much so, I didn't load mine."

Fitzpaine, clearly not believing, this tried once more. Several clicking noises, one after the other, confirmed Wenlock's claim.

"I'll bet you loaded yours though." The small, hard object trapped against his foot had been a snub-nosed revolver. It seemed Fitzpaine had also dropped his gun on the way down the slope. Wenlock reached back and plucked the snub-nose out of the sludge. He could tell by the weight and the expression on Fitzpaine's face that Wenlock would finally be winning a bet. He got to his feet and pointed the snub-nose at Fitzpaine.

"You wouldn't shoot," Fitzpaine sneered.

"For you, I'd make an exception. Now, drop the gun, hands where I can see them," Wenlock instructed.

Fitzpaine was finally rattled. Out of options, cornered and desperate. He was still holding Wenlock's revolver, too stunned to heed Wenlock's instruction.

"I didn't kill Kirby Grindalythe," he said in an almost pleading manner.

"I don't care," Wenlock replied.

Fitzepain almost staggered at hearing this. As if Wenlock had pulled the trigger. He looked over his shoulder at the outlet behind him. Wenlock didn't know how far the drop was but at the rate the sludge was falling it out it looked a long way. Fitzpaine turned to face the end of the tunnel.

"Don't do it!" Wenlock warned, catching his intention.

Fitzpaine, his face an emotionless mask, took one last look back at the ex-detective and then jumped.

Chapter 43

Ashby was fed up. She had been wandering the sewers for long enough that she could no longer smell whatever it was she was covered in. It was wet, dark, cold and she was certain to be missing out the scoop of being their during the raid. The cake-covered torch Acton had given her was dying and she had no idea if she was anywhere near the factory.

She was debating turning back when she heard first some shouts and then two large cracking noises echoing off the tunnel walls toward her. Feeling certain that it wasn't the rats, she pushed forward toward the noises. It certainly sounded like gunshots. In her haste to get to the sound of the noise, she did not notice how low the batteries in the torch had got and was soon left in near complete darkness.

After splashing around a few seconds longer, the smallest pin-prick of light showed up ahead. With nothing else to go off, she made her way toward it. As she got closer, and the light grew more, she saw that the sludge was moving toward the light as well. She heard voices, only just loud enough to be heard over her splashing feet and the rushing sludge. Unfortunately, what she didn't see, focussed as she was on the voices, was the sloping nature of the tunnel at this point and she fell down it.

At the bottom, with a few bruises and having lost Acton's now useless torch, she picked herself up. She had been correct, it was an outlet for the sewer. In front of the outlet was a hunched figure, slouched against the sewer wall and shaking, seemingly uncontrollably.

She immediately recognised the figure from his grubby coat and rushed over.

"Much?" she shouted as she reached him and turned him to face her "What happened? Are you hurt?"

As she did this, she realised he was indeed shaking uncontrollably, however not due to any obvious injury. It appeared that he was laughing.

He was laughing so hard he couldn't reply. He was wheezing, trying to catch his breath. Tears were rolling from his eyes, leaving streaky tracks down his grimy, sleep-deprived face. All he could manage was to point over the edge of the sewer outlet. Ashby gave a frown and duly investigated.

She peered over the edge of the outlet. Opposite her was the other side of a Anearby gorge. It seemed the outlet was dumping the sludge into Anearby river from a fairly great height. The outlet must have been 130 feet from the river itself.

Ashby's gaze moved to the river and then to what was directly below her. Whilst there was a steep drop, it no longer met the water. Years of cake-based industrial pollution had led to an artificial mountain of brown sludge. Presumably made of flour.

About 10 feet below the outlet was the beginning of this sludgeslope. Stuck up to his waist, and with sludge pouring from the outlet on to his head, was none other than Cheddon Fitzpaine. Aside from being covered in sludge, he appeared to be unharmed.

"Hello, Mr Mayor," Ashby called down, suppressing the urge to laugh. "What brings you here?"

Fitzpaine risked a glance upward at his tormentor, shielding his face from the torrent of effluence streaming from the outlet. He saw Ashby grinning back and groaned.

Afterward

"What do you think?" Ashby asked. Wenlock put the book she had given him the previous week down on the familiar table. It had been six months since they'd raided the factory and cornered Fitzpaine. This was the first time he and Ashby had actually met up since. The book had been posted through his letterbox a week ago with a note asking him to meet her when he had finished reading.

They were back in the linoleum paradise of Anearby Cafe in the seats they had occupied months before. Wenlock had ordered a cup of tea[58] and Ashby had just arrived. Both were sitting comfortably(ish) on their white, plastic chairs and framed by the net-curtained windows.

"I think it's a pretty good retelling of what happened," he replied. "It misses out quite a lot of the paperwork I did."

"I had to streamline some bits," Ashby explained. "Nobody really wants to read the tedious details."

"I see you left out all the lawyers we dealt with as well."

"The most tedious details," Ashby answered with a grin. "I've got a publisher, it'll be in print by the end of the year!"

"Great news," Wenlock took a sip of his drink that, if you were being charitable, you could call tea. "Do you think you'll quit *The Post* and become a full time novelist?"

"Absolutely not," Ashby snorted.

---

[58] He had received what seemed to be a cup of dishwater. He thought he saw a bit of sponge floating in it.

"Shame," said Wenlock, fortunately under his breath. "Did you hear about the first court appearances?" he added at a more audible volume.

"Yes," Ashby replied, "Minimum of twelve years each for the Cheneys on the kidnapping charges, seven for Fitzpaine for conspiracy."

"Seems a bit low for being caught red-handed with fifteen people you've held hostage," Wenlock grumped.

"And you can bet these weren't the first batch," Ashby added ominously. "This town has had more than its fair share of missing people over the years. I suppose the Cheneys & Fitzpaine still have some friends in high places."

"It was incredible the variety of people they were holding in there: journalists critical of Fitzpaine, opposition party activitists, anyone who owed the Cheyneys and couldn't pay."Wenlock added, "I'm a bit miffed we didn't make the connection sooner."

"It was a slick but horrible operation." Ashby agreed. "It shows how much running a racing team must cost if Fitzpaine had ot get a loan from the Cheneys in addition to the kickbacks they were giving him."

There was a pause between them as Ashby contemplated her luck that she decided to be a political correspondant.

"I thought it was nice they gave that Desk Sergeant a medal for apprehending them all and saving all the hostages," Ashby stated slightly hesitantly before driving the direction she was really interested in. "I didn't see your name mentioned in articles..."

"Oh, I'm still fired," Wenlock added, more casually than he felt about it.

"Really?" Ashby asked indignantly. ""Even with everything you did to find the factory and chase down Fitzpaine. That seems unfair!"

"I would agree, but apparently some of my actions preceeding the raid were not entirely professional... or legal." Wenlock replied, sipping his dishwater as nonchalantly as he could. The Chief had pointed out he was quite lucky to not be prosecuted himself. "They reinstated my pension - which was nice."

"Well, that's something I guess," Ashby knew how much Wenlock's pension had meant to him. "How's retirement then?"

"I won't get the pension for another fifteen years at least!" Wenlock shot back. "How old do you think I am?"

Ashby decided against answering that and instead gave Wenlock the good news she had.

"They gave me an advance for the book. It would've been unfair for me to keep it all, since you did a good bit of the work." She dove into her purse, pulled out a cheque and pushed it across the table. Wenlock could see his name on it. He could also see the sum, it was enough to cover starting the business he had in mind...

"Thank you, that is very kind!" he said, smiling nearly as widely as when he had seen Fitzpaine being covered in cake waste.

"It's the least I could do," she replied. Outside the cafe, it started to rain. Drizzle flecked the large windows which dutifully steamed up to cosy the atmosphere. "Did you hear that Woodford is getting better? Apparently he's started talking again. Mostly nonsense, but according to those who knew him he was like that before."

Wenlock said that he had not heard that but was happy to hear it.

"Did you ever get the dogs back off Turville?" Ashby asked.

"No, we're in business properly now. He pays me a fee to rent the dogs. It's what I've been living off to be honest," Wenlock replied. He wasn't really missing the dogs, they had taken up a lot of his free time and had mostly been the idea of his ex-wife. It seemed Acton was looking after them well enough. He passed Ashby the company business card across the table.

"If you ever need a taxi ride from a madman piloting a dog sled, call the number on the card. 10% discount."

Ashby thanked him and assured him that, should she ever need that service, she would ensure it was Acton she called.

There was a pause between them and Wenlock felt he should break the silence. He didn't really want to make the offer but did anyway.

"Do you want to get a drink? You know, something harder than tea... talk about what happened?" he asked.

Ashby looked at her watch and pulled a polite but apologetic face.

"Sorry, Much. I can't. I'm going to meet Lacey. Maybe another time?"

Wenlock breathed a sigh of relief with a breath he hadn't realised he was holding. He hadn't been keen on the idea and had offered just to be polite. Frankly, the last thing he wanted to do was talk about the case that ended his career, particularly not with the person who helped end it. Aside from the subject matter, they'd never had much chemistry as a crime-solving duo.

Deep down, Much Wenlock was rather hoping this would be the last time he saw Ashby de-la Zouch.

MUCH WENLOCK and ASHBY DE-LA-ZOUCH will return in

MUCH DE-LA-ZOUCH ABOUT NOTHING!

Acknowledgements

I'd like to thank a few people and organisations, without whom this book would not have been possible.

Firstly, big up the UK house purchasing progress, during who's infernally tedious and slow drudgery I wrote the majority of the book to take my mind off its horrendous inefficiency. Never change, you outdated, job-creating nightmare.

Shout out to Jordana & Dave for reading the earlier drafts, with the more depressing end, during your quarantines. Thanks for all your feedback and the cover quotes. I hope you like the new ending more.

Thanks to canva.com, who's software I used to make the snazzy front and back cover for next to nothing.

Thanks to spaceman Jeff, who made it so easy to publish any old crap such as this book. I appreciate it but please make the conditions for your workers better. Let's face it, you can afford it.

Finally, and most importantly:

Thanks to my Mum, who not only gave birth to me but also raised me and encouraged me every step of the way.

Thanks to my brother, for reading an early draft and offering thorough feedback that I mostly ignored.

Thanks to Lyd, who supported me all the way, put up with me twadddling on endlessly and who did all the boring proof reading & endless editing. You made this possible which I hope is a good thing.

Printed in Great Britain
by Amazon

65935985R00156